I0626684

ZOMBIE KONG

BOOKS of the DEAD

Zombie Kong

Graphic design by Derek Daley
Interior design by James Roy Daley
Edited by James Roy Daley
Copyedit by Ashley Davis
Cover Art by Daniele Serra

FIRST EDITION

For more information check out:
BOOKSoftheDEADPRESS.com

For direct sales and inquiries contact:
besthorror@gmail.com

1 2 3 4 5 6 7 8 9 10

BOOKS of the DEAD

Great titles from:
<u>BOOKS OF THE DEAD</u>

Table Of Contents

Dr. Steven Rutgers
UNDERSTANDING ZOMBIE KONG

The average size of a small intestine in an adult human male is approximately twenty-three feet long and three centimeters wide. It's not uncommon for an intestine to reach a length of about thirty feet if the person is considered obese. Once a person dies that same intestine can measure up to 50% longer due to the loss of muscle tone within the tissue. With such losses, a three hundred pound man that has been dead for a few days can have a small intestine reaching a length of approximately forty-five feet. A three hundred pound gorilla that has been dead for the same amount of time will have a small intestine that is similar in both width and length.

The average height of a male silverback gorilla is 1.7 meters, or about 5' 7''. A gorilla at this height typically has a weight of approximately 390 pounds, or 5.82 pounds per linear inch. Most experts agree that the gorilla, now referred to as "Zombie Kong," was slightly more than 52 feet tall and had a weight nearing 20 tons (40,000 pounds), or 64 pounds per linear inch. I have tried to find some facts and figures regarding the actual pre-death anatomy of the great beast but so far I have been unsuccessful. It should be noted that my own investigations have led me to believe that Zombie Kong's small intestine was close to 30cms in diameter and more than 400 feet long. 400 feet, for reference sake, is roughly 14% longer than the soccer field inside Wembley Stadium.

ZOMBIE KONG

SHELLEY ONTIS
Manny's Candy

Cesar wrung out his mop and swiped the last corner, not quite getting all the way into the crevice and not caring. They got enough work out of him, more than they paid. Break time, anyway. The mop sloshed water over the side of the bucket as he dropped it in, sending up the chemical smell that still made Cesar feel woozy after all these months.

"Man-*ny*," he said. "I know you've been watching me, buddy." Manny sat in the front of his cage, bouncing a little, looking as much like an excited kid as a gorilla. "Want something?"

Manny grunted and raised a thick black finger to his cheek, then twisted it back and forth.

"You want candy?"

The gorilla held his hands out, palms up. He pulled them toward himself, then repeated the sign for candy. He brought his fingers to his lips. *Want, candy, eat.*

"Yeah, I know, I know," Cesar said, pulling a caramel out of his pocket and unwrapping it. He slipped it through the metal grate. "You're a good little man, aren't you?" Cesar had noticed that about him from the beginning, how good he was, how he seemed so human sometimes. He'd started calling him Manny since he didn't have a name, just a number. He thought 'little man' was clever, since Manny was easily three or four times his weight, and at least a couple heads taller.

He glanced up at the camera in the corner to make sure it was pointed toward the exit and hadn't been moved. Lindstrom would have twenty kinds of fits if he knew Cesar spent so much time with Manny every night, but they only ever watched the

9

exits with the closed circuit TVs, never the animal cages. Cesar guessed it was more important for them to know who came and went than what they did while they were here.

Manny chewed the sticky candy slowly and Cesar felt a little pang of guilt. Lindstrom caught Cesar giving Manny a caramel one day and rode his ass about it, said it wasn't good for his teeth. "Gorillas do not find candy in the wild," he'd said. "Human junk food isn't good for him at all."

Cesar told Manny later not to worry—he'd still bring candy. They were going to keep the poor guy cooped up in that cage, poking and prodding him, he ought to have candy and girl apes and disco music and tequila if he wanted. Especially since whatever they did to him made him feel bad sometimes, Cesar could tell, and it wasn't because of any candy. It was whatever they shot into him. He had that sick look about him tonight, too.

"Poor little man," Cesar said. When Manny touched a finger to his lip and drew it down, *red*, Cesar gave him a piece of red, strawberry-flavored hard candy, another of Manny's favorites. "Teeth are the least of your Goddamn worries, aren't they?" He slipped his fingers into the cage and Manny leaned forward to have his forehead rubbed. "I gotta fuck around in the fish room for a while, but I'll be back."

Cesar hated the fish room. Fish shouldn't get that big unless they were dolphins or sharks or something. These were mostly the type of little fish that he might give his nephew or niece in a glass bowl, but they looked blown up enough they could eat half of him in one bite. He avoided their saucer-sized, dead-looking fish eyes as he cleaned the glass. One fish in particular––it looked like a huge goldfish that someone had boiled long enough for its outsides to bubble, but not quite burst—followed his hand a little too closely when he cleaned. He'd thought about dropping some sort of poison in the water more than once, just to save himself the creeps every night and put that poor, deformed looking thing out of its misery. But maybe it liked the way it was. Cesar couldn't bear the idea of hurting anything, not even a fish that probably wouldn't know it. But sometimes he didn't clean the outside of the aquarium. Too many nightmares about it breaking out the top and munching into the hand it had been eyeballing for so long.

By the time Cesar finished in the fish room, Manny was in the corner, his forehead against the wall. His back moved up and down a little as he breathed, like he couldn't get enough air.

"Man—"

The gorilla spun, its lip curled back, and lurched toward him, roaring. Cesar jumped back. "Manny! What the hell?"

Manny stopped, seemed to come back to himself. He sat, started breathing slower and leaned his forehead against the door.

"What's up, little man? You scared me." Cesar put his hand on his chest, his heart thumping. He felt the urge to pee.

Manny put his fist on his chest, swiped it down. *Sorry.*

"That's okay. Maybe you had a rough day, eh? Friends forgive," he said, but his heart still hadn't slowed.

Manny lifted both hands and hooked the fingers together, shaking them a little.

"Yeah, friends," Manny said, showing him the right way to do it, hooking the index fingers together then flipping them to hook the other way. Manny had never quite gotten the hang of that one, but Cesar figured it didn't matter since they both knew what he meant. He wasn't supposed to know any signs. He'd been sent here from another lab because of his inability to learn sign language. They'd called him a failure because he couldn't talk, which Cesar thought was a shitty thing to do to a gorilla that wasn't supposed to talk anyhow.

It still amazed him that all those educated highbrows in the white coats couldn't teach Manny sign language, with all their computers and their fancy degrees, and he'd done it in no time. All it took was a little patience, a smile or two and some candy.

Manny, with his big forehead against the cage and those woeful eyes, clearly wanted his forehead rubbed. But Manny had never acted that way with him before, like he could have just chewed his head off. Cesar lifted his hand, pulled it back an inch or so, deciding it might not be a good idea, but then looked into those sad, black eyes again and reached into the cage.

"All you ever needed was a friend, isn't that right, little man? A trusting friend."

Manny closed his eyes and hooked his index fingers together, while Cesar rubbed his head.

The vomiting started a few hours later, not long before Cesar's shift ended in the morning. He knew there'd probably be hell to pay—night people weren't supposed to be there for more than 10 minutes off the clock—but he waited far longer than that to make sure they knew exactly what had been happening with Manny overnight. He hoped it wasn't Rico. That bastard would probably put his own grandmother in a cage and poke her if someone paid him enough, so Cesar didn't think he'd care about a puking gorilla.

Dr. Lindstrom was first through the door. His blonde hair was slicked back so smooth he almost looked bald. His whole face puckered in on itself when he saw Cesar.

"I know it's past my time, but Manny's sick, he's been sick for hours."

"The proper thing to do would be to leave a note, not to break protocol."

"I know that, Dr. Lindstrom, and I'm sorry. But I-I don't write English so good, and I wanted to make sure you knew everything."

Lindstrom sighed. Cesar wanted to punch him and point out that he wrote just fine, thank you, but in their eyes it was a better excuse for not leaving a note, than for him to be simply worried about Manny.

He described Manny's symptoms, how he'd charged the front of the cage, how he'd seemed so sad and tired, and how he'd kept vomiting and wouldn't stop. He almost left out the caramels, but it might be important to Manny's health. He'd rather get in trouble again than not tell them something that could make a difference.

Lindstrom wrote on a clipboard, looking up at Manny sometimes, then scrawling away. He pressed hard and wrote with a scritch-scratching that sounded to Cesar like something trying to claw its way out of a box. Then Lindstrom thanked him and told him he needed to leave now.

"Is he going to be okay? Manny? Do you know what it is? Like the flu, or something?"

Lindstrom smiled—the first time Cesar could remember—and said that he'd be fine, *just* fine.

Cesar worried all day. Lindstrom saying Manny would be fine didn't reassure him; Lindstrom was the one making Manny sick. He didn't know exactly what they did or why, but he knew it was cruel. The most he was ever told was that it was important work that would save lives. He almost hadn't got the job when he'd asked who saved the animals lives. He saw the interviewer's eyes go dark with disinterest, so he'd backpedaled and said at least their lives weren't wasted like they would be in the wild, where nature was so cruel and they'd die for nothing. Here, they served a purpose, and he'd be proud to be even a small part of such an operation. He just needed the money.

That was before he knew exactly where the hell he'd be working. The compound was mostly underground, hidden from anyone who might wander that deep into the jungle like tourists from Puerto Madero on ATV or hiking tours looking for springs or ruins. Cesar and the other few people who cleaned during the nights stayed in a small camp about a mile away. They rode ATVs back and forth, and went home on their days off. They had to hike to a base a mile or so on the other side of the camp, and they were bussed to Puerto Madero where most took other busses home or had family pick them up. Two he knew of took trains home from there all the way to Guatemala. The bus ride sometimes lasted longer than usual because they took different routes all the time.

The whole point was to make it hard for the workers to find the compound on their own, Cesar guessed. He didn't want to find it, except… he missed Manny on his days off and worried about him being there with the doctors who didn't seem to care about anything but their charts. The *smart* people didn't even know he knew sign language. Manny didn't try it with them, only with Cesar. And they said he was too dumb to learn.

He opened his wallet and pulled out a piece of paper, soft with age and use, where he'd scribbled down the signs to teach Manny. His niece had brought home library books for him from school, one about gorillas and their habitat and one about Koko, the gorilla who knew more sign language than any other, with some of the most common signs included. She'd brought him an LSM book, the one that showed signs the deaf used in Mexico, but by then he'd grown familiar with the ones Koko used.

He'd written notes about the signs and made crude drawings so he could learn them himself before teaching Manny. He'd brought candy—caramels, butterscotch and the red, strawberry kind. When he talked to Manny in a sweet voice he'd come right out of his shell, moving from the corner where he sat at first, to the door. He was smart and gentle, and deserved much better than he had. Those eyes of Manny's, they could show as much feeling as any of them were capable of experiencing. More than some of them, no doubt.

When Cesar got to work that night, he went right to the lab where Manny was kept, even though he usually didn't get there until later in his shift. Manny sat in the corner, the back of his head against the wall. He stared up at the ceiling. And he looked different, darker or… bigger?

"Hey, buddy."

Manny turned his head and looked at Cesar. His lip twitched into a snarl.

"Manny, come over here, it's all right."

Manny roared and took a halting step forward. He tilted his head, shook it, and slowly made the sign for friend.

"That's right! Manny's friend, yeah, like always." Cesar reached his hand up, his fingers just poking through the door, trembling. Manny stepped forward and leaned his furry forehead against them. "That's good, little man."

Manny signed *candy, red*, but Cesar said, "Okay, but just one piece until we see if you're going to get sick." Looking into those gorilla eyes that seemed to have more caring and life in them that Lindstrom's or Rico's, Cesar doubted all the candy in the world could be the problem. The problem was whatever hellish experiments they ran in this place. That fucking deformed, huge fish in the other room stood as evidence to that.

He scratched Manny's forehead while Manny chewed the candy with so little enthusiasm, it broke Cesar's heart. What could he do but be Manny's friend? "Friends 'til the end, buddy," he whispered. The end. That might not be far off for Manny, thanks to that fucking doctor.

Manny groaned. His eyes closed. Cesar stepped to the side in case Manny was about to throw up again, but he kept rubbing the poor gorilla's head.

And he felt Manny's forehead *move* under his fingers. It *shifted*. Manny's eyes snapped open and he looked at Cesar in what he'd have sworn was pleading, *please…* Manny hit the side of his own head with his fist, grunting.

"Don't hit yourself, don't. You hurting?" Cesar rubbed his forehead a little harder, hoping to help, and he felt it again, as if the bones under the flesh were spreading out. "*Jesus H.*"

Manny threw his head back and howled. Cesar jumped back as Manny hurled himself against the door, growling like a rabid animal. *Or a madman*, Cesar thought. The door gave each time Manny slammed against it, something that shouldn't happen so easily, not with steel. Manny stopped, panting and groaning, and looked at Cesar again with those same pleading eyes, even though his teeth were bared.

Those eyes did Cesar in. What the fuck was this, keeping this animal in a cage, an animal that had never hurt anyone and just wanted to be loved? How was that right? Nature was cruel, he knew, but these men were worse. What if Manny did get out? He probably couldn't survive on his own, but Cesar could help him. How different could the Mexican jungle be from the African one? At least he'd have a fighting chance, and they couldn't hurt him this way anymore.

Cesar stepped back up to the door. "You're a good little man," he said, making the sign for friend. He slipped his fingers through the openings and pulled as hard as he could, throwing his own body backward in an attempt to help. Manny grunted and threw himself forward again and again. When the door finally gave Cesar was thrown back and slammed into the edge of a stainless steel table. The side of his face burned from contact with the edge of the door. He reached up and felt blood.

Manny loomed over him, teeth bared, but still with those pleading eyes. Cesar had never been this close to him before; metal always separated them. Manny reached down and grabbed Cesar's arm and the front of his blue, lab-issue jumpsuit, sending Cesar's heart tripping while he was lifted to his feet. Manny grunted a few times, banged his chest with a meaty fist and then brushed the fist downward. *Sorry, sorry.*

Cesar smiled and touched Manny's shoulder. "All right." He laughed a little and then had to wipe his eyes when Manny leaned down and pressed their foreheads together, his hands making the sign for friend between them. "Yeah, we'll always be friends, little man. God, I hope I'm doing the right thing. You've gotta know, I'm trying."

He half-expected a horde of white-coats to come rushing in because the cage door was opened without a key. That he heard nothing, no phone rang and no one was there with a tranquilizer gun, was a good sign.

"No alarm on your door, Manny," he said, straightening and rubbing his throbbing lower back. "That was poor fucking planning, huh?"

Planning. He couldn't lose this job. As much as he reviled the place and what they did, he had bills to pay. If he was on that camera opening the door for Manny to get out of the lab, he might even be arrested, forget just being unemployed.

"Let's hope this plan's better, buddy." He tried to impress it upon Manny, who sometimes still pounded his own head as if to stop whatever pain was tormenting him, to stay where he was. He used hand gestures and stepped away from him slowly. "Stay there until I give you the signal. You have no idea what the fuck I'm saying. But just stay, Manny." He stared into Manny's eyes, hoping whatever connection they had somehow made him understand.

Manny stayed in place while Cesar backed all the way to the door, hands in front of himself. Cesar thought it would look pretty good on the tape, him backing up as if he were terrified, trying to get out. He kept facing Manny even while he inserted the little card that disengaged the lock. He opened the door, backed up until he was in the doorway, then said, "Manny,

Manny!" waving his hands as if he were startled or scared to death while he really meant to signal Manny to come.

Manny raced toward him. Cesar pretended he was in a cartoon where the character's so scared he runs in place for a minute before actually being able to move. He knew Lindstrom already thought he was little more than Mexican trash, couldn't write proper English, sometimes didn't speak that well, probably a dope fiend. Hopefully, he also wouldn't expect Cesar to be particularly smart or brave when being charged by an angry-looking gorilla that appeared to be five or six times his weight, though up-close he now seemed even more than that.

As soon as Manny reached him, Cesar put his hands on Manny's arms as if he were trying to hold him back or push away, when he was really pulling, encouraging him through the door. God, he hoped it looked legit. And he hoped the cameras were video only. If not… it was too late to turn back now.

Cesar ran, leading Manny through the halls, hoping Manny stayed behind him like they were playing. If the gorilla got in front of him, it would look damn suspicious if Cesar didn't run the other direction. The other custodial staff would be spread into the other wings—he hoped they were where they should be, just this once.

The outer door—how was he going to get Manny through that without giving himself away? He stopped at the door and turned, his arms splayed against it as if he now might fear for his life. Manny roared and charged as Cesar slid to the side. Manny punched the panel by the handle, pounded it until his blood smeared the dented metal and the light went out. An alarm sounded then, and Manny swung his arms, his scream close to a man's, Cesar thought. Manny slammed himself against the door, bending the thick steel, buckling it, over and over again until finally it gave. Once on the other side, Manny stopped and looked back at Cesar. *Friend.*

Those pleading eyes. Cesar hadn't thought this far ahead. "Go. Hide, Manny, hide in the trees. I'll find you." He held his hands up and made a pushing movement. "Go, go!" He backed away as he did it, hoping to look scared on the camera, and hoping Manny understood. Manny roared, and ran.

* * *

"What the *fuck*?"

In all the times Cesar had seen Lindstrom upset, he'd never heard him carry on like he'd been doing for the last half an hour. He'd seen the security tapes, and Cesar knew the man hated that he hadn't sacrificed his own safety for the good of the work that was being done here. Contempt dripped from every look the doctor gave him. As long as he didn't lose his job, he didn't give a shit what this man thought.

Men had already been sent in search of Manny. And now Lindstrom and Cesar were alone in a small office, with Cesar in an uncomfortable metal chair and Lindstrom pacing, his hands clenched behind his back.

"Tell me again what happened."

For the fifth time, Cesar told him.

"Do you have any idea what all of this means? That he's loose out there? If we're lucky he'll get caught in some sort of trap and die, or he'll come back because he's hungry. But I probably couldn't *get* that lucky. What if he kills someone, and they have to put him down? They'll examine him for disease if he even just bites someone. I still don't understand how you didn't have time to alert anyone."

"Dr. Lindstrom, Manny wouldn't hurt anybody. He's not like that."

Lindstrom laughed. "I feel much better hearing that from you, an expert on gorilla behavior."

"I mean it. He's gentle."

"And gentle creatures often slam themselves against doors until they burst open?"

"He's gentle with people."

Lindstrom mumbled, and what Cesar thought he said chilled him.

"What do you mean, not for long?"

Lindstrom tapped his chin with his finger. "Come with me." Lindstrom led Cesar outside, hand in between Cesar's shoulder blades. The doctor looked around, then leaned toward him.

"Let me explain something to you, Mr. Ruiz. I need your help. I know you have a special way with the ape. I know you like him. I need you to help me get him back. If you go and start calling for him, perhaps he'll come to you. You don't want him to die out there, do you? I don't. I've spent too much time on this project. He can't be found by anyone else. And he *is* dangerous, now. You saw that he was bigger… you had to. It was clear to me on the tape."

Cesar walked slower, not liking the way Lindstrom's hand pushed against his back. He nodded. *Felt it, too. I felt it, you fucker.*

"My formula should be enhancing many things about him. His size, his intelligence, his strength—we've seen evidence of that already—and perhaps things like his… hunger. His general behavior, his instincts. I just don't know how that might manifest in the wild."

"I can't believe he'd hurt anybody."

"It's more than that, dammit!" Lindstrom stopped. "Look, I'll be clear with you, Mr. Ruiz. The experiments I've been running on Manny aren't exactly what the government had in mind. They're bolder, broader—government bureaucrats are small-minded, and I'm chasing greatness. Do you understand me? If he's found by animal control, poachers, anyone but my people, and they test his blood or tissue, let's just say that would be bad. I can't let that happen."

He smiled at Cesar then, and Cesar wished he'd stop it and never do it again.

"Neither can you, because if you don't help me you're finished. Your record will list the reason as drug use and violence toward a coworker. Or how about fucking the test animals? Who'll hire you with something like that in your record? And if you ever try to tell anyone about this conversation, I'll see to it that your record makes it clear you're not a man to be believed. Do we understand each other?"

Cesar took a few deep breaths. "Yes, sir."

"Then why don't you venture out just a little ways and see if you can get that Goddamn ape to come back."

He shoved Cesar hard enough that he almost fell. Cesar walked deeper into the jungle, felt warm blood in his hand where he'd dug a fingernail in as he made a fist and thought about plowing Lindstrom and running, not caring about the consequences. His back and face throbbed, and punching that fucker probably would have helped. But he couldn't. He'd shout for Manny half-heartedly a few times and hope he didn't show, or if he did, that he could see Cesar's face and know not to come.

He hadn't gone very far when foliage rustled ahead of him.

"Manny?" he whispered. A grunt came back.

"Run, Manny—*run*," he hissed. But Manny appeared out of the growth, shocking Cesar with his size. He looked unreal, like something out of a nightmare. Cesar could have sworn he was at least fifty feet tall. The huge ape signed *friend*.

Cesar heard shouts behind him, held his hands up toward Manny as the ape snarled and growled. Cesar turned to see several soldiers, weapons raised, shouting at one other to hold, *hold!* Manny charged, roaring.

Weapons popped—Jesus Christ, they used *grenades*—blocking out all other sounds. Cesar couldn't even hear his own screams, begging them to stop. The flashes and explosions overwhelmed him, but he ran in their direction to get to Manny.

The air shook with one large explosion, throwing Cesar down. He looked up in time to see Manny fall.

* * *

Cesar headed for Lindstrom when he'd composed himself enough to stand, but a couple of the soldiers held him back.

"You said you needed him! You didn't want him to die!" He kicked and struggled to get free.

Lindstrom shook his head. "I already have all the data I need. My serum works. The ape proves that. He'd grown too big, too dangerous. And I will admit a mistake in all this—I had no idea it would take full effect this fast. I thought I had time to gradually measure the progress. He's become a liability, Mr. Ruiz. Are you? You should think about that."

Lindstrom nodded and they started dragging Cesar back toward the compound. He heard Lindstrom order Manny's body burned after he took some samples. Cesar wept. "I'm so sorry, little man, oh my God."

Lindstrom kept him in an office for a long time, and Cesar started to wonder if they were going to take him somewhere and shoot him, claiming he knew too much. Which he did. But what good would it do him to tell someone? First, he might not be believed, and Lindstrom would ruin his reputation. Second, he might be believed. And Lindstrom would still ruin his reputation. Lindstrom was an educated American—he had the advantage in every way. That was probably the only reason Lindstrom let him go with a few more warnings. He knew Cesar was no real threat.

I'll find another job, he told himself. It would be okay.

He couldn't return night after night to clean Manny's old lab anyway. That would hurt too much. Christ, what had he done?

* * *

Cesar left, tears starting again at the idea that he'd never be coming back to see Manny, never talk to him again or scratch his head. He'd only gotten a few minutes away on the ATV when he decided he couldn't go just like that. He had to go back, back to where Manny died, and pay his respects. Mourn. Apologize. *Something.*

He rode in the other direction for a while, longer than he thought he should have. A burned smell in the air told him it was nearby, so why couldn't he find it? He drove into a little dirt clearing that seemed familiar and stopped, trying to figure out which direction to go. He sniffed and looked down for the source of the smell.

"Oh, Manny." What had looked like a mud spot now appeared to be a blood-soaked spot of earth. Manny's blood. Had they moved him to burn him? There was no way that many men could have dragged him. More spots led out of the clearing. He cut the engine and followed the trail. At the edge of the clearing, he pushed aside a leafy bush.

A leg sat in a dark puddle: a man's leg, torn mid-thigh. He lurched away and the leaves snapped back into place. Cesar tried to catch a breath but it felt like his throat was the size of a straw. He looked to the right. A hand stuck out of a patch of grass. Movement behind him. A growl.

Cesar turned, air finally filling his lungs. "Oh Jesus, Manny, oh Jesus!"

Manny, half his face and chest melted, fur scorched away in places, a chunk gone from his side and one of his legs, held a man in one mammoth hand. The man didn't scream, so Cesar knew he was dead. Manny's one eye was no longer black and soulful, but lighter. A thin, white film covered it now. Gore ran from gunshots and larger wounds in Manny's chest, his face, his legs.

Manny dropped the body with a thud and hooked his fingers together.

Cesar sobbed. "Friend, Manny's friend, oh *Jesus*." He signed back, his hands shaking so much he could barely make his fingers meet.

Manny signed again. *Candy, eat, candy.*

Cesar reached into his pocket and struggled to unwrap a caramel, his arms, his whole body shaking as much as his hands. Then he unwrapped the other three in his pocket. Manny reached down and Cesar dumped them into the huge, black— *bloody*—palm.

Manny tilted his head back and dropped the candies into his mouth, but then shook his head, groaning. *Candy, candy, eat, want, candy, red, red, red.*

Manny scooped the body from the ground—the broken, bloody, dead body he'd dropped—and bit into it, chewed, bobbed his head.

Cesar's throat was starting to tighten again. Candy. *Red.*

Oh God.

Cesar backed up until he hit a tree, shaking his head. No, not sweet, gentle Manny. This wasn't right; it wasn't *fair.* Lindstrom had turned Manny into some kind of monster. He remembered Lindstrom's words—size, strength, intelligence. The motherfucker never said anything about bringing Manny back from the Goddamned dead.

Or making him eat *people*.

The book he'd read said gorillas ate plants, fruits and vege-tables. They were herbi-something, which meant they didn't eat meat. Cesar was supposed to be sneaking his live, fugitive friend bananas and nuts and corn on the cob and caramels, not watch-ing his half-burned, dead, little man chew up one of the bas-tards who'd shot him.

The hulking gorilla dropped to the ground on his side with a thud, his massive head in front of Cesar. *Friend.*

Jesus, that eye, that wrong, milky eye. Cesar reached out and patted Manny's forehead, groaning as his hand slipped into a wound. "Friend, little man… we'll always be friends."

Manny rose after a few minutes and stood still, leaning, mak-ing no other movement. Like during so much of their relation-ship, unspoken sentiments seemed to pass between them. "See you later, Manny. See—see you tonight," he said, as he always did, and that seemed to satisfy Manny. He disappeared into the jungle.

Shaking, Cesar headed back, stopping once to vomit before he reached the compound. Once there, he didn't go to the camp. Instead, he went around it and kept going until he recog-nized the landscape, then hid the ATV in the underbrush. He found his way to the bus and rode home as usual, not quite sure how he managed it all.

Once home, he collapsed into an exhausted sleep filled with dreams of feeding candy to half-eaten soldiers' corpses and scratching Manny's head, the flesh squishing beneath his fingers and falling away.

* * *

He woke late, only a few hours before the sun came up, grabbed a flashlight and rushed out, cursing that it would be almost daybreak by the time he got back. He argued with him-self the whole time, his own fear warring with his feelings of responsibility toward Manny. He'd helped him escape—this was as much his doing as anyone's. If he hadn't helped, Manny might not have gotten out and gotten away before someone discovered him in the hall and called for help.

But if they'd recaptured him, would they have killed him? And would he have come back anyway?

It was a tight damn knot he couldn't unravel. What was done, was done. And he'd told Manny they'd be friends until the end. No matter what, he'd meant that.

The bus ride took forever, but once he was on foot he raced, hating the thought that Manny might think Cesar had abandoned him. He found the ATV and went as fast as he dared, then parked it in some dense brush not far from the clearing. Would Manny even be here, waiting? How long could a 50-foot gorilla hide in the jungle? How long before he wandered out into plain view? Manny was smart, but he was also *wrong* now. Cesar didn't know what to expect, but he sure as hell hadn't expected Lindstrom to be waiting for him, pistol in one hand, dim flashlight in the other. The morning was getting light enough to see now; Cesar had left his light at the ATV. Cesar wondered if the doctor had been out here with the flashlight all night.

Manny surely would have noticed him, if so. But maybe… maybe he truly understood how to hide. Maybe the soldiers died because they were hurting him, and he only hid from Lindstrom to avoid being hurt, as usual? He just didn't know.

"Disturbances today, Ruiz. The soldiers never came back, and I think you're responsible for that. At least… in part. Sounds, people seeing things… and no big, burned carcass for me to sample from for follow-up testing. I wanted to see how the tissue broke down, if it burned the same as gorilla flesh that hadn't been treated with my serum. Yet I have no body. Isn't that interesting?"

Lindstrom's normally flawless hair looked puffy, greasy instead of carefully slicked. One strand hung down over his forehead. "Let's you and I have a chat while we walk," he said. He motioned with the pistol, so Cesar started walking. And thinking.

"You might shoot me, you son of a bitch," he said, getting a rush from finally telling Lindstrom what he thought of him, "but that little pea-popper won't do you a bit of good if we find Manny."

Lindstrom laughed. "It worked, oh my God, it worked! So he *is* out there. And you've seen him, you've come *back* to see him… you may be the key to our ability to control the resurrected. That's the only part of the process I haven't figured out; I don't know how to control the soldiers once we bring them back. The size and strength were easy. Aggression, anger, hunger… getting them to devour the enemy, not much of a challenge. But we can't have them killing the wrong side, can we? Be glad you're still useful or *your* burned carcass would be out here, and here it would stay."

Soldiers… my God, he wanted to do this to *men*. Cesar wanted to tell him that if he shot him right now, it wouldn't be a terrible loss. He'd hate to leave Manny wondering what happened, but it would sure solve a lot of his own problems. And he would no longer be alive to feel guilt about the rest.

Lindstrom stopped, his hand clawing into Cesar's arm. "Is that him? Hear that?"

Something lumbered through the trees, snapping limbs. Animals squealed, chattered and flapped, clearly agitated. The dense growth before them parted and the smell hit Cesar, triggering his gag reflex. "It's him," Cesar said. "Oh, Manny… *Manny*." The rot was obvious and so much worse than before. Cesar wanted to bawl at the sight of Manny's eye, now a sick white-yellow where once shiny black and *alive* and *smart* and *gentle* had been.

Lindstrom stepped forward, something like devotion or awe on his face. Cesar chopped his wrist, knocking the gun away. Lindstrom pushed him down and looked back at Manny. "I did it—I did *this*. I made you, brought you back!" He laughed, but as Manny growled, his giant, darkened teeth showing in the growing brightness, Lindstrom's laughed choked off. He stepped backward, stumbling a little over Cesar's foot but not falling.

Cesar looked from Lindstrom to Manny and knew what was happening. Manny's growl grew into a roar. Cesar could push Lindstrom, tell him to run, distract Manny so the man could get away.

But why should he?

Giggling, Cesar stood next to Lindstrom who quickly got behind him, grabbed his arms and started trying to back up. "Tell him no, Ruiz! Make him behave—we won't hurt him, tell him, *tell him!*"

"All right, calm down," he said, giggling again, a manic sound that threatened to snap what was left of his reason. "Hey buddy, hey little man," he shouted waving his arms. Manny stopped roaring, tilted his head.

"Manny's friend," he said, hooking his fingers together. Manny touched his knuckles together, not right but Cesar knew what it meant. He laughed. "That's right, buddy. Hey, Manny, want some candy?" He twisted his finger in his cheek, lifted his fingers to his mouth. "Eat candy?"

Manny bobbed his head, his poor, misshapen, mangled head, and repeated the gestures, adding a finger brushing from his sagging lip to his chin, *red, red, candy, red.*

"Yeah, buddy, candy… red. I brought you some." He rolled away from Lindstrom, shouting, "Candy, Manny. Red!"

Lindstrom barely had time to scream before he was squeezed in the huge paw, the high-pitched sound squelching to an end. Cesar closed his eyes, flinching with each wet plop of gore hitting the ground, parts of Lindstrom dropping from Manny's hand or mouth. He pressed his fists to his eyes, laughed and had a hard time stopping it, in the same way he couldn't stop throwing up mid-retch. *I'm going mad right here on the jungle floor. This is it, oh fuck.*

He opened his eyes when the ground rumbled. Manny stepped toward him, stringy remnants of Lindstrom hanging from his chin. *Eat, candy, candy, eat, want, red, red, red.*

The laugh threatened again, until Manny's sign for *eat, eat, eat* became his hand hammering his own mouth, *EAT, EAT,* no longer a request, but a desperate demand.

Manny roared and reached for Cesar who rolled, scrabbled backwards on all fours. As Manny's hand caught him, he screamed, "Friend, Manny's friend, oh *God!*" and the pressure eased. Manny withdrew his hand, tilted his head, signed *candy, red,* and a knuckle touch that had become his sign for *friend.* Cesar waited, hoped, almost begged, but Manny never signed *sorry.*

"Friend, Manny, friend… I'll bring you… more candy. Just like I always have. Just like always."

Rico. He could lure Rico out here. That fucking bastard, this would be a right end for him. Tourists that might not be noticed right away. No, *no,* what was he thinking? He couldn't… he'd find drug dealers, pimps… promise them big paydays if they'd come out here for the score. Shouldn't be that hard. Most were the ones everyone else was scared of. They wouldn't see Cesar as a threat. And what kind of lives did they have anyway? They hurt people all the time. He could bring them here… but already Manny didn't seem easily satisfied. Lindstrom had said strength, hunger, size. What if he kept growing, kept wanting more?

Cesar knew a man who took money from people, transported them in the back of a produce truck across the border, and handed them off to another man who demanded more money from them before he'd let them go. A few had money sent from family for their freedom. Most had already spent everything to get there. Cesar didn't know what happened to them—he'd never wanted to ask. He couldn't stop the cruelty that went on in the world just by knowing about it, anymore than he could have stopped it in the lab or in nature. Maybe… maybe he could pay the man a little extra to take a detour…

"Jesus!" he cried out. What was he thinking, what was he doing? He'd gone from Lindstrom to imagining mass murders in the space of five minutes. But he was responsible for Manny. He was Manny's friend. He signed *friend,* but Manny only pressed his hands together now, a pale imitation of the gesture he'd known so well. The pressure caused a chunk of black flesh to burst and drop from the gorilla's finger.

"God, oh God." Cesar wept, his breath hitching. "I'll get you some candy, buddy, good red candy," he blubbered out, wiping tears and snot from his face with his sleeve, gagging at the smell on his clothes from Manny's hand. Christ, he'd left himself no choice. He couldn't abandon his friend now—wouldn't.

Anything could happen while he was away. Manny could be discovered, he could die from whatever they'd done to him, he could go on a rampage in a populated area and be all over the news. Cesar couldn't help that, couldn't stop it.

But if those things didn't happen—and Cesar sensed they wouldn't, but that Manny would wait for him as always, at least for a while—then the day would come when Cesar would die in this jungle. He knew it now as sure as he knew anything. Maybe a fitting end, he thought, for having a hand in this. One day, what he brought Manny wouldn't be enough and his friend would turn on him again, but this time he wouldn't stop. And when that day came, Cesar would try to understand that Manny didn't have a choice, any more than he did. Nature was cruel, but Cesar would be kind until the end, Manny's friend the whole way through, just like he'd promised.

DAVID NIALL WILSON
In Today's News...
(Meanwhile in Suburbia, Part One)

"Herman, would you take out the trash?"

The voice cut through the twenty pages of the daily paper and the silence of the kitchen like a well-honed blade. Herman Hislop had only two or three actual joys in life, and two of them were morning coffee and the paper. That knowledge in hand, Greta set out daily to deny them.

"In a bit," he said, knowing it was pointless. "I'm reading the paper. Did you hear about the new mall out near Lavender?"

"Just what we need… another place for gangs to hang out and people to waste their money. The trash men will be here soon. Can't you take it now? You know if you wait, it will be too late, and we can't go another week without…"

"Blah, blah, blah." Herman had heard it so many times he could have recited it like the litany. She ground her words through his concentration, banging the pots in the sink for emphasis.

If he took the trash to the curb, settled the can where it could be picked up, and came back, he would find that she'd poured out his coffee and the paper would be nowhere to be seen. She would tell him the coffee had gotten cold and bitter, and that she'd cleared the table for whatever craft project she had in mind for the day. More likely, he thought, she'd have one of a number of local delivery and repairmen in the minute he left for work, and she was trying to make the place look good for them. Never for him, of course. He was just the guy who stopped in to take out the trash and listen to her bitch. He was good at both, and that was enough for Greta.

With a sigh, Herman folded his paper carefully and placed it on the table. He took a long sip from his coffee, which, admittedly, was very good. He pushed back his chair and started to rise. As he did, the earth gave a shake, like a great shaggy dog trying to rid itself of fleas. Herman reached instinctively for the table, and his coffee. Somehow he managed to keep the latter from dropping to the floor, and as the room stilled, he gulped it down quickly, reveling in the tiny, momentary victory. He carried the cup to the sink and placed it inside.

There was a horrible grinding sound from outside, as if something heavy was being dragged.

"That's probably the garbage men," Greta said. She had hold of the counter firmly, and turned to glare at him, as if the earthquake could be his fault. Something he did to irritate her, like drinking fresh coffee and reading the paper.

Herman turned, tucked his paper defiantly under his arm, and grabbed the garbage bag Greta had placed by the door. He had barely hit the sidewalk when the second tremor nearly knocked him from his feet.

"What in the world?" he muttered. He stood his ground, and when the earth's shaking gave way once more to the loud, dragging grate, he lifted the lid on the rolling trashcan, dropped in the bag, and took the handle in hand. He started off then toward the end of the long, curving drive that led out to the street. There was no sign of the trash men, as he'd known there would not be. They never picked up before noon, as Greta was well aware.

Herman clutched the paper tightly under his arm, and with one hand managed to work the can into place beside their mailbox. He was having quite the morning. His paper was intact; he'd finished his coffee. Things were shaping up nicely. If he could just get out the door and off to work without another round of kvetching from Greta, he could actually mark the entire day in the win column.

He turned back toward the house, and he stopped. He stared. He glanced up, confused. As he watched in silence from the end of the drive, a massive foot covered in long, matted brown fur, toes tipped by broken, yellowed claws, came down firmly on the roof of his house. It landed with a sickening crunch of wood snapping, walls collapsing, and a single drawn out scream that cut off very quickly, and very suddenly. Herman stood very still.

With one foot firmly planted, the fifty foot tall gorilla slowly dragged its other foot through the Williamson's back yard, taking out their garage and their shed without slowing. The thing let out a deep, growling moan. It did not notice Herman, paper clutched to his side, and eyes wide. A couple of minutes that seemed like hours passed, and it lurched off toward the interstate, leaving a wake of screaming people, honking horns, and crushed homes in its wake.

As if in a dream, Herman walked back up the drive to his house. He stepped through the rubble that had been the outer door and into the remnant of the kitchen. The table was gone... crushed to splinters and rubble. There was a large red stain on the floor he knew must be Greta.

Unbelievably, the coffee pot was intact, standing beside the sink on the counter, which has not been touched. Greta had pulled one chair over to stand on so she could reach a high cupboard. Herman studied the chaos, and then, he smiled.

A moment later, fresh coffee on the counter, he sat back in his one remaining chair with a contented sigh. He flipped the paper open to the article on the new Lavender Mall, and he smiled. They were planning a coffee shop, and right next door––a newsstand. It was shaping up to be a very, very good day.

SIMON McCAFFERY
The Boys In Company Z

For Angela

After nightfall the jungle around us crawls with shadows and insects attack in clouds, but tonight something is wrong and everyone feels it. I slowly register the *silence* surrounding our campsite dug into the grassy hillside east of Phu Bihn Valley, illuminated dimly by red blackout lanterns. The trees and canopy above us should be alive with the screeches of birds, the rustle of hunters and the small shrill cries of prey, but I only hear the blood pulsing in my eardrums. Lieutenant Tompkins and his handpicked squad of soldiers stare into the blackness, pure coiled violence, locked and loaded.

It is August 1968. While others of my generation riot in the streets of Chicago at the Democratic Party's national conference, I am halfway around the world, realizing the sheer stupidity of volunteering to leave the Cambridge SOG labs to serve as a technical advisor in my first in-country field op. We have been hiking for three hot, uneventful days since insertion into Laos, a "cold" LZ east of Ban Muang-Èt. So far we've had zero contact with Victor Charlie or locals. Two "indigenous personnel" and seven Green Berets from the 5th Special Forces Airborne Group packing lethal firepower surround me, but this thought brings me little comfort. I am twenty-four years old, a newly minted chemical engineer. I have never fired a gun.

Something large crashes through the underbrush and staggers into the bloodshot light. SOG operatives use Soviet Block North Vietnamese Army weapons only, so Tompkins's men aren't carrying Mike One-Sixes equipped with night vision scopes. We're dressed in camouflage bearing neither American nor NVA insignias. No dog tags or other I.D. Flashlights strapped to AK-47s with electrical tape flare to life, converging on the mammoth shape blundering toward us. I hear Weller cock his Soviet RPK, a replacement for the standard M60 Hog.

"It's just a cow, you assholes," Tompkins says, his light reflected in the animal's large milky eyes.

It's a big tawny steer to be more precise, missing part of one horn. It looks precisely like the one we encountered the previous afternoon on the outskirts of the tiny nameless village we designated Agent Green-6 Test Case Number-One. The village is a known VC way station, and Tompkins's orders were to test Green-6's effectiveness on the enemy before we introduce it into the Black River, another day's trek from our current position. The Black River feeds thousands of gallons per day to NVA stationed all along the Trail through secret gravity-fed pipelines. After we dumped a canister of Green-6 into the local water supply—a gurgling serpentine creek—we crossed what passes for a small tropical pasture before melting back into the jungle. Fowler is the youngest of the Berets. His father was an Austin cattleman. He walked up to the domesticated steer, patted its broad chestnut head while it stoically chewed grass, and slit its wrinkled throat with an eight-inch sawtoothed Bowie knife. Stepping back from the gusher of blood, he'd quoted Napoleon. "An army marches on its stomach." I had had to look away, nauseated, afraid I might regurgitate my B-2 individual combat meal ration (beans with frankfurter chunks).

There's no mistake: the thing shambling into the edge of our camp is the same animal. It doesn't blink in the harsh beams of light. Its beautiful auburn coat is now a matted cape of flies. It raises its head and emits a horrible whistling bellow, baring gore-streaked teeth; the gaping sickle-shaped wound is stretched open like a giant blood-caked smile.

"What the f—" Fowler sputters, and the dead steer-thing charges into a burst of automatic fire and muzzle flash. Fowler's bullets crash into its skull and it collapses on top of the lanterns and compact camp stove.

Tompkins utters a string of profanity and orders Fowler to cease firing. The echoes of Fowler's gunfire roll away across the valley before being absorbed by the muggy night air.

Silence. Darkness, except for the bobbing spooklights.

Fowler stalks over to the steer's crumpled tent-pole body, prods its hide with the muzzle of his rifle. The body releases a belch of gas. The stench of raw rotted beef makes me slap a hand over my nose and mouth.

"Okay, which one of you fuckers put LSD in my canteen, because I *killed* this bag of meat deader than shit five klicks from here—"

Fowler doesn't finish. Something titanic steps out of the jungle, reaches down and lifts him high into the sultry air. One of the Berets screams. I glimpse an impossible black-haired nightmare face and hell-fired eyes.

Fowler shrieks once and I hear a wet crunching sound.

The attack commences.

* * *

In 1962, at a time when most Americans couldn't locate Vietnam on a map, President John F. Kennedy approved Operation Ranch Hand. This covert operation involved the airborne spraying of chemicals in an attempt to destroy the hiding places of the National Liberation Front. In 1969 alone, Operation Ranch Hand erased over a million hectares of forest and a few thousand civilians who dwelled in or near those forests. The chemical used in this defoliation program, Agent Orange, also caused chromosomal damage in survivors. Between 1962 and 1969, 700,000 agricultural acres were sprayed with another chemical called Agent Blue—a mixture of two arsenic-containing compounds, sodium cacodylate and cacodylic acid. The objective was to deny food to the NVA and NLF. But the civilian population suffered most from disastrous rice harvests that followed the spraying.

In 1963, a frustrated Kennedy asked the Pentagon to mount subversive operations against North Vietnam—a job he felt the CIA had been bungling in the same manner as their farcical attempts to unseat a certain vociferous Cuban dictator. JFK didn't live to see the fruits of his decision.

After his assassination Johnson ordered the Pentagon to form the Military Assistance Command Vietnam's Studies and Observation Group (MACV-SOG, often shortened to SOG, or to those who participated in its covert atrocities and mud-caked fiascos, SLOG). SOG ran America's covert war against Hanoi and the North from January 1964 until April 1972. Congressional oversight committees were told that SOG's mission was to rescue downed airmen, transport captured enemy prisoners, and conduct supply runs throughout Southeast Asia. The real mission was a long series of clandestine operations inside Laos and Cambodia to disrupt activity along the Ho Chi Minh Trail. Nothing was off-limits. SOG opened Pandora's Box, employing illegal and experimental warfare tactics throughout the region. They practically invented psywar—psychological warfare and the use of POW double-agents and captured civilians. They staged commando black-ops raids, not discriminating between military and noncombatant targets. They managed the insertion and running of spies and fabricated guerrilla resistance. They planted radio-equipped seismic sensors along the trail and flew cloud-seeding missions in the upper atmosphere to extend the monsoon season, hoping to drown Charlie inside his elaborate network of tunnels. They employed newly in-vogue "remote viewing" psychics to sit in small barracks rooms and visualize underground enemy movements and map the nightmare world beneath Cu Chi. And when aerosol rainbow herbicides like Agents Orange, Green and Blue didn't force a withdrawal, SOG command authorized the use of ground-water biologicals like Agent Green 6.

Many of SLOG's diabolical schemes fizzled like cheap Chinese fireworks, but not all of them. Over 3,500 pages of MACV-SOG's operational records were finally released in 1995, but all mention of Green-6 and the incident at Phu Bihn Valley was redacted.

Which is where I come into the story. My name is David Harris, MIT Class of '67, double major in biochemistry and chemical engineering. After graduation I was recruited by my master's advisor, a tenured professor who it turns out was consulting for the CIA. Don't forget that the CIA founded the infamous Massachusetts Institute of Technology Center for International Studies in 1950 and by the mid sixties was funneling millions of dollars into pre-DARPA weapons research programs. I was weary of my grueling academic life, and the thought of beginning a doctoral program made my head swim. I had worshiped JFK and wanted to do something important for my country.

By the fall I was supervising my own lab in an anonymous Brookline Street warehouse in Cambridge, lavishly funded by—you guessed it—SLOG.

* * *

Everything happens very quickly. At some point in the melee I turn to run and feel myself lofted into the air like a ragdoll, my stomach and sanity falling away. My head snaps back and I see an ocean of sharp stars stitched by white-hot tracers from Weller's RPK. Something in my left shoulder pops like a champagne cork. Something inhuman that smells a million times worse than the reanimated steer howls in ear-splitting pain and I pinwheel down and down into the thick elephant grass.

Then Tompkins is shaking me, turning me over. I feel wetness but it isn't blood, and I blush with shame like a first-grader.

Tompkins helps me sit up and I yelp with pain.

"Your shoulder's dislocated," he says.

He fixes that and I screech.

"Shut up," he hisses.

Tompkins pulls me to my feet and I stare at the destroyed campsite. All of our tents and equipment, including the communications gear, have been *flattened*. The three remaining canisters of Green-6 are scattered thirty yards away, ruptured, their deadly cargo spilling out into the soil.

"Where are the others?" My ears are ringing and it is hard to form sentences.

"Gone."

Underneath the Jackson-Pollock spattering of blood Tompkins looks gray with shock, but he is methodically gathering up ammo and weapons.

Tompkins hands me an AK-47 with a fresh banana clip. The stock is slick with human claret.

"Hurry up, Harris. Let's move out."

"Move out where?"

"They're not all dead." He's suddenly in my face, roaring. "My *MEN. THEY'RE NOT ALL DEAD*. Those things took them and we're going to *get* them."

"Who took them?" I say stupidly.

"The giant apes," Tompkins says. He stares at me with scorn.

Of course I saw exactly what he saw, but I find myself, an earnest young Man of Science, denying it again and again, like Simon Peter. Had the apostle pissed *his* pants when the Romans came for him?

It dawns on me that there are no bodies lying among the debris—man or monster. Including the carcass of the twice-dead steer.

* * *

Years later I understand that they weren't monsters. At least, not until we slipped them an Agent Green-6 mickey.

In 1935 a Dutch paleontologist with the tongue-tying name of Dr. Gustav Heinrich Ralph von Koenigswald purchased a yellowed molar among the "dragon bones" for sale in long wooden boxes in a Hong Kong pharmacy. For centuries Chinese medicine men had used the dragon bones—fossil bones and teeth—to create arcane powders with curative powers. Von Koenigswald had discovered the tooth of *Gigantopithecus blackii*, a ten-foot, 1,200-pound uber-gorilla that lived alongside both *H. erectus* and *H. sapiens* 100,000 years ago in southern China, Dhok Pathan in Pakistan and in limestone caves such as Tham Khuyen throughout Vietnam and Laos. "Black's Giant Gorilla." Over the years, intrigued scientists pieced together a description of these fearsome animals using nothing more than a set of jawbones and handful of very large teeth. Then in 1983 paleontologists unearthed a partial skeleton in the Sichuan provinces, and announced the discovery of a second primate species of even larger dimensions. Its height was estimated at fifteen to eighteen feet, drawing the predictable comparisons to a certain iconic Hollywood lovelorn ape. The team's claim was widely refuted and shots were fired back and forth in academic journals for the next twenty-five years.

These massive cousins of *Gigantopithecus* were undoubtedly the creatures we encountered in the vast Phu Bihn Valley on the way to Son La and the Black River (dammed to form the Ho Song Da reservoir decades later), where the Vietcong's buried pipeline delivered live preserving water to the deprived, half-starved troops living above and below the Ho Chi Minh Trail. Anthropologists later speculated that the giant primate's extinction was hastened by competition with pandas for their staple diet—bamboo—or perhaps it was their inability to compete with the more nimble-minded, tool-bearing human tribes once they began venturing beyond their traditional river valley dwellings and invaded the higher elevation jungles.

Located in the heart of the Phu Bihn Valley is another cave complex more vast than Tham Khuyen. These freakishly overgrown gorillas probably migrated south thousands of years ago after bamboo became depleted, abandoning their subterranean kingdoms and the rounded limestone towers at Liucheng. Perhaps they were driven there by bands of fire-wielding tribesmen. Perhaps the dense jungle and mineral-rich peaks around Phu Bihn reminded them of their ancestral Chinese home.

Clearly, Green-6's secondary effect on fatally disrupted mammalian central and peripheral nervous systems and neurotransmitters was wholly unintended. *Night of The Living Dead* wouldn't be unleashed upon drive-in movie viewers at home for another two months, so I had no reference point for what I had witnessed.

Unfortunately for us, *Gigantopithecus*'s larger cousins were not *entirely* extinct by the mid twentieth century, they *were* tool-bearing gorillas, and Tompkins and I were *not* the first modern men to discover their lair.

There were giants in the Earth after all, and thanks to SLOG they now felt an insatiable new hunger.

* * *

"You're making too much noise," Tompkins tells me for the second time as we track the creatures across the grass-covered valley. Like their NVA counterparts, the Green Berets move silently across the most treacherous terrain the trail offers, but I'm stumbling along like a scarecrow. The third time I trip and go down on my face with a grunt, Tompkins pulls me up by my soiled camo-jacket like a kitten.

"Get your shit together, college-boy. If you alert them, I'll let *them* pull your arms off."

We move on. The motto of the Special Forces is *De oppresso liber* (Latin: To Liberate the Oppressed). In the pit of my shaken, snow-globe stomach I feel we are on a forced march to liberate the dead and digested, but I cannot bring myself to tell Tompkins this for fear of what he might do. Under a three-quarters-full moon we don't need our two missing native trackers to follow the trail of crushed foliage, which is initially puzzling. A troop of giant gorillas would have long ago learned how to remain under the radar and not leave obvious trails crisscrossing the countryside.

We see the bodies of many birds of all sizes. Pigeons, swifts, owls, ducks, plover, and a large beautiful falcon. All stone dead. Apparently Green-6 has a different effect on avian species versus mammal.

We keep walking. A lone brown fox-like dog—a dhole—launches itself from the underbrush and Tompkins kills it with his boot heel.

"Just what in the *hell* was in the shit we dumped into the water?"

I say nothing, head down, miserable.

Exhaustion sets in. I try not to think of my warm apartment on the cheaper, rundown side of Beacon Hill, or Bethany, the long-legged girl I am dating. I concentrate on placing one boot in front of the other as quietly as possible.

Four klicks later we are ascending the far side of a deep ravine when Tompkins shoves me to the grass, knocking the wind out of my lungs. Despite my fatigue I'm furious and start to squirm and holler, but his hand clamps across my mouth. It stinks of sweat and the grease used to pack automatic rifles. He motions for me to be silent.

We huddle there for several minutes, and then I hear it—a soft whistling sound on the breeze. We can hear it because we have again entered a sphere of deathly silence. My heart begins kicking inside my ribcage.

Tompkins scrambles forward, motioning for me to follow. Ahead the ink-black doorway to hell awaits, the thick vines and foliage that normally obscure the cave's entrance carelessly pushed askew. Its damp abyssal breath flows over us, and my panic spikes. Like the mainly Hispanic grunts asked to assume tunnel-rat duty beneath Cu Chi, I cannot go in there, even if means Tompkins will slice my throat open like the steer. Dawn cannot be more than an hour or so away. I try to frame an argument in my mind that we should turn back and hike to the next village to call for reinforcements (like they will have a payphone). At a minimum we should wait until daybreak—

Tompkins unsheathes his serrated pig-sticker and cuts a ten-yard section of climbing cord from his pack. He ties one end around my waist and the other end to his belt.

"In case you slip or we get separated," he says. He grips my lower jaw where the nerve endings sing, fixing me with wild eyes that reflect moonlight against his grim, black-streaked face. "Try to stay right behind me."

Shaking but helpless, I shuffle forward into the creatures' lair.

As a kid I read all the Tarzan novels, and the pulpy adventures penned by H. Rider Haggard—tales of swarthy swashbucklers exploring caves filled with diamonds, ivory and gold. One look at the cavern system we are entering would have convinced Allan Quatermain and Captain John Good to punch out and beat a hasty retreat.

We half walk, half slide down a wide sloping incline covered in mud and leaves. Tompkins clicks on a small penlight with a red lens and plays it ahead as we carefully descend. After thirty yards we arrive on a broad ledge overlooking a larger cavity. Tompkins crawls to the edge and briefly shines his light below.

He crawls back and shakes his head—no creatures in sight.

We take a descending passage to the right, red lamp trained low, following the enormous gritty footprints. The air grows chilly and moisture drips down.

On the floor of the first chamber Tompkins shines his light skyward, illuminating a sizeable open space, the ceiling black with roosting bats sated from a night's feeding. We trudge into a cul-de-sac, than backtrack through a shallow, freezing stream and find a high-ceiling passage leading downward. No more muddy footprints are visible on the other side.

We descend through several cavities until we arrive inside an otherworldly cathedral vault filled with massive convoluted columns rising up to meet dangling rock formations seventy feet above our heads. A geologist's fantasy of flowstones, stalactites, stalagmites, soda straws, and helictites fill the chamber. Our breath clouds in the freezing air. I feel like a field mouse standing inside a giant Tyrannosaur's fleshless dagger-toothed jaws.

A muffled noise ahead from the next chamber. Tompkins clicks off his light and we crouch in the clammy blackness, waiting, not daring to breathe.

A hammering sound, and a muffled cry of pain.

Tompkins turns around and clicks on his penlight. His fearsome scarlet face floats briefly in the gloom, as if he is about to deliver the world's most terrifying campfire story.

"This is it," he says, his lips hardly moving. "They're up ahead. Make sure your rifle's safety is off and whatever you do, don't fucking shoot the men or me. If you panic and try to run, I'll leave you here and you'll never find your way out alive. Got it?"

I nod, my heart trip-hammering. In a second it will stutter out of rhythm and stop.

"When I give the signal, switch on the light under your barrel. Hopefully that will startle them long enough."

Long enough for what? I wonder.

Tompkins unties the climbing rope and stows it. We creep forward and round the corner. Tompkins whispers *"Now!"* and we fire up the lights strapped to our Kalashnikovs.

In traditional tales of the macabre, the author, if he or she is worth a damn, never fully reveals the monster. The more you *don't* see—the more your cranked-up imagination is forced to fill in drawing from its own reserve of childhood terrors—the better. But I wasn't spared the sight of them, so why should you?

What I see when we round the gigantic cone of slippery textured rock is a thousand times worse than any shaggy Lon Chaney Jr. Universal Studios creature or jerky Willis O'Brien animation.

There are five of them, hunched in a rough circle around a mammoth shelf of rock. They turn slowly to look at the sudden source of illumination and I see that they all wear the same vacuous avid expression as the butchered steer. Their cavern nightworld is obviously fed by tributaries of the same stream we laced with enough Green-6 to dose the population of a good-sized town.

In the moment before their roars ricochet off the wet limestone walls I gather some quick impressions. They are at least forty feet tall, with a gorilla's thick raven pelt, massive torso and large conical skull. I note the deep-socketed eyes—now soulless—and protruding jaws lined with powerful square teeth designed for chewing tough vegetation. Now those wide wrinkled vegetarian faces are smeared with gore and shreds of flesh and bone.

The stone buffet is littered with human and bovine body parts and bits of uniforms. One of the giant gorillas hoists one of Tompkins's wounded men from a nearby pit and dumps him onto the makeshift table. The soldier—I think it is Evans—tries to scramble away until a second gorilla pins him. A third gorilla brings down a huge flat ax-head of chipped stone, severing both of the soldier's legs mid-thigh.

Tompkins howls like a banshee and advances, opening up with the AK-47. The gorilla holding the large cutting stone snarls and pitches backward with a deafening crash. Tompkins adjusts his aim and fires another burst and a second gorilla topples.

"Harris! *Fire,* Goddamn it! Aim for the skull."

I brace the rifle stock against my shoulder and site on a third zombie gorilla. Squeeze the trigger and stagger forward. I scream above the roar of the gas-operated weapon as it sprays bullets into the beast and vaporizes a gallery of slow-drip millennium wall sculptures.

My wounded gorilla and the two remaining others retreat into darkness, probably into an adjoining chamber. I keep my rifle trained in that direction in case they charge. My breath comes in tight gasps and the barrel of my rifle trembles like a dowsing rod.

Tompkins scrambles up onto the stone shelf. Evans has bled out, both femoral arteries severed. Tompkins moves to the other side and peers into the pit.

"Harris, Weller is alive. Get your ass up here and help me."

I lower my rifle and jog forward, and that is when a sapling-sized stalagmite sails out of the darkness like a prehistoric javelin and skewers Tompkins. He staggers backward, eyes and mouth wide, and disappears into the pit with a thud. I fire blindly into the void and then my clip is empty. *And Tompkins has all of the spare ammo and grenades.*

Silence, except for my rasping breath. The most intense terror arcs through my nervous system.

I hear muttering sounds and the shuffling of feet from the dark anteroom.

I imagine them bursting into view, their powerful black fingers grasping me, transporting me to the cold stone shelf in their great dining hall, holding me down while one of them butchers me like a chicken.

I rip free the flashlight from my useless rifle, wheel and run. I hear—or in my panic imagine I hear—low hooting and grunts and heavy footfalls behind me.

I pass the body of the first gorilla and skid to a stop. I shine my light on the beast's neck below its blood-soaked face.

Impossible.

I see a large gray plastic collar with a bulge on the side, battered and cracked, bearing a thin metallic plate engraved with a long sequence of Vietnamese script and numbers. It looks like a serial number.

* * *

I kept my mouth shut about the effects of Green-6 and the incident at Phu Bihn Valley. Violating my nondisclosure could have meant a life sentence in a military prison. And who would have believed my story? Would you?

I was offered a plum job in agricultural sciences at Dow Chemical, but I resigned from SOG. I spent most of my adult life teaching chemistry at a quaint little university in a modest Midwestern city. The kind you might drive through and think is pleasant enough, but not enough to explore except for topping off your tank and a quick meal. I married my girlfriend and she bore us two sons. Barbecued on weekends and attended Friday-night football games. Professor Harris, a regular Mr. Chips to my students. I am still on the faculty today—department head, in fact. And yes, the company paid me a discreet visit in the summer of 1977, wondering if I was interested in helping re-cruit talented young men and women. I politely declined.

I did develop a serious case of adult claustrophobia and fear of the dark. And I had terrible night terrors for many years. Beth knew that I had served as a scientific advisor for the Army in Vietnam, and she didn't press me about details.

Many times when the dreams return I feel torn between slaughterhouse screams and hysterical cynical laughter. *Those giant radio-tracking collars with VC serial numbers.*

They'd had their own version of SLOG, too.

STEVE RUTHENBECK
Lyceum

The attack happened a little after 1:00 p.m. on a Wednesday.

Thomas Beckman slouched in the bleachers of the Oak Lake County Central Wolves Gymnasium, one body among the student body. A motivational speaker sat on the half-court line below. He spun a basketball on the index finger of each hand, another ball on top of his head and two more on the tips of his shoes.

"Follow your dreams," the man said. "I did!"

A vague tightness formed in Thomas's chest that might have been shame. Graduation loomed and with it the end of procrastination. Classmates talked about colleges they planned to attend and careers they planned to pursue. Thomas's dreams went no further than getting White Space 2 when it was released next Tuesday and asking Danielle to prom.

Currently, Danielle sat two rows below Thomas. Dark hair hung halfway down her back, and he could see the curve of her cheek. The feelings that rolled through him were as close to growing up as he felt. Otherwise, he viewed adulthood as some rough beast stomping closer. It had nothing to do with him stepping out on his own.

"And whatever happens in life," the man with the basketballs continued, moving the ball on his head to his nose. "Remember, put a positive *spin* on it!"

The gymnasium roof peeled back, and a gigantic simian face peered in, red eyes burning. The creature's matted black fur had fallen out in places and revealed mottled skin. A Volkswagen-sized hand reached, pushing a great stink and a cloud of flies before it. The paw picked up a clump of screaming students, and the beast bit into them like an apple.

"ZK attack!" Mr. Jablanski cried.

The rush for gym exits carried Thomas along with it, even as its undertow pulled others down, and cries of pain rose above cries of fear. The evacuation piled up at the doors, where teenagers bottlenecked into a mass of straining limbs and strident shouts. A basketball ended up among their feet and was kicked back and forth.

The ZK pushed its head and shoulders through the roof breach. The edge of the wall acted like the back of a chair when a person performs the Heimlich Maneuver on themselves, and the monster spewed vomit over the scene.

Drenched, students behind Thomas fell to the floor and writhed. The stink grew unbearable. Tears and gagging plagued the throng. Thomas stumbled through the door and into the hall. He unknotted himself from the kids around him and gasped for fresh air until his lungs and eyes cleared themselves of the foulness. He caught a glimpse of Danielle. She had made it out, as well. For a moment, their glance met...

What are you looking at?

That's what she asked him that day in Literature Class. Thomas arrived early and stood staring out the window. The sun shone on green grass. A breeze made the trees throw dappled shadows. Danielle came and stood next to him.

Nothing, Thomas replied, but his eyes were opened regardless. That moment was the best he ever had, standing there and looking out on a just-right spring day with a girl who was interested in knowing more...

Alarms pierced Thomas's eardrums.

A steel gate descended over the school's main entrance. Similar gates would fall over the building's other doors *and* windows, Thomas knew. All state buildings were mandated to be equipped with lockdowns in the event of Zmergencies. Since the early-warning system failed to alert them of the ZK's approach it didn't surprise Thomas that the lockdown would trigger in error. It was meant for Z sieges, not ZK attacks.

Now they were trapped instead of protected.

Something grabbed Thomas's shoulder. He spun and found himself face-to-face with Andrew Gardner. Soaked with ZK vomit, Andrew had turned Z. His bluish lips stretched wide as he lunged for Thomas's neck. Crying out, Thomas pushed his one time lab-partner away. Andrew was clumsy with death and toppled onto his back like a tree going over. His skull clunked on the tiles.

Other students who had been transformed by the ZK vomit (faster than normal it seemed) flooded out of the gym and pounced on their fellow OLCC Wolves with clutching hands and gnashing teeth. Their clothes hung in tatters, dissolved by the vomit that wormed its way through flesh and into bloodstreams.

"Look out!" Mr. Jablanski bellowed. The math teacher shoved a course through the jammed hallway. Sweat slicked his bald head and his tie hung askew. He fumbled a key out of his pocket and opened a cabinet marked with a flame symbol. He grabbed the red canister and twisted a valve. "Get down!" He pointed the flamethrower toward the Zs staggering through the hall, and a jet of fire blossomed into a cloud.

Thomas dodged down a side corridor and followed other teenagers seeking safety. Danielle was among them. Her hair flowed over her shoulder as she ran. Thomas put on a burst of speed, weaving in and out of people like a football player.

The ZK's hand punched through the wall, snatched Mark Muller and pulled him out of sight. The wall was a load-bearing structure, and a section of ceiling collapsed. Blocked, Thomas tried to go back. Flames shot through the hall he came from, and the shouts of Mr. Jablanski echoed. Meanwhile, students behind Thomas had been bitten and staggered toward him with a hungry gleam in their otherwise blank eyes.

Thomas picked his way through the hole made by the ZK's paw. The beast laid on its stomach, gnawing its meal. One of its legs still stuck out of the ceiling (its foot was caught in the rafters). Thomas tried to sprint past it, and a monster hand slammed down in his wake. The ZK attempted another grab. Its fist brushed Thomas as he dodged into the lunch-line hall. The force of the blow caused him to stumble. He rolled away from the seeking fingers and pushed his way into a bathroom. He shut himself inside the corner stall and locked its door. He sat on the toilet tank, feet up so they wouldn't be visible beneath the door.

How many doors had he passed through in the last five minutes?

Thomas thought of an essay by Siegbert Becker. God didn't carve a person's path through life in stone. He gave them freedom of choice, but sometimes directed their path through the opening and closing of doors. A person might try something and be shut down; or they might try something and make progress. If they found themselves in a place where a decision had to be made and they didn't know what to do, they considered their gifts, circumstances, right and wrong and made the best choice they could.

Outside the bathroom, muffled screams and roars reached Thomas's ears. A few gunshots blasted, probably from teachers.

What am I going to do?

Presently, Thomas worked for a commercial gardener, picking strawberries in the summer and chopping rhubarb plants into more rhubarb plants in the winter. It paid for video games and little else. It wouldn't work as a career.

As for college, Thomas hadn't applied to any because his grades weren't stellar, nor were his goals. He supposed he could attend the local community college, but that seemed like giving up—doing something just to do something. Still, it was an avenue to try, and filling out an application to see what developed wouldn't hurt anything.

Nor would applying at Agri-Verse.

The wheeze of a pneumatic hinge announced the opening of the bathroom door. Thomas froze as footsteps shuffled inside and stopped in front of his stall. Its door creaked as someone pressed against it. Thomas's heart pounded. A pair of hands appeared below the door as the person went to their knees to peer through the gap. The face belonged to a seventh-grader. Drool fell from his purple lips as he spotted Thomas.

Thomas erupted off the toilet tank, pushed aside a ceiling tile and pulled himself into the crawlspace. He managed to worm on top of an air duct, which squeaked and shook, but held his weight. An additional problem presented itself—the crawlspace was filled with smoke, which stung Thomas's eyes and made him cough.

Where there's smoke, there's fire…

The flamethrower Mr. Jablanski used was meant for the porthole at the front entrance, not the interior of the school. Thomas guessed insulation in the crawlspace ignited, and the fire would burn through the whole building, not reducing it to cinders but filling it with poisonous fumes. Even now, Thomas felt his head go light and nausea uncoil itself in his belly. He hurriedly worked his way down the duct until he guessed he was over the hallway. The smoke grew thicker even in those few moments. Holding his breath, Thomas rolled off the air duct, broke through the ceiling tiles and dropped back into the lunch-line hall.

Mr. Jablanski stood before him.

Speak of the devil, Thomas thought.

Mr. Jablanski had a hard time standing on his shredded right leg. The flamethrower's gun dangled from his hand, ending in a torn hose. The man once gave Thomas purpose. Thomas appeared in Mr. Jablanski's physics class at 10 a.m. Monday through Friday. Reading assignments and problems followed. Now the dynamic was reversed. Thomas gave Mr. Jablanski purpose. How quickly things changed. Mr. Jablanski lurched forward to take a bite. Thomas darted back and then around Mr. Jablanski's flailing arms.

The halls were starting to fill with smoke now. Thomas avoided three infected students and headed for the band room. It was a designated rally point. Coughing, he turned by the library and reached the goal moments later. Thomas banged on the band room door. A slot opened and a pair of eyes looked him up and down.

"Are you bit?" the owner of the eyes asked.

"No."

"Do the drill."

Sweating, Thomas dropped his pants and pulled his shirt up around his neck. He turned in a circle, eyeing the Zs staggering closer, closer…

"Okay, you're clean."

The band door opened, and Thomas ducked inside. The place was packed with perhaps forty kids. Thomas quickly scanned the faces and was grateful to see Danielle sitting on the far side of the room with a group of friends.

"Anyone else coming?" Larry Berlin asked.

"No," Thomas shook his head. "And we need to get going."

"The rules say we wait for help."

"We can't this time." Thomas pointed at the smoke that had started to spill out of the ceiling vents. "The crawlspaces are burning. We'll be poisoned."

Murmurs went up among the students.

"But we *can't* get out," someone said querulously. "We're in lockdown."

"There's a way," Thomas insisted. Before panic could spread roots into the group's psyche, he explained. Once he presented his idea, everyone agreed to it.

As a member of the Student Zmergency Council, Larry took charge and ordered the students to dismantle the room's music stands. This left them with narrow pipes about four feet long. Besides clubbing, the weapons could stab soft things.

"We'll move like a circle of wagons," Larry directed. "Everyone with a pipe will be on the outside. Unarmed people will keep to the middle. Before we go, does anyone have a gun? I know you're supposed to check them in at the office, but I won't report you."

Three boys raised their hands.

"Save your bullets for the target," Larry advised.

The group exited the band room in a serpentine line that tripled up in the hall. Drills allowed them to move fast even though the smoke made it difficult to see. Many of the students had removed T-shirts and tied them around their faces. Thomas tried to stay close to Danielle. She was unarmed; he held a pipe; and they were running the gauntlet.

Hands reached out of the smoke as Zs converged on their still-living classmates. Shouts. Moans. Flailing clubs. And screams as some were dragged into the smoke. Rebecca Meyer advanced, a pale apparition whose skin was almost invisible in the cloudiness. She snagged the shirt of the girl next to Danielle, and Thomas beat the clutching limb away. The train of them stayed in motion, to stop was to have their ranks overcome.

The group reached the gymnasium relatively intact. The ZK still lolled on the floor with the remains of its hunger. It had tried to free its ankle of the rafter, but succeeded in doing no more than breaking it; a bone jutted out of the joint like a snapped tree limb. Gunshots rang out as the armed students went for the ZK's eyes. Nine-millimeter bullets wouldn't penetrate to its brain, but maybe they could at least blind the monster.

Thomas joined the team jabbing their makeshift spears at the ZK's face. It reminded him of a Ray Harryhausen movie— *One Million Years B.C.,* where the characters fought a giant purple turtle. The beast's teeth chomped, and its great paws swept. One assailant was thrown against the wall with bone-crunching force. Somehow, Curt Johnson found an opening and charged. Instead of an eye, he stabbed a nostril. Thomas saw what was going to happen and dove out of the way. The beast, still governed by reflex even if it was dead, sneezed. Rotten snot doused several boys, and they ran screaming, trying to rip their clothes off before the fluid soaked into their system and infected them.

Meanwhile, the unarmed students stood caught between a rock and a hard place. The battle with the ZK happened in front of them while Zs simultaneously attacked them from behind. A few kids with spears tried to hold the infected teenagers back, but Thomas could see it was a losing battle. Danielle was tossed back and forth as the unarmed kids tried to move as one to stay out of the way of everything.

The clock in Thomas's head ticked into the red. Screaming, he ran forward, ducked a giant hand, rolled away from the other and come up in front of the ZK's face. The monster's breath seemed bad enough to sear his skin. Ignoring it, Thomas plunged his spear into the beast's eye and shoved it as far as he

51

could. The ZK roared, going rigid like bolts of electricity shot through its body. Then it simply went limp and stopped moving.

"Come on!" Thomas shouted.

The students scrambled onto the ZK's back. They climbed its snagged leg, using the monster's fur as handholds, and onto the school roof. By the time Thomas joined them, some were already filing down the fire escape.

Determined, Thomas sought out Danielle and budged into line behind her as she climbed onto the ladder. "Danielle," he said.

She looked up, all beauty and possibility. "Yes?"

"Would you go to prom with me?"

Danielle paused, and Thomas felt like he lived a hundred lifetimes in that few seconds of silence. Finally, she answered, "I guess that would be okay"

"Great!" Thomas smiled. "Call you tomorrow?"

"Sure," Danielle nodded and descended. She reached the street, walked toward home and disappeared around a corner.

Thomas remained on the roof. The sun shone down, and trees threw dappling shadows. There was the water tower, the church steeple, Main Street, the pool and softball fields. The town's volunteer militia was finally organized and heading toward the school in fire trucks and APCs. Surrounding the town were corn and soybean fields. Farm sites stuck up like odd rock formations, and ZKs wandered on the horizon.

As Thomas watched, another began to stomp near...

ADRIAN LUDENS
The Elephant In The Room

I.

"A Fly on the (Circus Tent) Wall"

"Hurry, hurry! Step right up friends! Beyond this point you'll find everything you've ever dreamed about and so, SO much more! Dare to meet the Human Piranha! Cast your eyes upon the Two Thousand Pound Albino! Arm-wrestle the World's Strongest Dwarf! Just five dollars ladies and gentlemen; don't delay!"

Simmons paused to mop his brow. The Louisiana humidity had soaked his tattered tuxedo and pasted it to his skin. He felt claustrophobic, constricted by his own clothes. He was about to renew his pitch upon the jaded masses when Hobart, a roustabout for the Freak Show, came hurrying up from his left.

"Mr. Simmons, sir, Mr. Quincy wanted me to pass along an urgent message."

"Well make it quick, man," Simmons hissed. "I'm making my pitch."

Hobart put his mouth up to the barker's ear. "Quincy says not to mention the gorilla act because the gorilla has up and died."

"Oh Christ!"

Plato the Gorilla was always a good draw. 'Smarter than most men' Simmons would say of the old silver-backed primate. Plato accounted for at least twenty percent of tickets sold. The wheels spun in Simmons' brain. As he rose to face the street again, those wheels found traction.

"Ladies and gentlemen, boys and girls, I have just been given some very sad news." He paused for effect. "Our beloved friend and performer, Plato the Gorilla is DEAD."

A few of the animal-lovers in the crowd murmured in dismay. Simmons felt the eyes of the crowd on him, waiting for an explanation.

"Smarter than most men, he was, and now he is gone! But today, ladies and gentlemen, today you may purchase your tickets for the first ever—" Simmons was going to say 'funeral for a gorilla' but one of the faded cloth banners hanging to his left caught his eye and inspiration struck like lightning. He felt the tingle of excitement from head to foot.

"The first ever resurrection of a dead gorilla!" Simmons raised his arms with a flourish. A few groans and jeers came from the crowd.

"I ain't payin' to see you wake up a sleeping monkey," one brawny man proclaimed loudly.

Simmons felt Hobart's incredulous stare but ignored him. "I assure you the gorilla is dead, my friends. Everyone who attends will have the opportunity to poke and prod the corpse until you are truly satisfied of the validity of my claim.

We shall call upon Lazarus Houngan on this day! Lazarus is the grandson of plantation workers from Haiti. He is a master of the dark arts of Haitian Vodou, created by African slaves. Lazarus serves the spirits known as the loa. He is a boker. My friends, I do not expect you to know what a boker is, so let me explain further.

A houngan is a vodou priest who serves the loa with both hands. That is to say, he performs sacred rites of healing and protection.

But Lazarus Houngan is NOT a houngan at all. Lazarus is a boker. He is a master of the darker arts. Lazarus is with us because he was cast out by his friends and family for performing forbidden rituals. Lazarus can use his knowledge of the taboo and his unholy power to restore life to Plato the Gorilla! You will witness this stunning miracle with your own eyes! One show only, ladies and gentlemen. One show only!"

For every one person who moved away down the street, nine others surged forward with money in hand.

* * *

"I won' do it." Lazarus said. He crossed his arms in a defiant gesture.

"The devil you won't!" Simmons growled back at the swarthy black man.

"I practice some little bits of hoodoo, dat's all. What you ask is too dangerous."

"I've seen you do some crazy stuff in your act. I don't know how you do it, and I don't care. As long as you keep the customers interested and coming back, that's all that matters. Now I promised the folks buying tickets tonight that you'd bring the gorilla back to life and by gawd, you're gonna do it."

"Mista Simmons, you ask me to dance wit' de devil this time. I can't do it."

Simmons grabbed Lazarus by the collar and yanked him so their noses almost touched. Then he unleashed a torrent of verbal abuse that would have made the cruelest plantation owner blush with shame.

With a peculiar gleam in his eyes, Lazarus agreed to raise the gorilla from the dead.

* * *

Lazarus Houngan's real name was long forgotten, even by him. But most everything else Simmons told the crowd that day was true. Lazarus was indeed a boker of great power, though he admitted the fact to precious few. Things were just easier that way.

But the ugly barrage of words from his boss reawakened old grudges within him. Some injustices run generations-deep.

I serve the loa with both hands, he thought. *But today one hand is tied behind my back by a white man. Today I dare to call upon Bondye, the Supreme God. Today I ask for vengeance.*

Lazarus fell to his knees and selected a stone from the dirt. He rose and hurried to his tent. He gathered a few small bottles of liquids and powders; poison extracted from a puffer fish, datura, human ash and other ingredients better left unnamed. Lazarus chanted and prayed as he smeared the mixture into the cracks and crevices of the stone.

Satisfied with the pwen—his object of power for the ritual——Lazarus set about fashioning an ouanga bag. The bag would hold the pwen and serve as a talisman that he hoped would house the spirits Plato captured.

The misguided man, driven by fear and anger, sought to bring Plato the Gorilla back to life as a sort of avenging spirit. He asked Bondye to give the gorilla the wisdom and strength necessary to kill and capture the souls of any man or woman who felt superior to another race, color or creed. But Lazarus was indeed dancing with the devil, as he had asserted to Simmons earlier.

By the time Lazarus stood in front of hundreds of people gathered to watch him bring the dead primate back to life, it was too late to turn back. Chanting a hybrid of dark spells, he made an incision in the gorilla's chest, close to the heart. Then Lazarus took the ouanga bag with the pwen inside and shoved it deep into Plato's chest cavity.

The result was instantaneous.

Plato the Gorilla, infused with a power from beyond, leaped to his feet and pounded his chest with both of his massive fists. He tipped his dome-shaped head to the heavens and emitted a roar that deafened the stunned crowd.

Plato wasted no time in carrying out the undertaking he had been assigned. He examined the souls of the men and women around him and found only hatred, fear and intolerance. The gorilla grabbed the closest offender's arm and yanked him forward. Then he crushed the man's skull to jelly between his hands.

Lazarus Houngan's lifeless body slumped to the ground, but his soul howled in surprise and rage and it was absorbed into the ouanga buried near Plato's heart. Plato grew in size and power.

He lunged into the crowd, judging hearts, crushing skulls and collecting souls.

Simmons somehow lasted for two entire minutes before his time for judgment came. His eardrums were shattered by the roaring of the beast and blood spattered into his eyes, lending a reddish hue to the unfolding atrocities. To Simmons, everything looked sepia-tone. His final thoughts were of a silent, grainy horror film he'd seen as a child.

II.
"Floating in (Cyber) Space"

CARNIVAL GORILLA
ATTACKS CROWD
Nonesuch, La. -Affiliated News Agency

Sources in the town of Nonesuch, Louisiana say that a gorilla believed to be a featured act in a traveling carnival has broken free of its keepers and attacked a crowd of carnival patrons. Authorities are unable to give the Affiliated News Agency a definite number of casualties. Various sources have reported between 3 and 35 deaths attributed to the rogue gorilla's violent spree.

Dr. Abraham Munn, an expert on primate behavior from Miskatonic Community College explains that an angry gorilla can tear a man's arm from his body without even trying, but goes on to say that a traumatic incident would be required to push the animal to rampage in such a primal manner.

Reports of the gorilla causing havoc on the highway north of Nonesuch are so far unconfirmed.

COMMENTS:

GenerallySpeaking—
This doesn't involve me directly so I don't give a sh*t.

Smitty—
I hated carnivals as a kid. Clowns are creepy and the games are rigged. Go gorilla!

Permanentguest—
This is why animals should not be trained for mankind's entertainment. Free the animals!

Mort69—
Animal control will catch that monkey and spank it for being naughty.

Gunner—
Spank the monkey! thought it was Shock the Monkey

Vinny26—
This could only happen down South. A bunch of inbred freaks… and I'm talking about the crowd, not the carnies (but probably them too)

GodiswhiteGodisright—
This is God working in mysterious ways to punish the wicked and unjust. It's in Revelation somewhere. 'A beast will be unleashed.' Look it up.

SolutionGuy—
Everyone just ignore it and it will go away.

Rationalatheist2011—
Don't even bring 'god' into this. It's an escaped gorilla who is seriously PO'd. End of story.

* * *

GORILLA'S BLOODY
SPREE CONTINUES
Summit Hill, Ky -Affiliated News Agency

Authorities throughout Louisiana, Mississippi, Tennessee and Kentucky have reported violent attacks to citizens carried out by a large gorilla. Eyewitnesses in Mississippi have told the Affiliate News Agency that the gorilla stood ten feet tall. Citizens in Tennessee reported the creature's height at closer to fifteen feet, while witnesses in Kentucky claim the rampaging ape is nearly twenty feet tall. Experts are discounting these reports as exaggerations brought on by mass hysteria. Experts are at a loss however to explain how the ape could have traveled so far so fast.

Raymond Gibbs of Portersville, TN said, "The monster seemed like it was actually picking out the people it killed. He'd crush the hood of a car to make it stop, then he'd pull people out of the car and crush their heads like grapes. I saw him crush this one guy's skull, stop and look into the car for a second, and go running after another passing vehicle. I ran over and there was a toddler sitting in the back screaming over what the thing did to his daddy."

Deputy Trevor Howie of the Mississippi Highway Patrol had a different assessment. "Even from a distance, I could tell this gorilla had completely lost its wits. It's rampaging. And it has a one-track mind. Like a zombie going after brains."

The governor of Kentucky has advised citizens to remain in their homes. In an unusual statement, the governor of West Virginia asked citizens to evacuate the entire state. The statement also asked that citizens choose destinations away from Washington, D.C.

COMMENTS:

Theo1972—
LOL its Zombie Kawng! It he throwing barrels?

Outlaw—

As long as the gorilla gets to killin knee grows I dont give a holy muslum she-ite

Smirky I—

R we sure it isn't just a pro b-ball player out on a tear?

Sadie89—

Now that's just uncalled for. I hope the moderator takes your post down. Prayers for the families who have lost loved ones today.

GOP4LIFE—

Why hasn't this thing been shot yet? Where is law enforcement, where is the military? This shouldn't even be news. Just kill it already.

OnionFan—

This has to be a prank story. Of course, I thought that when that doofus was elected to a second term.

Proud2BRedneck—

Agree with Outlaw. Beware the Ku Klux Kong

SecondAmendRights—

I also cannot believe we haven't shot the thing yet. Sucks that people died. Sucks more that we still have people whining every day about 'gun control'.

MikeD2011—

I'm betting that gorilla is making a beeline for DC. Gonna clean up washington or die tryin!

Meredith—

My friend Holly is such a lucky woman! She's earning six figures a year working from home. You can too! For information, visit www.nitwitclicks.com and we'll send you free information!

GunsNHoses—

Guns don't kill people, people kill people. Now someone with a gun please kill this damn dirty ape... and the spammers.

Gus M.—
Second that.

* * *

PRESIDENT DECLARES
STATE OF EMERGENCY
Rampaging Ape's Growth Confirmed by Military
Washington, D.C. -Affiliated News Agency

The President has declared a state of emergency for the states east of the Mississippi River this afternoon. The U.S. military has confirmed that the marauding gorilla has actually grown in size at an alarming rate. Official reports from the Pentagon confirm that the 'Zombie Ape' is now the size of an eighteen-wheeler standing on end.

"This defies all reason," a White House spokesperson said. "We are working around the clock. Our priorities are, first and foremost, to save the lives of our citizens. Secondly, we are calling in jet fighters from several air bases. Our intent is to destroy or incapacitate the animal. Finally, we are searching for the origin behind the ape's existence and, more to the point, how it can grow in size."

Citizens are urged to remain calm and to stay indoors at all costs.

"The Zombie Ape, as the media has taken to calling it, is still moving north at a high rate of speed," explained the spokesperson. "We can only speculate as to where it will head next."

Early estimates have the death toll at well over one thousand people.

The first report of the Zombie Ape came just two hours ago.

COMMENTS:

California Son—
What the eff are you losers doing on the east coast? Some-body's pi$$ed.

DonKeyKong—
This is happening because of the midterm elections. The gi-ant zombie ape is on our side and is targeting conservatives, I guarantee it.

GilbertG—
like hell this is a government project gone awry dont even pretend it has anything to do with political agendas it has to do with race the government created a black killing machine and will use it to turn public opinion against the black man in order to excuse enslaving him again

Mace—
yawn

Tyrell—
I hope Zombie Ape is crushing plenty of crackers.

Proud2BRedneck2—
screw you and your kind TY-RELL

Kristianna—
Want to increase the size of your penis? Find out how by following the link. Absolutely no harmful drugs. Natural herbs. FDA approval pending. You know what is important in your life… take advantage of this offer now!

TubaMan—
can you imagine the size of zombie kongs junk LMAO

III.
"Heads in the (Quick)Sand"

UNITED NATIONS DECLARES
STATE OF EMERGENCY
Military Efforts Have No Apparent Effect
New York City - Affiliated News Agency

The United Nations has declared a worldwide state of emergency.

Entire cities along the Eastern Seaboard reportedly decimated. Catastrophic losses as death toll mounts. Government estimates put the number of dead at over one million. Independent figures estimate higher.

Size of the Zombie Ape is estimated at 300 feet tall. Weight unknown. The growth of the creature increases with the number of deaths it causes. As a result, the larger the ape grows, the more quickly it can take lives. The growth and potential for further destruction multiplies with each passing minute.

The first reports originated only five hours ago. Some scattered early survivors who called in to nationally syndicated radio shows imply that the attacks are somehow racially motivated, but citizens of every race, color and creed have perished.

Military attacks using Air Force jet fighters, Army tanks and an arsenal of ground to air weapons have been deployed and have yielded no discernible results.

Update:
Scientists warn that if the ape continues to grow at its current rate, the sheer weight of the creature will tilt Earth's axis, causing catastrophic earthquakes and tidal waves. At the current rate, the integrity of the earth's orbit could be affected in as little as 19 hours. Size of the ape has nearly doubled since last report. Satellite images show the ape without needing magnification.

Update:

UNITED NATIONS ORDERS TACTICAL NUCLEAR STRIKE

A series of nuclear missiles will be armed and ready to fire within the hour. The missiles will come from multiple locations in several NATO and non-NATO affiliated countries. The size and speed of the rampaging 'Zombie Ape' poses targeting problems.

"One nuclear warhead could potentially miss the intended target. In a span of ten minutes, the creature traveled from New York state in the United States to the northernmost tip of Quebec in Canada. Should the creature continue to increase in mass as it nears the North Pole, the effect would be cataclysmic. A series of nuclear strikes may eliminate most of the population of North America, but there will still be hope for the rest of the world."

COMMENTS:

Snarky—
Effing towel heads have been waiting for an excuse to bomb us. screw them

WakeUpCall—
The ape is not the zombie here, people. WE ARE THE ZOMBIES. Wake up before it's too late.

USAUSA—
Terrorist sand monkeys are behind this. Fire off the warheads on their asses NOW

hockeyfan—
thanks alot USA because of your arrogance and stupidity we have to pay the price. See you all in HELL

Uncle Sam—

screw you stupid canadians and your hockey pucks and stocking caps and bacon you guys are morons ey the mcken-zee brothers are gay fags and you all are too

Kristi—

Want to increase the size of your penis? Find out how by following the link. Absolutely no harmful drugs. Natural herbs. FDA approval pending. You know what is important in your life; take advantage of this offer now!

Margine C—

This is why I don't care for the internet news. So much negative stuff going on that I don't care to know about.

TutoneFan—

did anyone see that movie with the gorilla that climbed the sears tower i think it was, what was that called again because thats what this reminds me of

Amazing!—

My friend Sally is such a lucky woman! She's earning six figures a year working from home. You can too! For information, visit www.nitwitclicks.com and we'll send you free information!

Richie—

Donkey Kawng is still a fun game my high score cannot be beat. the games out now cant compare to vintage stuff

MurryCasala—

can you imagine the size of this giant ape's unit? lol

Spinner—

This doesn't involve me directly so I don't give a—

AMANDA C. DAVIS
Escape from Ape City

At some point our first question—the keening, desperate "Where did the giant zombie gorillas *come* from?"—became moot. It was merely academic. The origin of the giant zombie gorillas was as useful to us as the number of angels who could dance on the head of a pin. Less useful, in fact—pinprick-sized angels might be somehow brought under our control. Building-sized undead gorillas left us no option but to run.

"They're like any silly fashion," said Bradbury to me, one day in the bunker. "One turns up and before long they're on every street corner."

"Fashion!" spat Lillian. "Who cares about fashion?" Before the giant zombie gorillas she had cared very much. "Only a month and they've turned us back into cavemen."

"Minus the advantages vis-à-vis cavewomen." Bradbury really was a card.

Lillian, giving him a vicious look, went back to sharpening a curtain rod into a double-ended spear.

Jenny squeezed inside then, through the trapdoor that used to be a basement window. She fell neatly to the ground and landed on her feet like a cat. "Listen to this, you Morlocks," she said. (She's a card too, a good match for Bradbury, I always thought.) "Get your things. Get everything. There's a boat. We're getting out."

We ignored everything but that penultimate sentence, and the shock of it drove us to our feet. "A boat!" said Lillian, for once losing her scowl.

"A warship?" said Bradbury.

"All I know is it floats."

66

Lillian said, "It can't be. Who's still got a boat?"

"Astor. Rockefeller. Who cares?" said Jenny. "The Laurel Street bunker says there's a yacht or something not far out to sea and it's coming toward us at a quick old clip. They think it'll be here by dark. It must be a rescue. It must be."

I said, "It's nearly dark now," although I had no way to know other than one page torn out of an almanac and a watch I kept faithfully wound.

"Then pack fast," said Jenny.

We didn't need to be told twice. We scattered. Everybody had a corner, and we all went there. Lillian had the corner nearest to mine. She laid out a bed sheet and started throwing clothes and tinned food and tools into the middle of it.

"Do you suppose we'll have to live on the boat," said Lillian, "or do you suppose they can take us somewhere nice? Tom, I couldn't live on a boat."

"I expect we'll live there," I said. I had salvaged precious few belongings compared to her and they all went into my cardboard suitcase without trouble. "I hope you know how to cook a fish."

I hauled myself and my suitcase across the room before she could work up any kind of a retort.

If I had any proper luck, I'd have never met Lillian; I'd have been hiding in an underground bunker with Bets, my sweetheart and best girl. But I had been at the college the day the giant zombie gorillas popped up, and she had been at Macy's. Of course everyone knew what happened to Macy's. By the time I discovered where she had been, the giant zombie gorillas had turned the city into their own dead iron jungle. There was no getting anywhere. I'd never made it as far as the ruins of Macy's. And there had been no sign of her since.

I didn't like to think about Bets. But it was better than actually talking to Lillian.

* * *

They used to say all kinds of things about this city. To hear people talk nobody liked any part of it, although a whole bunch of people lived there. To be honest, the accusations of squalor were never far off. Now they were dead on.

I didn't like to go out in the daytime, so I never did it. The destruction was simply too enormous. We squeezed out the basement window of the tailor shop and all the ruin and squalor of our little room expanded as far as I could see: cars under buildings, buildings under cars, clothes and papers strewn wherever the wind took them, body parts too small for the giant zombie gorillas to notice. I kicked a crushed baby stroller. I had no way to know whether it had been occupied when the crushing took place.

Jenny beckoned, and we followed her over the mountains of debris. I could see giant zombie gorillas sitting on their rubble thrones not too many blocks away. One put the end of a steel beam in his mouth and tried to chew it like a stalk of celery. The metal creaked under the strain of his vast flat teeth.

Lillian moaned. The giant zombie gorilla paused his chewing and sniffed the air. He dropped the beam—it made a terrible clatter—and began to heave his enormous, rotting simian form onto its knuckles.

"It's Tubbo," Bradbury hissed. He really believed he could tell the giant zombie gorillas apart. He ducked to the nearest building and gestured us all to join him. We picked through debris and jammed ourselves into the door he held open.

It was the old post office. I couldn't believe the place still stood. The inside walls were plastered with notes and posters so that you couldn't tell whether there was any wallpaper underneath. One of them caught my eye: fresh paper, and large letters. I pulled it off the wall.

YOU ARE NOT ALONE
OUR BUNKER IS SAFE BENEATH THE SITE
OF MACY'S DEPT STORE
YOU ARE WELCOME

And beneath that were about thirty or forty signatures in blue ink, all kinds, women's and men's and some so scrawly their makers must be either very old or very young.

And I knew one of them.

Bets.

"Look at this," I said, thrusting the note toward Jenny, not quite willing to actually give it to her. "Have you seen this?"

"Oh, sure," Jenny said. "All over the city. I guess they're recruiting. Bradbury, that isn't Tubbo. Tubbo's only got one arm now."

"Do hush," said Lillian, watching through a bullet hole.

"It's Bets," I said. "That's her name, her signature. It's her. She's there. I have to find her."

Lillian turned to me and said, with icy emphasis, "*Do. Hush.*"

I stood there with the note in my hand, no doubt looking as stupid as I felt. I never had made it to Macy's. I hadn't found Bets, earthly remains or living ones. I simply hadn't gone looking.

I said again, "I've got to find her," as if it was the only thing I knew how to say.

Now Jenny turned too. "Find someone?" she hissed. "In *this*? You've got to get out of here, is what you've got to do!"

"She's right," said Bradbury. "I know you love her and all, but think of the odds. And come on, Tom, how often does a boat come by?"

"Exactly that," I said. "Exactly that. What if I leave her and it's the last boat ever to come by?"

"REALLY," said Lillian, through her teeth, "YOU MUST. HUSH. RIGHT—"

She could not finish before the opposite wall came crashing in.

A vast, rotting hand lunged inside, groping with enormous black-and-green fingers that twitched with infestation at the bony tips. The hair on its knuckles was thick as wire.

Jenny shrieked. Lillian threw herself into the front door and was on the street before any of us. We followed in a mob.

"Stay together!" shouted Jenny. "Head for the docks! Find a bunker!"

I skidded and stopped. The giant zombie gorilla roared behind us, finishing off the post office for good. Bradbury, without breaking stride, turned his head: "Tom! Move!"

"I have to find her," I shouted. "I'll see you on the boat."

"Wait!" cried Lillian.

I didn't wait. I ran. I ran like I hadn't run since grammar school. I cleared obstacles like a show horse. The whole city opened to me, a block at a time, and I owned it yard by painful yard. Behind me I heard the giant zombie gorillas stomping and chewing and tearing apart buildings floor by floor. I couldn't even hear myself breathe.

And there it was.

Macy's, which used to reside between a bank and an apartment building, now resided under them both. Its impressive storefront was a pile of bricks—not a very big one, and difficult to distinguish from the bricks around it. Painted right on the side of the pile of rubble were letters in whitewash, tall as I was: WELCOME. There was a big arrow pointing toward a makeshift door.

The door said KNOCK TWICE so that's what I did—softly, because I knew the giant zombie gorillas were never far off. At once, the door cracked open. Someone's hand took hold of mine and I was hauled inside by a man in a welder's helmet. The door closed silently, carefully, firmly.

"Bets," I gasped. "Where's Bets?"

The doorman raised his helmet. His face was filthy. "You know Bets?"

"Tom!"

Someone broke from the cluster of people in the dim corners of the bunker, and came flying into my arms.

The doubts evaporated the moment she spoke.

"Gosh, here you are!" she said. "I thought—that is to say, I didn't think—oh, come here, you." And she tried to break all my ribs at once.

I reciprocated. But there wasn't time to enjoy it. I pulled back and took hold of her arms.

"Bets, there's a boat coming in to port. Our bunker was going to try to catch it. We think it's—well, something like a rescue."

"A boat!" she said. "It can't be. Not after the—"

"It is," I said, "and I mean to be on it when it leaves this lousy city. Come with me, Bets. Life on the open seas. Away from the giant zombie gorillas. What do you say?"

She hesitated. "But Tom… we're doing all right here."

Her words struck me cold. I never expected them. "What do you mean?"

"We're doing all right." She gestured around. "We have enough food for a while, and sometimes new people come by—like you just now. We're safe enough. Safer than most. We thought we could make this a sort of town hall when things settle down. Do you really want us to leave this? A boat might be dangerous. It might not be a rescue at all."

I took a hard look around. The ceiling was low and the walls damp. People sat or paced. But I could smell food cooking (the same humdrum tinned stuff we lived on) and I heard talk and laughter. Even with Bradbury and Jenny around, we had rarely found occasion to really laugh.

"I… I said I'd meet them at the boat."

Bets took my arm. "Let them do what they think is best. Now you know about us. You do what you think is best."

"Bets, are you… "

"I'm staying," she said.

All my imaginings about my future had been shattered before, a month ago, with one great blow breaking my dreams like a window and then a series of little ones to shake the last few chunks of hope out of the frame. The boat put a few of them back and Bets broke them out again. Could I live underground forever, always on the end of my nerves, with her at my side? Could I live on a free, open vessel without her?

I watched the possibilities of my future wind out in twisty strands before me, wild and fragile. My vision shook. Then I realized it wasn't my vision at all: that things around me, the walls and ceiling, actually *were* shaking. The building quivered around us. We quivered within it.

"Tubbo!" I gasped.

"What?" said Bets.

"He's the one—never mind, it's too foolish. One of them. He must have followed me. We have to get out of here!"

Bets took a firm hold of my hand. "No, we don't. The giant zombie gorillas find this place once or twice a week. We're underground. All they can do is shift the rubble a bit and maybe block off an exit. Then they all grow bored and leave. It's like I've been trying to tell you, Tom. We're safe here."

The walls shook again.

"Bets!" I said.

She frowned. "It *does* seem different than usual. I wonder…"

As she spoke, a young girl in an oversized hardhat came tearing inside from a door in the back. She got hold of the man who had let me in. "It isn't the giant zombie gorillas!" she cried, taking him by the sleeve. "We're being shot at!"

"What?" said the man. "By who?"

She spread her arms wide. "How should I know? There's fog everywhere! But it was coming from the ocean. It was cannonballs! Hitting this, that, and everything!"

Cannonballs! I went to the pair of them. Bets came along. "We heard that the Laurel Street bunker saw a boat of some kind coming in to port not a few hours ago," I told him, since he seemed to be in charge.

"Great Scott!" he said. "Where'd anyone get a boat nowadays?"

"Search me, sir," I said, adding the sir because his tone demanded it. "Some of my friends were going to try to board it. They think it's a rescue."

"Sounds like an invasion force instead!" he barked.

"Well, we ought to find out for sure," said Bets. "Is the radio picking up anything?"

The girl in the oversized hardhat went dashing off. She returned in an instant. "No sir," she said. "Just white noise. But I've got them listening close!"

"Sir," I said, "I'm Tom, by the way—maybe the giant zombie gorillas can't break your bunker and you'd know that better than I, but I'll bet a mortar shell could. And if somebody is shooting at the giant zombie gorillas, shooting something big enough to sting, you know, these monsters will be kept busy for a while. This might just be the time to make an escape."

He tilted his lid a little to get a look at me. "Tom, you may not like this particular frying pan, but I promise you the rest of the world is the fire."

"Then I'll go alone," I said. "I'll check out the ship. I'll try to keep them from shooting at this place, and I'll try to send word back if it really is a rescue."

Bets said, "Oh, Tom!"

I took her by the shoulders. "Listen, Bets, please. Two hours ago I swore I was getting out of this town, and my only regret was leaving you behind. Now I've got you. I can't stay here and live like a rat underground any longer. But I can't be happy without you. Please, Bets. Please come with me."

She bit her lip. I worried she was going to cry.

"Oh, all right!" she said at last. "Damn you, Tom Findley. I can't stand this hole any longer either. I'll come with you. Because it's you. But you'd better not leave me again, now or ever. Do you hear me?"

"I hear you," I said. "I hear you. I'm so glad to hear you again."

She kissed me. It almost made the whole terrible situation worthwhile.

* * *

The Macy's bunker lent me a hardhat; the man in charge said it might bring me luck, and hoped I'd try hard to return it. He said it as a sort of joke. Bets gathered her own things and a helmet for herself. It only made her look more adorable.

Hand in hand we crept through the ruined streets. We steered clear of any loud noises, whether gunfire or the shrieks of a giant zombie gorilla. The girl lookout had been right about the fog and smoke. We could tell we were headed toward the docks, but only just. At one point Bets grabbed my arm and jerked me behind a building.

"One of them," she mouthed to me. I craned my neck around the corner. One of the giant zombie gorillas strolled past. I swallowed and felt pale.

Bets nodded gravely. We set off again.

The streets were not so devastated that we couldn't pick a path through them, though it was neither fun nor easy. For every building that stood, another was strewn across its neighbors. I had not been out scavenging for some time, and it made me ache to see the valuables—what had once been valuables—tossed among the bricks and debris. I stopped to scoop up a small, flat food tin with the label burnt off. It's never prudent to leave food behind.

"There," said Bets, in a low tone, just at the edge of my ear. "There they are."

We had reached the docks. Not far out over the fog-riddled water, we could make out billowing sails.

"Sails?" I murmured. "Where did they—"

"It doesn't matter," she murmured back. "I won't be happy until we're on board. Please let's go."

Sailing ships! I couldn't imagine anything that old could still float. But as we crept closer, I could just see the black ends of cannons extend from the side of the ship. They burst with a roar of cannon fire. *Perhaps,* I thought, my spirit rising, *perhaps the giant zombie gorillas have knocked our civilization back hundreds of years, but mankind was fairly dangerous back then as well...*

"I see a lifeboat!" I said, as we crested the last mound of rubble. I held out a hand to help her. "We can row out! Bets—we're going to make it!"

The earth heaved. As I tumbled down, I saw that we had been climbing not a pile of rubble but a giant zombie gorilla nestled deep in the fruits of its own destruction! I rolled down his knee and across his vile foot. Bets skipped back, eyes wide as plates. The giant zombie gorilla stood. His left arm ended in a bony, green, gangrenous stump at the shoulder.

"Tubbo!" I gasped.

Bets and I clung to one another, ducking behind his great heel. The monster rolled to his knuckles and paced toward the shore, sniffing deep. Just then a cannonball came roaring through the thick mist: it passed not a hundred yards from Tubbo and sank into the side of an abandoned factory.

Tubbo reared. He loomed above us. His good arm pounded his chest in sluggish arrhythmia and the scream from his torn throat was the ungodly rasp of dead flesh and broken teeth. I recognized his behavior at once. He was posturing—not at us, but at the *ship*, the floating thing twice his size spitting boulders at him. He challenged it as he would a living thing. He would attack it like one, too.

I clutched Bets. "He's going to tear that ship plank from plank!" I hissed in her ear. "We must stop him."

She looked at me with dull, sad eyes. "Okay, Tom," she said. She put a hand in her bag. "You'd better run."

"I won't run!" I said.

She drew a pistol and aimed high. It lurched hard in her hand.

Tubbo reared forward. Bullets were not enough to fell his type, but this one lodged in his skull, and he noticed it. He made a huge swooping turn. His knuckles pounded down yards from us. Bets took my hand and began to back away. Her mouth quivered. "I'm sorry, Tom," she whispered—or maybe she couldn't quite get the words out. I knew what she meant.

"It's just all right," I said. I knew this was my last chance. I had to make it count. "I'm glad I'm with you. Bets… I love—"

I finished the sentence in a howl as Tubbo swiped his giant hand toward us, took hold of me like a child holds a crayon, and swept me into the sky.

I would have been sick if I'd eaten anything that day. I heard, faintly, Bets calling from below, but the whoosh of wind in my ear covered it. In seconds I was face to face with the beast. His vast eyes were large as my head, and scraped white as wool. His breath reeked of the death he had eaten and the death he had become.

I became suddenly very calm. *Just avoid the teeth, Tom,* I told myself. *They're barely held together, they're decaying flesh. Some have clawed their way out of the gullet and lived. Only be sure to avoid the teeth. And take a deep breath.*

I took a deep breath.

Tubbo roared again—that rasping scream, that insane alarm that heralded our demise and broke down our city. I cringed between his fingers. I forced myself to straighten, to go down aware, alert, like a man. I could see so far from here. The city stretched out to my left: not quite lifeless. The sea stretched out to my right. I saw the ship clearly now. It was not one, but many. A dull, far-off *boom*. And then, to my terror, I realized that what I had taken for cannons emerging from below deck were, in fact, cannonballs—and they were getting bigger—I heard them whizz through the air, all around—and one struck Tubbo's ear and burst out the other side with a massive spray of white bone and black flesh.

And then I was falling.

And then I was not.

Darkness and stars warred in my vision. I thought I heard Bets calling my name, although I must have been addled from the fall, because it sounded like there were three or four of her. My head reeled. I rolled to my elbows and crawled across the spongy black palm toward the pad near the thumb. I thought I saw someone coming toward me, but my vision made multiples of him. He reached me—got me under my arm—one on each side—could it be that I was not so addled? Were there many, after all?

"Got you, old boy." It was Bradbury, on my left. "Nice adventure you had, didn't you?"

"It wasn't nice at all," said Bets, on my right. "Can you walk, Tom? They have a lifeboat."

My vision cleared. I saw Jenny and Lillian before me, and Bets and Bradbury at my sides, supporting me. "I can walk," I croaked. I wasn't sure right then that I could, to be honest. But I had the desire to be useful.

"They're warships!" said Jenny, as we went, as quick as we could, to the docks. "They're going to shuttle us north where there aren't so many of the you-know-what's. We've been taking people back and forth. There are more than you can imagine, Tom! This city isn't as dead as we thought."

Bets helped me into the lifeboat. She stroked my cheek. "And neither are you."

I thanked my Maker it was true. As we rowed away from shore, I realized it didn't matter where the giant zombie gorillas came from—or even where the rescue ships came from, although I certainly intended to ask. All I had to know was that they *did* exist, and that I had done everything I could with them. As I held Bets in my arms, gazing out at man's last army fighting nature's most hideous one, I realized that I had everything I needed right here: my girl, my health, my friends.

Giant zombie gorillas or not, it wasn't such a bad life after all.

MARK ONSPAUGH
Dear Fay Wray, We Need Your Help…

It came chittering and moaning from farm country in Iowa.

Easily fifty feet tall, its vast size made it visually incomprehensible, an enigma the mind simply refused to reconcile. Even films of the creature could only resolve that it was a massive primate, and that what had been thought to be mange was instead, decomposition.

The thing was rotting as it traveled toward the east.

Farmers and hunters in the area, the sons and daughters of pioneers, shot at it with rifles and shotguns, pistols and hunting bows.

Nothing slowed the creature as it shoveled vast quantities of livestock and people into its gaping, fanged maw, chewing them into a bloody mass of muscle and fur, skin and bone, its copious, foul-smelling drool leaving small toxic ponds in its wake.

The Army joined in the fray as well as members of law enforcement and local gangs, each bringing high-tech weaponry and sheer bravado to the fight.

They were crushed underfoot or swept into the crushing jaws of the thing, while bits of corrupted, furred flesh the size of Persian rugs dropped into the streets, one such loathsome cast-off smothering a mother and her newborn.

The President called in fighter jets, perhaps thinking back to a movie his grandparents had told him about. Following that line of reasoning, he tried to contact Fay Wray, only to find out she was dead, and her estate refused to have her exhumed.

As if getting into the spirit of things, the oversized simian clambered up the side of a skyscraper with the practiced ease of all primates, evacuating its bowels and bladder as it climbed, claiming another ninety lives in that awful tide.

The press, having little to offer in the way of weapons beyond the metaphorical, gave it names like Prince Primate, Astounding Ape, and The Mighty Monkey.

Scientists were called in as it began to lay waste to Illinois.

Probes were shot into the thing, dislodging huge parasites, fleas the size of corgis and ticks the size of schnauzers. These fed upon hapless grad students and pets, adding dozens to the death toll.

The probes revealed that the creature had no life signs beyond locomotion, vocalization and feeding.

No heart beat, no respiration, no cellular activity of any kind.

Clearly this was impossible. After all, this wasn't a world of wizards and witches.

Probes were recalibrated and re-launched, more grad students were sucked to withered husks by oversized vermin.

The new probes confirmed the impossible.

The thing was dead. The rotting flesh was consistent with death, although a more rapid rate of putrefaction would have been expected.

The stench of the thing became so great that its coming was known several miles distant, and some people succumbed to the foul odor. One old woman left a suicide note under a plaster bust of Lincoln: I would rather be dead than smell that *(expletive deleted)* critter any more.

The press tried names like Stinkosaurus Rex and Stenchzilla, but the public wouldn't accept them. The reporters went back to their Zim's Zoo Book and thesauri for new ideas.

At the White House, nuclear options were discussed and discarded.

Pheromones as bait were discussed, but what was the gender of the beast, and would it be attracted to the opposite sex? And where to find another creature, preferably undead?

Meanwhile, in Addison, Iowa, Doctor Emily Grange made a remarkable find.

Under an enormous red tent, trimmed in gold, she found the remains of a carnival, and a barrel of toxic waste labeled An-775.

The toxic waste had gone inert by that time, which was a small blessing. It was traced to a small Iowan trucking company and from there to a shell corporation called "Goosie Juice." This proved to be a front for a black ops, off the grid, unofficial and unsanctioned research arm of Medusa, the team first commissioned by FDR to fight Nazi zombies in World War II.

Further digging by journalists and Iowan Senator Ken Farley revealed that An-775 was called "Anubis gas," and had been developed by Doctor Helmut Waschbär to fight undead Nazis with good old American Nazis (plus some Brits and maybe a few Aussies).

An-775 did reanimate the dead. It also turned live things un-live.

Unfortunately, An-775 also had problematic side effect: it enlarged the organism twenty-five times its former size.

While an army of one-hundred-and-fifty-foot undead Yanks might seem like a real advantage in a fight with puny six-foot Aryan zombies, there was the question of control, feeding, and transport.

Project Anubis was scrubbed and Dr. Waschbär went on to the highly successful "Red Rover" program, turning Russian soldiers into werewolves.

In the time it took to track down the possible source of the ravaging zombie primate, it had reached the Appalachian mountain range. Here brave hill people fought with a tenacity and ferocity still celebrated in songs like "Monkey on the Mountain," "Critter Ruined My Still and Ate My Grandpappy," and "Stinks to High Heaven."

Thanks to a flaming barrier of old tires, strip mine leavings and moonshine, the creature was held at bay for two days, giving the President, his top advisers, and key members of the populace—senators, doctors, scientists, entertainers, and sports figures—time to evacuate to a secret underground bunker code named "Bedford Falls." From there the President could coordinate attacks against the Behemoth Baboon in safety, along with the Constitution, the Bill of Rights, and Sammy Alcala, the MVP of the recent World Series.

(Editor's note: It should be noted that the fire that saved the President rendered the Appalachian range, arguably one of the nation's most beautiful, into a charred and stinking mire of burned trees, homes, people, and livestock. Efforts by Dolly Parton and Billy Ray Cyrus have already raised two million dollars for aid and reclamation, thanks in part to the release of their duet, "Monkeyshines.")

Once past the mountains the creature consumed an entire fleet of tour buses (nicknamed "Zombuses" by All-Star Tours and featuring "Tours of the Zombie Primate and Other Undead Horrors") pausing only to pick some large clumps of tendon and muscles from its teeth with a telephone pole.

In Virginia the thing hesitated as if trying to get its bearings. It was unmindful of various attacks by American and UN forces, even though one lucky rocket strike took out the monster's left eye. Unfortunately, the rogue eyeball destroyed most of CIA headquarters in Langley, something the FBI gleefully posted on YouTube (with the caption, "Suck on that, spooks") and tweeted to their fellow domestic law enforcement agencies throughout the free world.

The creature headed north, straight for Washington, DC. Government officials decided to move the President even further down, to a sub-sub-shelter known as "Satan's Rumpus Room." Though well stocked with plenty of gourmet foods and wines (plus Cheeseburger Macaroni Hamburger Helper, the President's favorite), a private movie theater, game room, nine-hole golf course and a theme park recently confiscated from the estate of a dead pop star, accommodations were more limited than they had been in Bedford Falls. Certain sacrifices had to be made. (Editor's note: The wisdom of leaving the Vice President and his family behind in favor of the cast of the President's favorite sitcom "Cheez-Heads" is not something we will debate here.)

The colossal beast reached the nation's capital and a curious thing happened.

It spent two entire days seemingly obsessed with manhole covers. It would see one from several blocks away and rush over, or through, several buildings to get to it (see side article, "Ape Destroys Lincoln Memorial and Most of DC's Starbucks in Mad Rush to Manholes"). It would then pick up the manhole, examine it closely with its one remaining eye, then bite it.

"Like a feller checkin' a silver dollar to see if t'were any good," observed homeless squeegee jockey Donald "Gummy" Olberstein, former Western sidekick of the popular 1950s series "The Sons of Doc Holliday."

Unfortunately, whatever the primate was looking for was not to be found in any of the manhole covers of Washington. After biting the one hundred pound cast iron and concrete treat the gorilla would roar and hurl the disc. This resulted in several more thousands in damages (negligible in the face of the billions already run up) and the decapitation of the entire DC Jammerz street gang (see YouTube video, "Fronters Loose (sic) Heads" posted by Li'l Diablo).

A number of DC's finest, hoping to get a jump on the military and the Secret Service, filled the streets with SWAT vans and weapons confiscated from cartel minions and gang members.

A number of them, taking in the miasma that surrounded the creature, fell violently ill and collapsed in the street, where they were consumed by maggots the size of piglets dripping from the ruined eye socket of the beast.

Others, wearing gas masks, did not succumb to the foul stench of the undead thing, but found that their bullet-proof vests and heavy wool uniforms were no barrier against the questing proboscises of the giant fleas and ticks searching for fresh blood in the streets of Washington.

The creature, unmindful of the bullets, tear gas and rocket fire, filled its putrid maw with squirming victims and its own parasites. Their screams became muffled and were soon lost in the din of battle, while partially-chewed officers rained down upon their fellows, one leg still kicking, a head and torso screaming for a full five minutes before a grizzled desk sergeant put a bullet in the man's head.

Though it was not the worst encounter with the gorilla, the DC police came to call it "The Everett Avenue Massacre," and it was made into a TV movie with Miley Cyrus and John Stamos.

In Iowa, Doctor Emily Grange woke up in a cold sweat on her cot, shouting "Petroglyphs!" Without delay she made a call to local law enforcement for a chopper and found that all aircraft in the area had been either stepped on, or grabbed out of the air and chewed on by the creature. She eventually found a crop duster willing to take her up and over the carnival site, and perhaps beyond, if her suspicions were warranted.

She prays they are not.

In Satan's Rumpus Room, the President appeared in a mock-up of the Oval Office and assured the beleagured nation that he has "not left his post." This claim was shown to be a rather transparent fiction when the backdrop behind him collapsed and revealed an impromptu bowling tournament between the President's family and several well-known 80s musicians, including Hall & Oates.

Enraged, much of the population of Washington stormed the White House, not realizing the President was safely underground in Nevada. The protesters were mowed down by the Secret Service and the police, delighted to finally have a target they could take down with bullets, tear-gas, and rockets.

Though the action would later be whitewashed and the body count chalked up to the rampaging gorilla-ghoul, people would come to call it "The Pennsylvania Avenue Massacre," and it would be made into a big budget Michael Bay movie with James Franco and Anne Hathaway, with WETA providing a motion-control zombie ape, played by Andy Serkis.

As bodies were piling up outside the White House Rose Garden, the gorilla took this moment to put in an appearance. By this time the Army had mobilized Project Coconut, and had instituted an emergency draft to beef up its decimated ranks. A warhead with a low nuclear yield (called an "Oppenheimer Junior") was deployed from an M1 Abrams tank and fired by Corporal Scott "Scooter" James, the President's nephew.

The missile slammed into the creature's mid-section and exploded, sending putrescent flesh and some of the larger undigested human bones flying. These destroyed the White House Rose Garden and made a charnel house of the Lincoln Bedroom, which, at the time, was occupied by the Vice-President and one of the docents from the midday tour.

The creature halted as its entrails spilled out in a foul, fetid mass. Its stomach acids ate through several tanks including the M1 Abrams, and Scooter James died a messy and agonizing death.

Several hundred brave men and women closed in to finish off the creature, when five undead tapeworms, each nearly a quarter mile in length, broke free of the rotting intestines and attacked the troops. The tapeworm, generally an annoying but somewhat passive creature, had been transformed by An-775 into something like a moray eel crossed with an anaconda on meth—a really huge moray eel and anaconda, on a really huge quantity of high-grade meth.

The tapeworms strangled, poisoned, and devoured over fifty percent of the troops before the gorilla began scooping up vast mouthfuls of its own innards, parasites and hapless humans. (Editor's note: Video of the event showed the living dead primate healing while continuing to decay, a contradiction that scientists are still investigating to this very day.)

The President and his staff were considering more extreme options (move the U.S. to an offshore territory, annex Canada, relocate to the moon) when Dr. Grange called in from Iowa. "Mr. President, I believe I have a way to lure the creature into the sea... however, we do have a bigger..."

"How do we lure it, Doctor?"

"We need to fabricate a quarter the size of a manhole cover. If you contact the mint, I'm sure..."

"Say again, you need a large mint?"

"No sir, a really big quarter... you know, the coin?"

At this point, the President hung up on her. "Crackpot," he said to his staff, and they went back to discussing the feasibility of a space ark.

Dr. Grange, to her credit, did not give up. She contacted a cousin in the scrap metal business and he was able to create a reasonable facsimile of a twenty-two inch quarter using fenders from a 1960 Ford Galaxy. Dr. Grange was able to secure a helicopter from a local news station in Washington. Joining the pilot, she dangled the giant coin in front of the undead simian and waited.

The results, to all watching, were remarkable.

The creature stopped eating, fixing its one eye on the faux two bits. It let out a roar and grabbed for the coin. The pilot, a veteran of the war in Iraq, deftly kept the coin just out of reach of the creature. In this way they led it far out into the Atlantic, where it sank and presumably drowned.

As they landed on the helipad Dr. Grange heard from the crop-duster, Joe Kittinger.

"Mr. Kittinger, did you find anything?"

"Yes, ma'am. 'Twere at the bottom of McFarland Lake… it's comin' out now…"

He sent her photos from his cell phone, and Dr. Grange put in a call to the President.

The President took the call, intent on making her quick thinking part of his re-election campaign.

"Dr. Grange, I'd like to present you with the Medal of Honor, just as soon as the White House is habitable again."

"I appreciate that, Mr. President, but we have a bigger problem."

The President chuckled. "Larger than a fifty-foot zombie gorilla? I seriously doubt that."

"It's not a gorilla, Mr. President, it's a capuchin monkey… The tail was a big giveaway. And its been spotted on Roanoke Island."

"Monkey, ape, aren't we just splitting hairs here?"

"Sir, the red 'tent' we found was no tent… it was an enormous cap and vest…"

"I don't…"

"The Anubis gas reanimated and enlarged a trained monkey - an organ grinder monkey. Not only is that monkey still alive… um, undead, but…"

85

"Out with it, Doctor!" the President barked.

"At this moment, a one hundred and fifty foot organ grinder is making his way to Washington."

In the background of her call, the President could here the first strains of "The Beer Barrel Polka."

And screams; lots of screams.

GUSTAVO BONDONI
Shadow of the Gorilla

For a moment, Verstappen found himself believing that, just maybe, Conrad had been right about the place. Night seemed darker here than anywhere the Belgian freighter captain had ever been in his life, despite the life he could feel buzzing and flittering just beyond the reach of the electric lights. The illumination was weak, as if it knew it didn't belong.

The *Étoile Ostend* didn't belong there either. If it had been entirely up to its captain, the ship would have left Verstappen and his men to fend for themselves in the jungles of Congo—or was that Zaire, now? Mugabe's soldiers would have little doubt about what to do with a group of white men unaligned with any of the major power blocs.

The captain's attitude was understandable, the cargo hold was almost completely laden: copper from the inland mines—the supposed reason for their trip—and a container-full of chemical drums lifted out of South Africa just before a UN inspection, which were to be dumped in the middle of the ocean for a tidy profit. But the money would only be paid if they managed the operation unobserved. If they left now all of them could retire wealthy men, but if the American or Belgian special force troops that seemed to be so prevalent since about 1965 spotted them, they would likely spend the rest of their penniless lives in prison.

What the captain didn't know was that the final piece of cargo had a price tag that made the South African money seem like pocket change. If he'd known that he wouldn't have been so anxious to leave, but he would certainly have demanded a cut.

Finally, the truck, a twenty-year-old Saab, turned onto the potholed loading dock, right under the only functioning crane in the entire port of Matadi. Thierry, the driver, climbed out of the cab and made a beeline for Verstappen.

"I swear, if we hadn't been through three wars together, I'd beat you to a pulp."

Verstappen grinned. "Tough trip?"

"I can't believe they call these things roads. Even the paved parts look like they've been bombed."

A shrug. "They probably have. How is the cargo?"

"It woke up a few hours ago. Dented the container." Thierry pointed to a massive bulge on the side of the ribbed box. "We just opened a hatch and hit it with elephant tranquilizers until it shut-up. If it's dead, it's dead."

"Unlikely."

"Yeah, I heard. The chief made me pay a huge blood price. He says he lost half his village squeezing that thing into the container."

"It's peanuts, Thierry. We'll be rich men when we get back to Brussels. But I'm still amazed that they managed to get it in at all."

"It's a pretty tough squeeze, but anything much bigger than a forty-foot container was going to look suspicious when we unloaded. We made it a little wider and a little longer. Let's just hope no one measures the thing."

"We'll worry about that when we get there. Just get it loaded. The sooner I get out of Congo, the happier I'll be."

* * *

Carolina checked her phone and smiled: a dancing iguana figure with tropical music blaring told her who the message was from with no room for doubt. Felipe might be unreliable and capricious, but she was totally worth it, especially in bed. And the fact that he'd actually come all the way down to Tapera to see her—a bit of a hitch-hike from the center of Florianopolis––meant that she'd actually managed to get far enough through his armor to avoid becoming the latest in his series of one-night tourist girls.

She walked across the road, removed her sandals and felt the sand on her feet. The guy at the caipi-bar smiled at her hopefully. "Later," she told him in Spanish—he was actually from Uruguay, she'd learned—and kept walking. A single dark-skinned man was sunning himself, clad only in a zunga, about fifty meters down the beach. She knew that body.

"Hi."

He smiled up at her, dazzling white teeth nearly blinding in the sunlight. "Hello, there *garotinha*. I didn't think you'd be here so quickly."

They both knew that was a lie, but Carolina ignored it and sat down beside him, enjoying the caress of the warm sand on her buttocks. "And I didn't think you'd be up so early. When I left, I wasn't sure whether you were alive or dead."

He shrugged, barely moving on the sand. "I'm used to not getting much sleep. It's par for the course."

"What's that?"

"Can I look later?"

"No, look now!"

He grumbled a bit, but moved. "I have no idea." He made to lie down again, but she stopped him.

"Is it a Tsunami?"

"We don't get Tsunamis in Brazil," he replied laconically. "Wrong sort of climate for it."

She counted to three, reminding herself that if she wanted intelligent conversation she shouldn't look for it from surf bums. "Look, there's a huge lump of something dark over there. It might be a wave." Ever since the Southeast Asian Tsunami she'd been anxious about giant swells.

"Not a wave. A wave would take up the whole horizon. Looks more like some kind of tall boar."

She stared out onto the bay, trying to make out further details. "Grey and green? And shaped like that?"

He shrugged. "If it's coming this way, we'll find out what it is. Relax a little." He reached out a hand and caressed the inside of her thigh.

She decided that the ship, or whatever it was wasn't so important after all and bent over, pretending to kiss Felipe's forehead with a move that pushed his hand into a more favorable position.

* * *

Verstappen wasn't happy with the delay. They could have dumped the South African chemicals the day before, but the captain hadn't wanted to do it. He'd said that the only other craft on the water, a fishing boat under Angolan registration, was probably a Soviet spy-boat in disguise.

Verstappen had responded that the Soviets couldn't care less if a Belgian ship dumped a load of South African chemicals, but the man had refused to see reason and had sailed deeper into international waters. It hadn't made anyone happy, especially since the most precious container on board was perched precariously on top of two others, right at the summit of the pile of metal shipping boxes.

When the storm hit, the Belgian went below in disgust, while the captain began the procedure to unload and sink thousands of yellow drums—some marked with biohazard warnings, others with radioactivity labels, and all with large, stenciled 'DANGER' signs. And though it wasn't the first operation of this kind they'd put together for some government or other, it was always nice when the evidence was safely at the bottom of the sea. It made for much more relaxed cruising.

He'd just closed the door that separated his smallish cabin from the rest of the ship when he heard a clatter from above, as if some of the drums had gotten away from the crane operator. Verstappen smiled. If the pompous bastard of a captain had splattered his ship with radioactive tailings, it was going to be fun watching him try to get through a Geiger check on his next port of call. The cold war seemed to be making everyone paranoid—and the seventies were probably going to be the worst decade yet. They'd certainly started off badly enough.

Footsteps on metal alerted him to someone's approach, and Thierry poked his head in without bothering to knock. "You need to come quickly, boss," the soldier-cum-driver said. Another crash sounded overhead.

Verstappen didn't waste time arguing. He'd chosen his men well, trained them better. If they said he had to come, then he had to come. They ran along the passage and up to the deck.

The expected scene—drums of chemicals rolling over the container deck—was absent. Instead, Verstappen found the crew desperately trying to curb the movement of a single oversized container, the container holding the gorilla.

The enormous gorilla-like creature they'd tracked and captured had somehow managed to push a leg through the corrugated steel of the container—forcing one of the door hinges—hinges that were as thick as a man's leg. The free leg was pushing the container across the planking on deck, straight towards the crane. More ominous, though, was the fact that the movements weren't designed to move the container: the gorilla was trying to get its arms free. That was unacceptable.

"Quick, bring the tranquilizers!" Verstappen shouted. Thierry ran off to get the gun crew, and Verstappen joined the captain, watching helplessly as a team armed with poles tried to immobilize the container. They seemed like flies trying to maneuver an elephant. Every once in a while, they spilled across the deck as an unexpected lurch threw them off their feet.

A single fist, almost as tall as a man, suddenly shot out of the box and flattened a pole-bearer against a bulkhead with a sickening crunch. As the man—instantly turned to jelly—slid slowly down the wall, the rest of the sailors fled.

It was just as well that they did. With a deafening roar, the fifty-foot gorilla inside the container flexed its muscles and tore the container to shreds like a horrendous black chicken hatching from a rectangular egg. A scrap of discarded metal flew over the captain's head and broke the forward window on the bridge tower.

"Where's that gun?" Vertappen screamed.

Small-arms fire erupted from the deck—someone, it seemed, had managed to locate a gun or two. Verstappen wanted to tell them to stop, that they would only succeed in enraging the beast, but remained silent. Their gnat-stings would serve to distract the thing and it would concentrate on the immediate irritants while his own team prepped the tranquilizer gun. And who knew. Maybe they would get lucky and hit something vital.

Thierry arrived with Jan, the chemist. "What dose do we need?"

Verstappen sneered. "What do you think?"

"I'll give it everything we have." Jan set to work on loading the glass cartridge, full of a viscous yellowish liquid, into the wide barrel of the modified elephant gun.

Some reflection must have given them away, because suddenly, the huge gorilla turned towards them. It took less than two huge strides—maybe three seconds—for the creature to reach them.

"Shoot it! Shoot it!" Verstappen cried as a huge hand descended onto them from high above. Jan fumbled once, twice with the unwieldy firearm before managing to press the trigger. It was the second fumble that killed them all, since that was the one that insured that they were flattened before the dart left the muzzle. It was a pity, actually, since Jan made a beautiful shot, managing to ember the dart in a blood vessel just outside the gorilla's right eye socket.

But, though he was dead, Verstappen missed little that would have interested him. The captain watched with satisfaction as the drugged gorilla fell overboard to sink to the bottom of the cold, dark sea. He ordered the crew to keep dumping barrels into the ocean, little knowing that they were landing on the unconscious—soon to be drowned—gorilla. Then he had the bodies thrown off the ship.

The *Étoile Ostend* sailed off to disappear into the murk of cold-war record-keeping, never to be heard from again. The barrels, meanwhile, were breaking under the pressure of the fathoms.

* * *

"No, no!" Felipe shouted. "This way!"

Again Carolina shook her head. The guy was trying to lead her into a structure that seemed to be made of straw and thin sticks. That… thing… would tear it away like so much paper. She ran into the cylindrical concrete structure in front of them. Felipe, cursing, followed her through the dark opening.

The first thing that hit her was the smell, as though a mammoth had died in an open sewer. "What is this place?" she whispered.

Felipe looked around, illuminated by the sunlight from the outside, and shrugged. "Utility of some kind. Probably a pumping station."

"So that's why it smells? This is connected to the sewer?"

Felipe, despite his obvious fear, laughed. "No, that is the smell of the *Sem Terras*. They sleep in here."

The *Sem Terras*. As far as she knew, they were a political movement, but most Brazilians seemed to hold them in contempt, as though they were leeches on an otherwise productive social system. Carolina had her doubts—but that certainly wasn't the time or place to express them. "What is that thing?"

He shrugged again, and again made her remember that she'd selected him more for the shape of his pecs and the washboard beneath them than for his mind. "Some kind of sea monster. First time I've seen it."

"It didn't look like a sea-monster. It looked like something from land, something that shouldn't have been in the water at all. And it looked like it had pieces falling off."

He shrugged and said nothing.

"I'm going to have a look." Carolina walked towards the rectangle of blinding light that marked the entrance, blinked a couple of times and then stared. The thing approaching had to be fifteen meters high, vaguely humanoid, with slimy greenish-grey skin on which small, matted clumps of fur seemed to be barely hanging on.

Felipe had come up behind her. "It's a gigantic monkey," he said. "And it smells terrible!"

The creature was tearing up the beach bar that Felipe had wanted to hide inside. The screams that had been coming from that direction died down after one of its blows landed with a particularly sickening crunch. "That's the smell from the sewage," Carolina said.

"No way. Look, we're downwind from the thing. It's the monster's smell."

Trust a surf bum to know precisely where the wind is coming from, she thought. But the guy was right. The smell—worse than the stink from inside the concrete bunker—was definitely coming from… well, from whatever it was. The stench was completely out of place on that beach, which should have smelled of cool breezes and coconut-scented tanning lotion.

"It sees us!" Felipe ran back into the darkness of the cylindrical building.

Carolina hesitated for a second, thinking that she had plenty of time, and thinking also that a round structure with no back door might not be the best place to avoid a charging monster.

The hesitation almost cost her her life.

Moving amazingly quickly for something so big the creature took two strides, and in the same motion, drove its gigantic fist towards the doorway. Carolina jumped back just far enough to avoid being crushed, but not quite far enough to avoid the spray of noxious slime that sluiced out of one of the fingers. She ran back towards the opposite end of the building and, forgetting for a second that Felipe was nothing but a bit of fluff, she grabbed hold of him for dear life.

The monster, the giant, the monkey, whatever it was that pursued them, began to attack the small utility building. The walls shook and dust fell in clouds from the ceiling, but the builders of the building had apparently decided that the integrity of the sewage inside was paramount and had designed the bunker to be able to withstand anything thrown at it. A mere overgrown monster wouldn't faze it.

"You need to go out there!" Felipe shouted.

She pushed him away. "What? Are you out of your fucking mind?"

"No, really. You know how it is! These huge monsters are always weak where women are concerned. Especially beautiful women. As soon as he sees you, he'll become as tame as a puppy."

His charm was nearly enough to make Carolina smile, but he was as dumb as a brick. He probably didn't have much experience with puppies, either. "He already saw me. Don't you remember? It was just before he tried to flatten me."

"Maybe he didn't see you well. You were standing in the shadows."

"I'm not going out there, and that's final."

The building had stopped shaking, but they could still see the monster's shadow cutting off the bright light from outside. A huge eye, bloodshot and grey suddenly filled the hole, followed almost instantly by a huge hand which squeezed through the opening and groped around, trying to catch them, to squeeze the life out of them. Carolina screamed, knowing it was a stupid thing to do, and still completely unable to make herself stop. At least she could take some comfort in the fact that, right beside her, Felipe was screaming in counterpoint.

They'd pressed themselves back as far as they could go, unconcerned about what the pool of foul-smelling liquid they were lying in might be made of. Despite cramming themselves into the deepest corner, it seemed that the fist would inevitably turn them to jelly. The monster was pushing it further and further into the opening. It was three meters away. Two.

Less than an arm's length out, it stopped. The twists of the bunker's interior had finally thwarted any further attempt to thrust the arm inside. They could hear the creature's enraged grunts, feel the building shaking all around them as the monster raged.

And though she hated herself for it, Carolina buried her face in Felipe's chest. She knew it was pathetic, but there was no helping it. She heard him chuckle: "I can't believe you brought your purse," he said, his typical male obliviousness not allowing him to spot the difference between a purse and a beach bag.

A pause ensued, as if the creature was distracted by something. The giant hand menacing them stayed suspended in mid-air, quivering slightly, smelling like rotten fish.

Suddenly, without warning, it retreated, leaving the opening free. As sunlight poured in they could feel the building vibrating—not violently, but as though giant footsteps were moving away. A bellow of absolute rage reached them from what was unquestionably a good distance.

"It's gone," Felipe said. "Let's go!"

"Go? Where?" But it was too late. Felipe had already sprinted for the door. Carolina followed a bit more cautiously, popping only her head out of the bunker in order to look around. There seemed to be no sign, seemed to be no threat, so she stepped all the way out to try to see where the creature had gone.

Its path wasn't difficult to deduce. A line of palm trees had been pushed aside like matchwood directly behind the little building, and the destruction led all the way to the two-lane road that ran parallel to the beach. The monster could be seen, sitting directly in the center of the tarmac, tearing apart a container which had been on a truck. The truck itself was lying on its side on one shoulder, looking like a discarded plaything. It raged at the container itself, as if blaming it for some terminal misfortune. Scraps of steel painted hull red flew until there was nothing left.

A small figure caught her eye, then. Felipe had instinctively run for the road, but, on finding his path blocked, had stopped like a rabbit in headlights. He stared at the creature in his path as if wondering what sauce it would go best with. Carolina reasoned that that probably wasn't the best way of dealing with it, but she didn't want to call out in case the gorilla—it looked more and more like an gorilla, the more she looked at it—heard her.

In the end, it made no difference. Finding that the last pieces of the container had disappeared, the monster looked up to see Felipe standing motionless as if in challenge. It bellowed again and Felipe ran. Carolina was relieved to see that the creature was far enough away that Felipe would make it to the bunker long before the gorilla would.

But Felipe panicked. Instead of running towards the safety of the concrete box, he headed for the sea, perhaps in some instinctive "back to the womb" reaction. What he hoped to achieve by this was unclear, but he never made it. The gorilla, eating ground efficiently with its enormous legs, caught him just as he was about to reach the edge. A single swipe of an enormous hand lifted Fellipe high into the air. Carolina could hear his screams as he reached the apex of his parabola, braced herself for the bone-crunching impact that would come when he hit the sand.

But Felipe never made it to the ground. A huge mouth intercepted his descent, and the jaws closed on him. Even from that distance, Carolina could see the spray of blood as his body burst.

The enormous eyes fastened onto her, and a second later, they were back to their original position: she was huddled in the corner while a huge fist groped blindly for her in the dark. Now that she was alone, she found her urge to scream had gone. She cried to herself in the semi-darkness, going over Felipe's last seconds again and again.

After what seemed like an eternity, the gorilla tired. The hand retreated, but instead of bright daylight shining through, there was little change in the quality of light. Carolina understood that she'd spent the entire afternoon stuck in a round concrete building—and had it not been there, her day would have ended badly indeed.

Where is the army? she wondered. *The cops? Someone has to have been told about this by now.* But that, like the origin of the creature, seemed to be just another mystery. And she really, really had to pee.

That last was easily solved, at least. A few seconds after removing its hand, the creature once more obstructed the entry, but this time, it was neither its hand or its face in the opening. It was just a big bit of rotting fur with some kind of huge warts. Thus unobserved, Carolina allowed herself to crouch in one of the smellier corners to relieve herself.

Spurred on by this act of bravery, she walked towards the door, her eyes able to make out some kind of pattern on the fur, roundish, elongated and…

She screamed and skittered back into the far corner.

Fused to the skin of the gorilla, melted and deformed, but easily recognizable, was a human face. No, there were two human faces, melted together at the chin like monstrous Siamese twins. And the other mounds, the bigger ones, could only be their bodies.

She could probably have taken that, she felt, had it not been for the fact that, on one of the horribly grimacing figures, she could clearly make out a single eye, staring at her with a madness she'd never imagined possible.

But what could she do? She moved forward, slowly, afraid that the human figures would jump off the creature and kill her—or worse. They stayed where they were, however, with that single baleful eye the only sign of movement. But what movement it was: the eye followed her around like a spotlight, pained and malevolent at the same time.

The face the eye belonged to contorted, grimaced, pulled, and finally, with a gush of foul-smelling black bile, opened. The only sounds that emerged were gurgles and clacks.

She stared, and then, impulsively, touched the cheek of the other face, the one without eyes. There was no human suppleness to the skin, just hard, cold and dry parchment. Like fish scales left out in the sun. The rotting fur that framed it didn't help, either.

The eye followed her hand, rolling unnaturally around as it did so, and widening in obvious fear as she reached towards the face. She could see muscles working in the jaw, trying to free the mouth from some other obstacle that she couldn't see. They stood out like thick cords. With an audible snap, something let go, and the face emitted its first sound, a tortured keening unlike anything a human being should be capable of creating. There were no teeth in the mouth.

The sound made Carolina step back, still followed by the eye. Since it had managed to break through its chains, she hoped the face would be satisfied and stop contorting, fall back into its previous torpor.

But she had no such luck. Its mouth continued working, its eye kept revolving, and sound kept pouring forth. She imagined it was trying to speak, but all that emerged were moans and sobs, punctuated by an occasional screech of superhuman pain.

Night fell. The gorilla's shadow had been replaced by the true dark of tropical night. Stars gave no illumination, and the new moon never would.

But the sound didn't cease. Eventually, by dint of what sounded like supremely painful efforts, the face began to gain coherence, or at least the semblance thereof. Now, instead of sounding like the grunting of some big cat, the noise was that of a foreign language being spoken in slow motion. Moans echoed around the bunker, making the warm tropical blackness feel like a lonely Scottish moor in the dead of winter, complete with howling-wind sound effects. She huddled in her corner, afraid to move lest that single, mad eye should report her presence to the monster above. Sleep was fitful, but, surprisingly, not inexistent.

She woke with a start. In a groggy state, she thought the sharp pain in her side, consequence of the position she'd been reclined in, was the culprit, but then she realized that the voice had become almost recognizably human, and that was what must have woken her up. It seemed to be a stream of some kind of Germanic gibberish whose meaning she could almost make out—some of it seemed similar to the English she'd learned in school.

"Hallo."

This was sudden, unexpected, out of the blue. For a second, Carolina thought that the Brazilians must have finally gotten their act together, that the army had been mobilized and the threat removed. People must be combing the beaches for missing tourists. But then, she heard the same voice, this time spouting the gibberish from before.

"Wait, hello," she whispered without thinking.

The voice stopped. Silence echoed through the bunker more powerfully than the earlier sound. "Hallo… English?"

Should she respond to this? Should she interact with the monster? "Yes, some English," she said.

"I… need… help…"

The first thought that crossed her mind was that whatever else might be happening, the owner of that face, that voice, was beyond all human help. "How can I help you?"

There was a pause, long enough to make her wonder whether she'd dreamed the whole thing.

"Kill me…" Another pause ensued as Carolina processed this. "Please… *please*…"

Still she said nothing.

"Please…"

"But how? You're a part of this huge thing. How can I kill something like that? How?" Desperation lent her a fluency that she could never recall having had when taking her lessons.

The voice gurgled. With one final wet sound, it seemed to disappear. And then, with a final effort, more of a series of coughs than real words, it said: "Fire… the chemicals… use fire…"

"But how? I don't have any fire! I don't even smoke."

But all she got from the face was a series of gulps and wheezes. More snaps and pops showed that the figure it was attached to was still moving, but its capacity to speak seemed to have disappeared.

At dawn, it was no longer creaking and popping. But it wasn't dead. That single, insane eye revolved in its socket and reminded her of her promise to help—a promise she'd never made, but one that the revolving orb seemed determined to hold her to.

I don't even smoke, she thought, but the eye didn't seem to care.

With the rising sun, her giant adversary stirred. The gorilla stood, letting the blinding morning light—reflected off the white sand—into the bunker like a searing flame. The very same flame that she didn't have. Her heart thumped as the beast took three steps away—could it be leaving? Would she be able to escape none the worse for wear?

No such luck was forthcoming. After its short walk, the rank-smelling creature returned to the utility structure, and the tiny, rolling eye of the thing fused to its back was replaced by the enormous, evil orb of the creature itself—followed in short order by the grasping hand. Carolina, seated in her corner with the bag that had caused Felipe so much amusement, barely even flinched. The growling in her stomach seemed louder and more threatening than the giant gorilla she'd already grown accustomed to.

She opened the bag, hoping against hope that she'd remembered to pack some cookies, a cereal bar, something, but no such luck. All she had was a thermos full of now-cold water and the implements to make and clean the maté—her single concession to infusion addiction—she went nowhere without, some money and her cell phone. That last was useless there in Brazil, but she lugged it around anyway, feeling naked without it.

No lighter, no flare gun. No hope.

She tried to get into a more comfortable position. Maybe if she ignored it, the thing would go away.

But it didn't, and after hours, there were no comfortable positions left, and there was no question of moving into a different spot to pee. All she could do was to try to stay as far from the small puddle beside her as possible.

If only I had a box of matches, she thought. And that thought brought back a memory. A cold spring night camping in Patagonia, and the discovery that the lighter they'd been relying on to light their nightly fires had somehow broken. One of the guys in the group had managed to get a fire lighted using only a cell phone and something in her maté kit. The *virulana*, the steel wool. And she'd brought that very same chunk with her—it was still inside the bag.

But how had he done it? She recalled that he'd taken the phone apart, so she did. Then she stopped to remember the guy himself. As far as she could tell, just another Felipe: good looking, hair too long, and better in bed than in the daytime. She clearly had to change the kind of guy she fell for—but, to be fair, he'd known the cell phone trick, and she didn't. Even now, with the cell phone battery and the steel wool in front of her, she had no clue as to how it would work.

The battery was a featureless flat rectangle as long as her thumb, and the only thing about it that didn't look completely inert were a few tiny strips of copper on one edge, with the positive and negative signs beside them. She pressed the steel wool to the edges and nearly dropped the battery into a pool of her own urine when a small spark flew inside the black piece of *virulana.* She did drop the steel wool, but luckily, it landed on her foot.

Carolina studied the steel wool. Tiny singe marks scarred it, barely visible in the dim light of the utility bunker. But the verdict was clear: the wool had burnt, and it was time for her to make a decision.

Should she attack the monster, try to set it alight? Would that even work? It seemed much too large to be flammable. Maybe her best bet was to sit tight and wait for the authorities to do something about it.

But that could take days. There was no question that the government knew about the creature, but they were probably waiting to see what happened. Without thinking about it, she pressed the steel wool into the battery again, this time, making sure she kept it there even after smoke began to pour from it. *Didn't these batteries have acid in them?* She just hoped it held out long enough to get a decent fire.

A tiny dot of light appeared on the *virulana*, and she moved without thinking toward the gigantic hand resting on the floor. She reached out and tried to press the smoldering steel wool onto a finger.

Carolina realized almost immediately that it was a big mistake, that she'd stepped well inside the beast's reach. But almost immediately wasn't good enough. Moving with lightning speed, a huge fist wrapped around her legs and pulled her out of the building. Only quick reflexes allowed her to duck in time to avoid leaving her brains splattered all over the top of the concrete doorway.

The gorilla placed the fist right in front of its face, and studied her for a second. She thought she could see malicious gloating in its eyes, but soon the stench overpowered her other faculties—it made the putrid interior of the bunker seem like a flowery meadow.

A second later, panic kicked in. This monster wasn't going to keep contemplating her forever, and soon, she would follow Felipe's lead and become a shower of blood and bone, to be washed off the beach by the next high tide. She frantically pressed the steel wool to the battery, pressing the smoking concoction against the fist with trembling hands.

A small patch of flaking, rotting material came alight, and she had hope for a second, but it was too little, too late. She was already being conveyed to the giant maw, and the monster wouldn't even notice a flame that size.

But in the instant before she was consumed, the flame suddenly spread as if the creature had been made of gasoline. The hairs on her arm were singed with heat, and the beast screamed like a banshee with a bad headache. Before she had time to react, Carolina was dropping to the floor from thirty feet up. Only a glancing blow against one of the gorilla's knees, which slowed her descent, saved her from being killed by the impact with the sand. It didn't save her from hearing several bones break.

She lay there, determined to watch until the beast was gone. It took a surprisingly short time to be consumed, but that time was employed in running to and fro—nearly crushing her with a giant foot in the process—and screaming. When it finally fell into a smoking, ruined heap, she allowed the darkness to overcome her.

* * *

She woke to screams in Portuguese. Hands, arms placing her on a stretcher, lifting her over the sand at a run to a running helicopter. A doctor telling her that she was going to be all right, a guy in a uniform apologizing, saying that they'd had no idea that anyone was left alive, that they were observing the creature to decide what to do with it. Another asking if she knew any of the victims.

The doctor told her not to answer any questions.

But what could she have said? She really hadn't known Felipe—or at least not anything about him that was anyone's business. But as she drifted into the fog of the painkillers, she knew this particular version of the dumb guy would be her last––but it would also be the only one she remembered.

REBECCA SNOW
Monkey See

Diamond-shaped, primary-colored flags fluttered from poles staked around the lot. A gust of wind made them sound like television machine gun fire. A concrete block building stood at the center. Blotches of white paint had peeled making it look like an overweight Dalmatian. Through the plate glass windows I saw a small group of men in cheap suits playing cards. One of the men tossed his hand to the table and pushed back his folding chair when he saw me. He tapped one of the other men before walking toward the door. I spun in a circle taking in all of the shiny used cars parked in rows. Another breeze ruffled my hair and flapped the streamer-flags that anchored an inflatable monkey to the roof of the building. A black and white banner told me that I would *GO APE!* over these prices. I caught a whiff of something foul. Someone must have hit a deer on the highway.

"Can I help you?" the salesman said.

I squinted at the man through my sunglasses. His rumpled suit hung on his frame as if he'd lost some weight but hadn't replaced his wardrobe. From the greasy red stain on his tie, I guessed he'd had fast food for lunch. His black hair was gelled back except for a wayward piece jutting straight out from the side of his head.

"I'm looking for a used car. Nothing fancy," I said. "I'd prefer one with good gas mileage."

"Well, you've come to the right place," he said, thrusting his hand toward me. "My name's Warren. I'm sure we can find the perfect car for you."

His hand was sticky when I shook it. When he turned to look across the sea of vehicles I wiped my hand on my skirt. I glanced back at the monkey as I followed Warren to a line of cars close to the highway. Its colossal arm flopped in the breeze.

"Here's a little beauty, just like yourself, if you don't mind my saying," he said, stepping up to a metallic red sports car.

"I don't want anything fancy," I repeated.

"You know you'd look great in this one. It's got all leather interior, automatic transmission, cruise control, built-in GPS." He caressed the front fender in a way that made me want to mace him.

"This car isn't even close to what I'm looking for," I said. "I don't want an automatic."

"Ah, you're a stick girl," he said, leering at my blouse.

"I want a small, fuel-efficient, reliable automobile with manual transmission. I've got a strict budget and would prefer something in dark blue or black."

Warren's eyebrows drew together in a scowl, and his lips pinched into a straight line. He slid his eyes sideways to look at me and nodded his head.

"I'll tell you what I'll do," he began. "I'll go get the keys for this hot little number, and we can take her for a test drive."

"Sir, I do not want this car," I said, trying to stay calm. "I have no interest in this car. None whatsoever. If you won't show me something closer to what I've requested I'll ask another salesman, or get that big monkey to sell me something."

I motioned to the monstrous hulk perched on top of the showroom. Warren's gaze followed my gesture. His mouth fell open as he lifted a hand and pointed behind me. Glancing over my shoulder, I saw what I had mistaken for a giant monkey sales balloon open its mouth and groan. Its arms strained against the ropes of flags. When I turned back to Warren, the man was gone. I thought I caught a glimpse of his ill-fitting suit slithering into a boxy motor home as I ran for the showroom.

I pressed on the door and banged on the glass until I realized I had to pull the door to gain entrance. Stepping into the freezing cold, air-conditioned showroom, I was enveloped in a new car smell so strong it made my eyes water. The men were still playing cards.

"Hey," I yelled and pointed out the door. "Your monkey's mad."

My comment was met with four bewildered gazes and one wide-eyed stare.

"That's impossible," the staring man said. "He's sedated. They come back every night and sedate him again."

The bewildered gazes turned to gape at the speaker.

"What monkey?" one of the other men asked.

"The one on top of the building," I said. "He's about to go ape shit."

The staring man jumped to his feet and sent his folding chair clattering to the floor. I grabbed his arm as he tried to run past me.

"I don't know what's going on here, but you're about to have a pissed off primate stomping all over your inventory," I said.

He shrugged off my hand and ran behind the counter. He picked up a small metal box topped with a red button and set it on the counter. Looking up at me, he smiled before pointing one dirty-nailed finger toward the ceiling and lowering it to press the button.

"There, that should do it," he said, as a loud crash rocked the building.

All five men dropped to the ground. I rushed out the door to see what had happened. The gorilla was still standing. His glazed eyes rolled in their sockets, and he stomped on the roof of the building as he beat his chest with his bound arms. Ribbons of flesh hung from his wrists. One of the flags was tearing, so I knew it wouldn't be long before he got loose. When the big monkey moaned, I smelled the aroma of his rotting innards. It hadn't been a dead deer after all.

"What's going on out there," the staring man asked popping up from under the counter when I returned to the showroom.

"Before I say another word, you'd better tell me what's going on and why that ape smells dead," I said, placing my hands on my hips and tapping my foot.

The man, still on his knees, swept his eyes around the room and motioned me to the counter. I took two steps and crossed my arms over my chest.

"Spill it," I said, in my 'mom's caught you lying' voice.

"Well, ma'am, I purchased a giant ape online. It was cheaper than renting one of those inflatables."

The building shuddered; a ceiling tile crashed to the floor. The man threw his arms over his head to protect his bald spot.

"Continue," I said, lifting an eyebrow.

"Well, after I'd placed the order, I got a phone call. The guy said that it would be even cheaper to use one of their undead apes since I only wanted it for a few days. He said that they'd keep him sedated, and no one would know the difference. Once I was done with the monkey, they'd take care of disposal."

"What was the button supposed to do?" I asked.

"It was supposed to fry his brain," the man whimpered as the building rocked again. "But I guess it didn't work."

I shook my head and stared at the man. Didn't he know how dangerous it was to play with dead things? Hadn't he seen the warnings on commercials and plastered all over billboards? Only trained specialists could be trusted with the dead. And lucky for him, I was one of the specialists.

"Stay here," I said, before stepping out the door. I looked back through the window and didn't see a single person. They must have gone to ground under the counter.

I turned towards the giant stinking gorilla and waved.

"Hey, fella. Are you okay up there?"

The mammal stopped straining against the ropes.

"Yeah, that's it. You can calm down. I'm going to get you loose and take you home." At least that was my plan.

I continued soothing the savage beast with peaceful words as I backed toward my aging blue compact. When my hand touched the hatchback, I fished my keys from my skirt pocket. After unlocking the trunk I lifted the lid and retrieved my tattered leather handler's bag. Before I could pull my hand free of the trunk the lifters gave out. The hatchback crashed down on my forearm. I grimaced, lifted the hatch, removed my arm and the bag, and let the lifters slam the hatchback. The concussion

I'd gotten last month caused by the broken lifters was one of the reasons I had come to get a new-to-me vehicle.

The humungous primate had resumed his struggle against the restraints. I watched in horror as a flag ripped and the gorilla staggered from the roof. His tumble crushed a tan minivan like a recycled soda can. The ground shook as his skull cracked on the asphalt. He stood up from his misstep, threw back his massive head, and groaned. The odor almost made me lose my lunch. As he began to beat on his chest, I saw some of the torn sinew rip from his wrist. His clenched fist loosened as the muscle snapped.

"Over here," I said, as I waved my arms over my head.

The great gorilla ignored my flailing and stagger-loped to the motor home where Warren had disappeared. The monkey pressed his enormous opposable thumb to the windshield and popped it free like the lens on a broken pair of glasses. Then he picked up the vehicle and tried to shake Warren out like a cereal prize. I could hear Warren's wobbling screams as he was thrown around his hiding place.

"Warren," I yelled. "Are you okay?"

"Are you kidding?" he screamed back. "I've never been less okay in my life."

The giant gorilla took this opportunity to bash the end of the RV with his flopping hand as if he were trying to pour unwilling ketchup from a bottle. I admired Warren's ability to stay inside the motor home as it jerked around until I saw his face fly past the little bathroom window. He had locked himself inside the small cubicle. As long as the door held and he protected his head, I figured he'd be all right.

Opening my bag, I reached in and pulled out a small rubber object. It was shaped like a banana. I squeezed it, and it squeaked.

"Lancelot, I've got a present for you if you put down that nasty old thing," I said, as I squeaked the banana again.

The crazed gorilla turned his head in my direction, and I squeezed the banana a third time. He stopped shaking the RV and looked like he was on his way to releasing it until Warren shrieked. There was no way my little banana squeaks could compare to a shrieking man, especially to the ears of a giant gorilla. I dropped the banana to the ground and rummaged through my tools as the beast crammed the fingers of his functioning hand through the opening left by his thumb.

"Okay, George," I said, setting a remote-control helicopter on the ground. "Maybe this'll distract you."

The little helicopter lifted off, and I maneuvered it to hover in front of the gorilla's face. He swung his floppy hand and sent the toy copter flying over a line of trees. That gorilla had done it. I was mad. The chopper had been my favorite weapon.

I grabbed my dart pistol from the bag and aimed.

"Hey, Magilla," I shouted. "I'd rather you cooperated, but if I have to, I will take you by force."

Hearing my voice, the huge gorilla lowered the motor home and turned. When he saw the pistol he let out a guttural grunt, hurled the rear end of his wheeled toy through the showroom's window, and charged me. I aimed and fired, hitting the crack in the center of the hulking monster's forehead. It was a perfect shot, and I breathed a sigh of relief when his large thighs quivered and crumpled. The gorilla's head crushed the cab of a pickup truck as he dropped.

I had reached down to pick up my bag when I heard a snuffling noise from where the beast had collapsed. Trying not to make any sudden moves, I inched my head up and saw the huge dead gorilla sit up and toss his head back and forth. The sedatives had been my last resort. My bag of tricks was empty and it was too late to call for backup. Then, I had an idea.

"Warren," I shouted. "The monkey's stunned, get out of there!"

I heard movement from inside the motor home before the side door swung open and fell off, clattering to the pavement. Warren was covered in blood and cradled his left arm. When he saw where I stood he stumbled toward me. The gorilla was still shaking his own head from side to side.

"Can't you kill it?" he asked. "It attacked me."

"Only as a last resort," I said, as I led the shaken man to my car and made him sit on the hatchback. "I've got one more idea, but I'll need your cooperation."

He flopped his upper body back on the car.

"What do you want me to do?" he screeched. "Haven't I done enough?"

I smiled to myself as I unrolled a length of duct tape and secured Warren's shoulders to the car's back window. He didn't have much strength left to struggle, so it wasn't difficult to affix the rest of him to the car.

"What the hell are you doing? Stop!" he screamed. "I'll sue you! You're endangering my life!"

"Keep yelling," I said, with a smirk. "We'll need your screams to lure the ape out of town."

By this time, the huge gorilla had gotten to his feet and had taken a stumbling step forward. I started the car and beeped the horn. Right on cue, Warren screamed. The gorilla turned toward us and followed the noise in halting, shuffling steps.

With Warren baited on the back of the car and the primate stumbling after us, I called dispatch with one hand and drove with the other.

"Hey, Shirley," I said.

"Hey, girl. Did you pick up that snazzy new ride?"

I heard her laughing on the other end of the line.

"Not yet," I said. "Look, I've got a situation here. Are any of the extra-large holding facilities free? I've got a giant undead ape in tow."

"Let me check," she said.

I heard her fingernails clicking on the keyboard.

"Yeah, what's your location?" she asked.

"Right down the street from the sleazy used car place. The one across from where the mini-golf place used to be."

Glancing in the rear-view mirror, I saw the gorilla had gathered himself together and was gaining ground. I sped up; Warren screamed louder.

"What's that noise?" Shirley asked.

"Just the bait," I said. "Do you have anything?"

"Hold your horses, this ain't rocket science," she laughed.

"Hey, lady," Warren shouted. "I think you'd better go faster."

"Sorry." See No Evil was gaining on us. I had to speed up.

I looked back. The gorilla was reaching for my car, trying to pinch the bumper with the fingers on his good hand. I pressed the accelerator to the floor. The car demonstrated another of my motivations for its replacement by jerking forward three times before surrendering an extra five miles per hour.

"C'mon," Warren screamed. "Is that all this piece of crap can do?"

The gorilla groaned behind us.

"Here's one," Shirley said surprising me. I almost dropped the phone. "It's down by the docks. Is there a way you can bypass the center of town? You know the boss wouldn't appreciate his view disrupted by your friend there."

I laughed at the thought of Henry seeing us pass in front of his seventh-story corner office.

"Okay, I'll try to go around," I said. "Once I get to the docks, where do I go?"

"Just drive straight through the gates. I'll call ahead and have the guys open them for you." Shirley laughed again. "You be careful, and when you get that new car, you better let me borrow it."

"Will do. Thanks, Shirley."

I tossed the phone on the passenger seat and cursed as it fell through the hole in the cushion. I figured there would be enough change in that hole at least to make a down payment on another car.

I took the lumbering gorilla on a tour of the outskirts of the city. We passed the dump. Hungry gulls surrounded the gorilla. From my training, I knew the undead virus didn't affect birds, so I wasn't worried. When the flock circled back to their home turf, seagulls from the dock swarmed. I drove through the open gates and made a mental note to thank Shirley for her diligence. Several men in orange vests and hard hats waved me toward a large hangar.

"When you drive through the doors, go to your left," one of the vested men said as he jogged next to my car. "When the ape gets inside, keep circling around the wall as fast as you can until you make it back to the front. We'll close the doors when you're out."

I nodded, and he dropped back with the others.

The hangar bay was dark. I held my breath and flipped the switch for the headlights. Nothing happened. Ever since driving through a shallow river to outrun a zombie rhino, my car lights had been less than predictable.

"Hold on," I yelled to Warren. "This might get bumpy."

I squeezed my eyes shut to try and acclimate myself to the darkness before I drove inside. When I opened them, I had to squint hard to see the outline of the room. A desk chair went flying over the hood. Warren squealed. I tapped the brakes so I wouldn't cause more damage than I had. I felt another bump and heard a crash. It sounded like a metal table had met its end.

"The monkey's in," Warren screamed.

I sped up and turned the wheel toward the lit opening. As soon as the car cleared the door, the orange-clad men began sliding the giant doors closed. I saw the gorilla floundering toward the light as the door shut and the locks engaged. A muffled moan seeped through the barrier.

"She'll be okay," one of the vested men said. "Once the carrier docks, we'll ship her off so she can decay with others like herself."

"She?" I asked.

"Couldn't you tell?" he laughed. "Why do you think you had to strap that guy to your car to get her to follow you? That is why he's there, isn't it?"

The man stopped laughing, tilted his head, and looked at me with questioning eyes.

"Of course that's why he's there," I said. "Do you think I'd drive around with a used car salesman taped to my car for kicks?"

The man's face lit up with a smile.

"I don't know about you, but it sounds like a fun evening to me."

I cracked a grin and turned back to the used car salesman.

"Well, Warren. What do you say to a spin around the block for old time's sake?"

MEGAN R. ENGELHARDT
The Beast That Would Not Die!

In the rainy months of 1883 my brother George came to visit me on the Dark Continent. I had been in Africa for nearly a year, recovering from a slight disease of the brain in the warmer climate, and as George was in need of some recovery as well, especially from a bit of scandal he had gotten into, he put himself on a boat and shipped himself into my care. I did not want him there, having quite enjoyed being far away from my wayward and intemperate brother, but as I did not know he was coming until he showed up on my doorstep, I was forced to welcome him with open arms.

I had grown fond of the long hunting expedition for which the African bush is particularly suited, and so when we tired of conversation (as we quickly did, having very few interests alike), I suggested a trip to show my brother the local fauna, and to acquire what trophies we were able. He agreed to the suggestion and after hiring a few hunters to go with us we set forth. George never knew how to pack for things and insisted on buying a large wagon, nearly twenty feet long, in order to carry what he referred to as *the goods*—the ivory and other trophies he anticipated returning with. He also bought eight donkeys to pull the wagon. It seemed a ridiculously cumbersome thing to me and I tried to talk him out of it, but he persisted.

We had been tracking a herd of springbok. On the third day we found ourselves at the edge of some deep jungle that grew denser the more we tried to make our way out of it. After several hours of struggle we came out into a clearing with a wide lake, surrounded on all sides by the thick forest. We could see the sky from that clearing, and I was surprised to note that the sun was nearly gone. Night was fast approaching.

"Well, George," I said, "how do you fancy roughing it again?"

"Not well, Simon," he said, "but I suppose if you can do it, so can I."

This was not strictly true, for there were plenty of things I could do that my brother could not.

George might have been willing, but the hunters, who had been acting nervous since we had entered the clearing, refused to camp at the spot.

"Not here," the hunters begged. "This is a bad place."

"Come now, what do you mean by that?" I asked.

"This is near the home of a white monster," they said. "We should not disturb it."

I was curious about this "white monster."

"It is tall," the hunters said, "taller than the mountains, and whiter than you. It will kill us all. We are mighty hunters, but this monster no man can kill."

"What manner of monster is it?" I asked.

"Like an ape," they said, "but larger than any ape could be. It has a heavy brow and roars like a lion, and when it walks it shakes the earth."

"I suppose it *is* some sort of ape," I told George, but when I questioned the hunters further they would say no more. I assumed it was just a story with no legs and disregarded it as such. I do not approve of encouraging superstitions, so I refused their request and determined that we would camp there. It was a likely spot, and I did not relish stumbling through the dark searching for another place that was more acceptable to the hunters.

While we were setting up camp, George scared a flock of a sort of bustard and the hunters made quick work of them, laying low three brace. I dropped one as well, but George pulled a little high and missed his mark.

We roasted the birds over the fire. The fat falling into the flames made little pops and sizzles that were quite pleasing to me. We ate well that night and soon fell into that companionable, comfortable silence that comes from being full in the night air. Only the donkeys were restless, nosing each other softly and walking around and around their tethers.

We settled down to rest with one of the hunters tending the fire. George fell asleep quickly, right in the middle of protesting that he would never be able to sleep. It took me some time longer to get comfortable. I had the feeling that something was amiss. The hunters' warning loomed large in my mind and I couldn't shake it, not even as the night wore on and we remained unmolested.

At first I thought it was just nerves and berated myself for getting shook up by all that superstition nonsense. But then the moon rose and, in the shafts of silvery light that cut through the trees, I saw something glinting in the bush.

I turned over very slowly, so that I could get a better view. My blanket scuffed slightly on the rough ground and I froze. At that very moment, the lights in the bush blinked out and back on again, and I realized, to my horror, that the lights were *a pair of eyes*.

I reached out my hand, my fingers groping for the rifle I kept at my side. Another set of eyes joined the first, then a third. They glared out at my sleeping companions, and I may be forgiven for ascribing a certain malevolence to their steady, piercing gaze. I suddenly felt very strongly that I should not be in that place. Never before in my time in Africa had I felt so unwelcome, so much apart from the natural rhythm of the land. I wished desperately that I had listened to the hunters and found another camping spot. But we were there now, and I pulled my rifle to me and determined to see it through.

"Simon!" George whispered. "Do you see it, or am I going as crazy as you?"

I hadn't realized my brother was awake.

"Keep still!" I said, sharply. "I see it. I don't know what it is but I don't think it likes us much."

"It is the white monster!"

The hunters had woken, too, and I spared a glance around to see them huddled together. One or two had the presence of mind to take up their rifles or assegai. The spearheads reflected the same firelight that glinted in the eyes in the bush.

"It's probably just a springbok," I said, but I knew it was not.

"We should not be here," one of the hunters moaned.

"Nonsense," I said, trying to be tougher than I felt. I cupped a hand around my mouth and shouted into the bush. "You there! We see you... come on out!"

The brush rustled. There was a low grunt, a series of deep *uhks* and snorts. I could pick out three separate "voices." They went back and forth, and then the bushes parted and the watchers stepped into the light.

It was a gorilla... or rather, three gorillas. They were terribly huge, not a one less than fourteen-feet tall. Their enormous fists pounded the ground, kicking up clouds of dust as they landed. They were all impressive beasts, but I confess I paid the most attention to the creature that led the way. The other two were black, but the third—he was a white monster, indeed. He was a devil of a beast. His hair was pure white. Not a single dark spot adorned his muscular frame. His eyes bored into me, pale pink but deep and brooding. He flared his nostrils at us and curled his massive lip. I have never before or since seen an animal as impressive as that giant white gorilla.

"Hush," I whispered, motioning for George to keep still. The gorillas, catching my voice, swung their large heads to look at me. I had risen to my knees, but I dared not stand. So I knelt there, staring up into the great pink eyes of the beast.

The theory has sometimes been advanced that animals are capable of emotions as deep and varied as those that plague you or I. It was never as believable as when I was face to face with the white monster of the jungle. I must be clear that I saw no anger in his face—irritation, perhaps, that we were intruding on his place, and curiosity, and a sort of stern lordliness. That beast was more regal than any lion I had seen in my travels. But there was also something youthful about him, as if he were a princeling investigating for the first time the extent of his future kingdom.

Something passed between us in that moment. I felt a sort of kinship with the beast. Slowly I stood, gaining my feet, all the while keeping my eyes locked with the gorilla's. When I had reached my full height, which seemed nothing compared to that of the creature before me, I reached out very slowly with my empty hand. I'm not sure what I intended by this gesture, but I was so drawn into that moment of communion with the beast that it felt the thing to do.

I truly believe that the situation would have resolved peacefully if it wasn't for George's big mouth. As I reached out to the white gorilla, my brother opened his mouth and said quite loudly, "Ho, Simon! Watch it doesn't bite your hand off!"

The beasts swung their great heads to look at him.

"Keep still, George," I hissed, but my brother was never very good at following advice. When the giant gorillas fixed their eyes on George, he yelped and stumbled back, raising his rifle and letting off a wild shot into the canopy. The sharp retort echoed through the brush.

The giant white gorilla started, then with an ear-splitting roar, he charged.

I would not have been able to get my gun up in time, but George had never let his guard drop. Through a rain of assegai thrown by the hunters, I saw George drop his rifle, raise a second gun, take aim, and fire.

The shot hit the white gorilla full in the chest. It stumbled in its charge, one massive knee hitting the ground. Several of the assegai had hit the beast in the chest and some of the hunters, who had smaller rifles on them, had also marked its broad breast with gunshot. It was bleeding from several wounds, but still it was fierce. It roared its defiance at my brother, who acted as coolly as I'd ever seen. He dropped the rifle, reached out his hand, and grabbed an assegai that had fallen near him. He lunged forward and thrust the spear into the broad chest of the beast and buried it up to the hilt. The monster roared a final time and collapsed.

I tore myself from the astounding scene and whirled around, afraid that the other two gorillas would charge to avenge their leader. I was faced with an empty jungle—they had faded back into the bush, without even the glinting of their eyes remaining.

Behind me, George started hooting and hollering like the damn fool he was.

"Did you see that shot, Simon? Whoo-ee!"

I was about to answer when I felt the earth shake beneath us. The hunters, already unnerved by the charge of the white beast, fell to their knees, moaning and crying out.

"The white monster!" they cried. "The white monster comes to avenge the death of its child!"

That shook me. I had assumed that George's gorilla was the white monster. The thought that that beast was only a child, and that its parent, by necessity even larger, was coming after us—well, that put a fear into us. We bundled up the camp as quickly as we could. I was all for leaving the corpse behind, but George wouldn't dream of it. He bullied several of the hunters into helping him load it into the wagon. The donkeys pulled the wagon behind us as we fled.

It was this delay that almost cost us our lives. The shaking had grown worse as we struggled to move the corpse—we later found it weighed nearly two thousand pounds!—and just as we finished securing the donkeys and started off, a roar like thunder echoed from above us. I glanced back and saw the most terrifying thing it has been my misfortune to see.

The corpse we had in the wagon was an infant, and its father was pursuing us.

This giant gorilla was tremendously tall, fifty-feet if it was an inch, and must have weighed several tons. It was still far away, but the very size of it ensured that we could see it coming from far off. It, too, was an albino, and the white of its hair shone in the moonlight. It was as if a snowy mountain had grown legs and was bearing down on us.

"Run!" I yelled. "Run for your lives!"

And we ran, George upon the wagon creaking after us.

I have had many frightening experiences since that night but nothing has yet compared to those hours we spent crashing through the dense jungle, falling and rising again and again, afraid to rest lest the enormous beast catch us. Once it was so close behind us that I could see, even in the dark, its enormous broad chest and large head, pink eyes gleaming like a devil's. It was a curious thing—I thought I could see, in the light of the moon, a network of gashes that ran all down the beast's breast, open wounds that were not bleeding and injuries that should have killed even a monster of that size.

We ran until we reached the edge of the jungle and tumbled out onto the plain. It was a relief to be free of the roots that grasped at ankles and the slick undergrowth that threatened to make us lose our footing at every step, even though I knew that the open plain would allow the monster to gain ground more easily, as well.

Strange, then, that as the giant gorilla reached the tree line it stopped. It would not step foot onto the plain, though we were within sight and it could have had us in two strides of its long, long legs. It beat its chest and roared and shook the trees with a sound like a storm, but it would not follow us. I could even more clearly see the monster now and saw its dead eyes and the blood around its mouth where it had eaten an unlucky hunter. George wanted to stop and take a shot at it—I think his earlier success had gone to his head—but I refused. We pushed on at a slower pace, though we were all exhausted, wanting to put as much distance as possible between us and the beast, just in case, as I said, it decided to venture out of the jungle after all.

It did not come, though, and when we were far enough away that we could no longer see its head towering over the canopy or hear its shattering roars, we rested, and two days later made our way back to civilization, having suffered only one casualty in the unfortunate hunter. I paid the other hunters double what I had promised them, for the encounter with the giant white gorilla was more than anyone had anticipated when we set out.

George had his smaller white gorilla stuffed and, when he left for home a month later, took it with him. I was relieved to see it go. Every time I looked on that still, giant body, I remembered the intelligence and majesty I had seen that night in the clearing. It made me sad and it was also, to some extent, unnerving. George had set the beast just outside the study windows, on the veranda, and sometimes on a quiet night I would have sworn I'd seen the corpse move. It stood there, a white shadow beyond the dim lights of the study, and its arm would seem to twitch, or its head to turn. It was nonsense, but I almost hoped it would move, or come alive again. Its corpse upset me, for I much preferred the way I had seen it, alive in the moonlight.

The night after George departed I went to the village and found an old hunter who no longer went out, but sat by the fire and told stories. After some money and some shared whiskey he imparted to me surprising information about the mysterious giant gorillas of the inner jungle. Perhaps I should have shared my new knowledge with George but, to tell the truth, I was angry with him for shooting the young gorilla. In my few moments of communion with the white beast I felt more brotherhood than I had in years of life with George.

Sometime later I received a letter from George. He indicated that he had arrived at home safely and that the previous troubles, which had driven him to Africa, had been satisfactorily resolved. He begged me to come celebrate Christmas with him. Since I had been home, and I felt I had recovered sufficiently from my previous illness to chance a trip back to colder and wetter climes. I sent a quick note in return accepting and began to arrange for the journey. I was not much interested in seeing George, but I did miss England, and I must admit that I was also looking forward to seeing the white gorilla again, especially considering what I had heard from the old hunter.

It was snowing when the train pulled into the station. I stared out at the large white flakes and thought of the snowy white hair of George's gorilla. He met me at the station—George, not the gorilla—looking very fat and merry and chattered the whole way home, about people I had forgotten and gossip I had never known.

"Do you ever think about that gorilla?" I asked as we rattled down the dark country roads. George looked at me curiously, then laughed.

"Of course, old boy!" he said. "It's standing in my study, the first thing visitors see. I tell the story at every possible opportunity! I'm practically famous for it! Some of the girls think it's haunted and they flock to see it."

We arrived at the house and I was surprised to find it dark and empty. George explained, somewhat embarrassed, that he was between housekeepers. When I pressed him he reluctantly admitted that no less than three sets of housekeeping staff had quit their positions in his service since he had arrived at home.

"I've never known you to be a harsh taskmaster," I said, disapprovingly.

"It's nothing like that," George said, flushing a bit. "You know me, Simon. I barely asked them for hot water once a day."

"Then why would they take their leave so quickly?"

"Nonsense, really. Talk of ghosts, strange noises, moving shadows… and I suppose there is that maid that disappeared. But I am sure she just ran off with the groomsman, who also disappeared around the same time. They were both fine looking young folk."

We were in the house by then, and when we had the lights on I turned around and looked up to see those same pink eyes that so haunted me on our first meeting.

The gorilla looked as alive and majestic as he had in the clearing the night my brother shot him. I could almost imagine that I saw his nostrils flare and the hair around his mouth rustling gently as he breathed. It was just the flickering of the light, I told myself to still my leaping heart, and turned away. But I kept a close eye on it from that moment on, and each time I entered the high-ceilinged study I spent some time near it.

Several days after I arrived, George held a Christmas party. It was a lavish, decadent occasion and one that I had very little intention of attending. George's friends were annoying and trite and often quite offensive to me. They were of that set who finds it pleasurable to make a mockery of all things, quite cruelly, and among them there was not one person who had any sort of honor or redeeming quality.

I made an appearance at the party, for George's sake, but after an hour of watching his guests act deplorably, I was content to call it a night and retire. The last glimpse I had of my brother was as he drunkenly acted out the killing of the giant white gorilla, knocking into the beast as he staggered to and fro. He leapt towards a similarly inebriated young lady with a roar—she jumped with a little shriek and spilled her glass all over the gorilla. The wine dripped red stains down his white fur. I frowned and spent the rest of the evening in my room, where I fell asleep over a book in front of the fire.

I was woken several hours later by screams.

Leaping to my feet, I grabbed for my gun, which of course was not near me, as I had left it in my house in Africa. I took up the heavy iron poker from the fireplace, instead, and, carrying the lantern in my other hand, ventured down the stairs. I walked into a scene of utter carnage.

Bodies were strewn everywhere. The young lady who had spilled her wine was near the door, hand outstretched as if to escape. The top of her head was ripped open, her brain missing, and her head was torn from her shoulders. Near her was another young man, his head equally ruined. I saw, in fact, that among their different wounds each victim had suffered the same treatment—the head torn open and the brains removed. I knew at once what had happened.

Stepping gingerly over the bodies, I entered the study. There was George, held tight in the arms of the giant white gorilla. There was blood all around his mouth—the gorilla, not George—and it was clear that he intended the same fate for my brother as he had for the other guests.

"Simon!" George yelled as he saw me approach. "It's come to life! For the love of God, help me!"

"I thought that perhaps you were still alive," I said, but I was not addressing George. The white gorilla watched me walk forward and snuffed gently. "Or rather, un-dead. That's why I came here, you know. Not for these people. But to see you and, if possible, to take you back home, if you'll let me."

"Simon!" George cried. "What in the hell are you—?"

The gorilla moved his two strong hands and cracked open my brother's head like a nut. I looked away as it ate his brains for, as much as I despised my brother, I did not wish to observe that moment. When the terrible noises had ceased, I turned back and saw the white gorilla approaching. I stood very still as it sniffed around me. Then I reached out one hand and waited.

The un-dead beast looked at me with its unblinking pink eyes, and I again felt that sense of communion, of brotherhood. I knew in that moment that this monster—for monster it truly was, I will not deny that—wanted only to go home, to be once more in the place where it was prince, and it knew that I wanted nothing more than to aid it in its return. It took its large white hand and touched mine, very gently.

It was an easy task, to clean up the house enough that the courier, who was to take the large package to the docks for me, would not be suspicious. We arrived home on the same ship, the gorilla and I, and soon enough we were heading for the deep jungle. I did not hire hunters this time, and I did not bring a wagon and donkeys. It was a strange journey, the two of us alone in the bush, but never once did I fear for my life.

Soon we reached the clearing with the lake where our adventure had begun. We waited for the night to come, and once darkness fell and midnight rose, we felt the stirring steps of the giant white beast approach. The reunion between father and son was gladdening for me to see. Once he had assured himself that his son was, more or less, unharmed—for that must be a very different standard among a species that does not die when killed—the gigantic gorilla reached down and picked me up. I was swallowed up in his hand like a feather in the hand of a man, but again I felt no fear. Snuffling happily, the gorilla grabbed up his child in his other hand and began heading further into the jungle.

I do not go back to civilization these days. I am content in the jungle with the gorillas. Also I understand that the British government would like very much for me to be apprehended so I can answer for the deaths at my brother George's Christmas party. I doubt they would believe me if I told the truth, so I believe I will avoid them for as long as possible. And in one or two hundred years—for I have tasted of the river of un-death that flows through the country of the giant white gorillas—I do not believe the government will remember me, anyway.

TONIA BROWN
My Life Was Saved By Coffee…
(Meanwhile in Suburbia, Part Two)

Seated, alone, at the kitchen table, in a wrinkled shirt and trousers, I stared at my cold bowl of bran flakes with a sigh. Muriel always made me eggs and bacon. She ironed my shirts too, just the way I liked them. If she could've just seen my need for the occasional nip every now and again… but what's done is done I suppose.

Her letter said she wanted out before our marriage went to hell.

In a hand basket, of all things.

Who even says that anymore?

I didn't really have time for sighing, seeing as how I was already an hour late for work. At first, when the swimming numbers of the alarm clock came into focus this morning, I thought the boys had set it ahead for a lark. Then I remembered. They couldn't have set it ahead because they were gone to North Carolina, with Muriel. Gone a week now. They weren't on vacation neither, no matter what I told the neighbors, the guys at work, the mailman or my parents. Shaking off the melancholy of missing my kids and my woman, I turned my attention to the only thing that remained rock steady in my life, there through thick and thin, there forever and always, amen.

Coffee.

The machine sputtered the last bit into the pot beneath, and that sound had me salivating more than Pavlov's dogs at a bell ringer's convention. I jumped up, ignoring the lingering effects of a week's drunk, and scrambled to the counter to pour my cup of addiction. Muriel might have been able to wrestle liquor from me, but coffee? Never!

I grabbed the only clean cup in the house from the top shelf of the almost empty cabinets—yeah, Muriel did the dishes too—and watched with glee as the dark brown, nay, almost black liquid swirled into the bottom of it's porcelain offering vessel. Forgoing the squat canister of sugar and the tall container of non-dairy creamer, I lifted the cup to my nose and inhaled its pure coffee goodness. Keep your fancy creamers and low calorie sweeteners, strong black coffee was a man's drink, even more so that straight bourbon or cold beer. For me, coffee was nirvana, and I wasn't even sure what nirvana was.

I turned the cup up, downing that first blessed mouthful. God how it burned! My tongue was dry as sandpaper and my throat was raw from far too much drinking. And before you point out how the bitch was right let me explain that no matter what the woman claims I do not have a drinking problem. I drink just fine.

It's the vomiting that I have trouble handling.

Anyways, that first sip slipped down my throat in a warm ooze of caffeinated splendor. The second went smoother than the first, hydrating my dry mouth and filling my empty belly. The third, fourth and fifth were just as good, each gulp bigger than the last as I got used to the fresh from the pot scorch. I held the cup away, smacking my lips and feeling more like a human being than before. It was when I reached out for the pot again, to pour my second and slower cup of glory, when I felt it.

That familiar, warm, wet slop running all down the front of my chest.

I glanced to the cup in my hand, and winced when I saw it was that old "World's Greatest Dad" coffee mug. The one with the huge crack down the middle. The one we kept way in the back of the cabinet because you couldn't actually use it but the boys gave it to me so we couldn't throw it away either. I then looked down with a grimace, finding just what I hoped I wouldn't find.

"Shit," I said, to no one in particular.

My shirt was covered in coffee. My last, clean, button-down, has a collar so I can wear a tie for the office dress code shirt. I only had five of the bastards to begin with, and the other four had suffered similar food related fates earlier in the week. Mustard on one. Grease took another. Chili all down the third. And mustard again on the last. (What can I say? I eat a lot of hotdogs.) Now coffee. I didn't even know how to get coffee out of a shirt. Could you even get it out? Maybe Muriel...

Okay, so she wasn't here to help. What could I do? No clean shirts and I was already an hour behind. I would have to stop on the way and pick up a new one, which would make me well over two hours late. It was either that or call out for the day.

No way! That's what everyone expected. I could hear their tongues wagging now. It was only a matter of time. His wife leaves him and he falls apart. But the fact of the matter was simple: if Muriel had been here to do the dishes I wouldn't have had to use that cup in the first place.

I would just go to work in the coffee stained shirt and explain it to the guys.

Really, Jon? You're going to blame her for this, too?

Still clutching the offending bit of ceramic, I growled under my breath as I stomped back into the bedroom at the far end of the house. The empty house. The quiet house. I set to digging about in the dirty laundry hamper—or as it had come to be known since my wife abandoned me, the floor—searching for the least stained of shirts. It became a sword in the stone moment for me; if I could locate the cleanest of the dirtiest shirts, perhaps I could redeem my pathetic life.

That's when I began to feel the tremors.

At first I thought it was just the lingering effects of a week's worth of drunken pity parties, but no, it was external. They ran through the floor, making my already unsteady stance even more exaggerated as I doubled over rifling through dirty clothes. Within moments, the furniture was shimmying and the photos on the walls were dancing and I was doing my best to keep from going ass over elbows into yea olde lande of filthy clothes. An earthquake? In this quiet Floridian suburbia? No, it couldn't have been because the shudders were too steady, and had a distinct pattern to them.

Thump. Thump. Thump. Thump.

The house shook with a groan just as a shower of plaster rained over me. I fell to my knees and crawled into the doorway of the bathroom, holding my arms over my head as I braced for the worst of whatever this fresh hell was. The thumping continued, growing louder and stronger. A terrible crash and screech sounded, as the house shook to its very foundations. I saw the light of the morning through the seams of the walls; they were so close to bursting wide open! This was followed by a moan of epic proportions. I swear it sounded like a million howler monkeys got their privates trapped in a million vices while screaming into a million loudspeakers.

And the smell.

Oh my god, there came this smell in the air. I had never in all my life smelled anything like it, and I hoped never to again. In a word it was rotten. Rotten and decayed and festering and decomposed and you just can't imagine how bad it was. One time a stray cat got under the house and died and Muriel made me crawl under there and pull it out three days later. I ended up puking all over her shoes from the smell alone. Well, I would rather coat the insides of my nostrils with three-day rotting cat carcass for the rest of my life rather then smell whatever the hell I smelled as I held onto the doorframe and waited for the house to fall down around me. Or on top of me, preferably.

But no, the house held firm and just as quick as it started the shuddering passed. The thumps faded. The smell lessened, but didn't go away completely. I was left as white as a sheet on my hands and knees, gripping my nose and trembling like a wind driven leaf. I took a moment to make sure that was all there was, that there wasn't an aftershock on the way. No. The world seemed to return to normal. Well, normal as it was all things considered.

I got to my feet and tiptoed around the wreckage of my house, or rather what was left of it. The north end of the house was somewhat okay. I mean it was trashed, sure, wires popped and sputtered and pipes sprayed water all over the place, that sort of thing. But it was better than the south end of the house. I poked my head through the remains of the hallway, and into the open air that was once my beautiful kitchen. And there I stood, slack jawed and wide eyed, surveying what was left of my kingdom.

The south end of the house was flattened. Everything, and I mean everything, was crushed into the earth beneath, as if something had squashed it like a bug. The stove, the fridge, even my precious coffee machine was ground into a mulch of useless bits. That smell was stronger here too, lingering in a miasma of gut twisting putrid stench. And to make things even stranger, as if things weren't already weird enough, there was an oval print over the remains of my house, including the distinct shape of toes at one end.

Yes, I said toes.

I turned my gaze to the horizon, and watched the hazy form of some enormous thing lumbering away in the distance. I swear to god—I swear by all that is holy and good and right—it looked just like a big ape. A big dead ape. Only it couldn't be dead, because it was up shambling about. Each step of its huge feet crushed anything beneath, and the moan of it echoed enough to make my walls tremble once more. I tried to rub at my eyes, to clear this vision of a giant, putrid smelling, dead looking ape lurching across my neighborhood, but found it was hard considering I was still clutching that mug. The same mug I had cursed only minutes before. The same mug that dribbled coffee all down the front of my shirt and forced me from my cold cereal, back into the bedroom. Away from the kitchen.

The now crushed kitchen.

I stared at the cracked coffee mug and thought about Muriel, and my boys. Any normal morning we would have all been in there. Bitching and moaning, passing the salt and the milk, just carrying on with a regular suburbia day. And had we been there... in there... had my kids... my wife... me.

Muriel. I always suspected I couldn't live without her and now that I had seen my life flash before my hung-over eyes I knew I didn't want to. What good was I without her? Maybe she was right. Maybe I did drink more than was good for me.

Maybe I should call her and apologize. I mean, after all, it isn't everyday your life is saved by your wife having the foresight to leave you.

Or by a leaky cup of coffee.

MICHAEL O'NEAL
Kooking With Kong

Thank God It's BRAINS! Coming up is Zombie Television's Must Eat TV line-up!

Out of the hundreds of nameless faces wandering in the dark, one zombie grunted. It steered toward the voice and its lights, the only light in the dead city.

Set in a protective electrified kiosk, the television towers—flatscreen stacked over flatscreen, crowned with a row of overhead speakers—wailed into the night. Through the iron bars protecting the boob-tubes the announcer begged for the crowd's mindless attention.

Got a hunger that won't stop? Got a hankering for more than subhuman slop? Get ready for a show that'll blow your mind... without the bullet!

More of the undead trudged away from their endless stroll. Soon dozens surrounded the caged stall, hypnotized by the pretty colors.

Premiering in less than a week, ZTV presents: Kooking with Kong!

The screens flashed with pictures and shapes that none of them recognized anymore. Yet when they saw the image of a giant gorilla with two fistfuls of goop wearing a chef's hat, they cooed in unison. The camera zoomed in on the gorilla's cranium, its skull the size of a pick-up. At the scale of such a brain, those with saliva leaked it through their cheeks; those without, simply pawed at their mouths, wondering where the hell they'd misplaced their tongues.

That's right!

Kooking with Kong—ZTV's newest show that tells you simple bastards there's more than one way to cook a cat!

The commercial had barely been on a full minute but already the zombies filled the street. Some got too excited and dared to reach their fingers through the bars to grab the gorilla's head. Their hands sizzled and popped free at the wrists. It did little to deter the hungriest. Without hands, they tried their faces instead.

Don't miss it! It's not like you idiots have anything better to do.

So stick around!

And for all of you too stupid to understand what I'm saying, remember our catch phrase:

Brains! Brains! Brains!

That's TGIB programming! That's Z-T-V!

* * *

Zeek ducked his head to get through the double-garage doors that led into his dressing room. It was a tight fit. He had to admit to himself that he'd put on a few pounds in the last year—over 700 to be exact, though most were insect larvae and worms, but who was counting? Thankfully, the zombie execs at the studio had refashioned an old sound stage to accommodate his "upscale" requirements.

A team of make-up artists and designers waited by his vanity mirror, swiped just for him from the telescope at Mt. Wilson Observatory. Astronomy was so out of vogue; the only stars given an ounce of interest these days drank serotonin lattes, got Botox to keep their flesh from dripping off their skulls, and walked around like their maggots weren't as creepy as the next guys. Most zombies don't look up, or so he was told, so who cared that they stole it?

Of course, they needed to tilt their heads skyward now if they wanted to see him. The point was really moot.

Somehow the idiots had managed to find enough brain-power between them to rig the mirror at an angle through a series of scaffolding and ropes. The mess appeared ready to collapse if he didn't tiptoe around it.

After he glimpsed his reflection, he thought about stomping.

Holy hell, you're falling apart Zeek. Some moneymaker you turned out to be.

The bright lights from the commercial shoot had begun to peel the buckets of plaster they used as concealer. Holes large enough to dig a finger through opened in his cheeks. The glue that secured his wig had slipped, exposing bald patches like mange on his furry scalp. Even his glass eye (the damn thing was bigger than a workout ball and made of solid marble) tilted in its groove to give him the mug of a retarded chimp.

Careful not to squash them underfoot, Zeek sat in the middle of his make-up crew and let them crawl over him to do their best to fix him proper. They certainly couldn't make it worse.

They better be saints because I need a miracle. If not, I'm as good as meat. Truckloads of it.

The human-sized door by the garage entrance opened. Out of it, his manager slash agent, Hollow H. Eston, strode in a beeline toward Zeek's feet.

"Kong, baby! You're a making your daddy proud!" Eston said.

He slapped the bottom of Zeek's heel and walked between his legs, head and plastic nose cocked high to the point his spine might snap.

Zeek could only wish.

The weasel of a zombie contained all the trimmings of his kind: flashy silver suit the color of douche, immaculately greased wig that seemed to have been parted by razors, a set of veneers the size of Chiclets. He was one of the elite, those wealthy enough to keep himself fed with the drugs that helped to maintain a minimal level of intelligence, and a former star himself of the big screen, though well retired before the Apocalypse hit.

He was a master of his game. And he owned Zeek like his dog.

"A cooking show?" Zeek said.

Eston shrugged. "Yeah. Why Not? Got to give the people what they want. And the people are hungry."

"I don't know anything about cuisine."

"You'll learn. Besides, it doesn't really matter what you cook." He flipped open his cell. The device was more like a laptop than a phone. "We're already getting the numbers returned from the initial pitch commercial. Our C3 Nielsen rating is at the top of the charts. The undead masses have lined around the block to catch a peek at you. I mean, literally. I had to rundown more than a dozen in my armored Ferrari just to get in the studio gates."

"You mean this." Zeek pointed at the huge dome of his skull. "That's what they care about. The size of my brains, not me. Not my talent. You think it'll be enough? I don't."

Zeek glanced at his make-up team while they struggled to fix his face. He couldn't be for certain, but he swore they were staring at his head with way too much drool on their decomposing lips. There was no hiding the fact that he was well-endowed (in terms of what turned on a zombie) more so than every possible human counterpart.

"I mean, I'd like to say, *'Hello? My eyes are over her'*," Zeek said.

"Don't be that way, Kong. You're a head above the rest. Several, in fact."

"And Kong? Did you have to go that route? I have a real name."

"No flash, no gas. Besides Zeek doesn't rhyme with cooking."

Neither does Kong, Zeek wanted to add. Instead, he kept his big mouth shut.

Eston clapped his hands together angrily. "And where the hell is my boy's hors d'oeuvres?"

"I'm not really hungry."

"Nonsense. You eat, you'll be happy. Besides, I'm starving."

Several of the production assistants that had been loitering immediately broke into a sprint. Within minutes, another set of doors to the far side of the studio opened, and they wheeled an over-sized candy bowl that could've doubled for a millionaire's Jacuzzi into the room. Inside lay half a dozen bound, uninfected humans. They struggled only mildly against their bonds. Most were too drugged to put up a fight; their resistance consisted of little more than a mild seizure.

Eston snapped his fingers until a PA lugged a small one from the tub, cracked it over the head, scooped out its brains, then neatly placed them in a saucer with a sprinkle of oregano and a dash of paprika. Eston ate them with his pinky poised in salute.

When the PA yanked a second human from its kin, Zeek waved them to put it back. The morsel looked tempting but his stomach wasn't in the mood.

"I don't know if my heart's in this, Mr. Eston," he said.

"Of course it is. I can see it right there."

Eston pointed to the gaping hole in Zeek's left side that exposed his ribcage and part of the sternum. One of the make-up crew had crawled inside and was polishing the ribs with a steel-toothed brush to make them shine. Above his head, Zeek's blackened heart didn't beat—it quivered, most likely filled with grubs. This time of year the pests always established a residence in the worst possible places.

"That's not what I mean, Mr. Eston—"

He paused, not really sure what he meant, or what he might get away with saying. Eston acted casual at the moment, yet rank would be pulled upon a single wrong word. If that happened, the conversation was over; all hope of escaping this mess, dissolved.

Carefully, he chose his next words, "I'm worried I won't do a good job."

Despite his caution, the battle was lost. Eston's face finally soured and he tucked his phone into his jacket pocket. He only did that when he was about to lay down the law.

"Listen, ape. You're my property. And you got two options. You'll do exactly what I tell you to do, and you'll do it fantastic. Or option *numero dos*—you'll make one hell of a barbecue. Either way, I hop the wave to the top. Whether you ride my coattails… or my entrails… I leave you to decide."

With that, he turned his back, flipped open his cell again, and began to scream at someone more important. Zeek watched him stride across the sound stage as if he owned the place.

Eston stopped in the doorway. "We start shooting in two days, ape. Get your act together. I got some cooking books for you to peruse and study 'till then. My assistant will drop them off within the hour. Prepare to be a star, baby boy!"

And he left.

When Zeek was sure the prick was gone, he growled and beat his fists against his chest.

"Hey!" The polish guy, still stuck inside his ribs, flipped him the bird.

"Sorry," Zeek said.

He had less than forty-eight hours to figure out how to be a master chef. Or if not a master, at least entertaining enough to keep a million mindless zombies enthralled for sixty minutes, minus commercials. Maybe the miracle workers laboring on his face had a spare one stowed in their sleeves.

Two days.

Two days until either fast fame or a slow roast.

* * *

They'd left him locked in the sound stage overnight, though an unlucky PA lay a button press away if he needed anything urgently. His crew had long gone, leaving him alone to prepare. Thankfully Eston's assistant had indeed dropped off a few books on cooking.

From one of the hors d'oeuvres, Zeek retrieved a hand attached to an amputated arm and used it to flip through the pages, his massive digits far too clumsy on their own.

"I'm never going to learn this before the show airs," he said.

There was nothing but cookbooks—lists of ingredients and recipes, a few glossaries of cooking terms, and pictures of beautified foods he'd never hope to understand. They all showed *what* to cook, not *how*. And what the hell was a *colander?*

Zeek rubbed his face, then scratched his noggin. It sent a flurry of maggots tumbling from his fuzzy scalp like dandruff. One by one, he absentmindedly picked them off the ground and pitched them into his mouth. He always ate when he got nervous.

Mr. Eston's going to feed me to the masses.

It was that simple. This endeavor, this lunacy of making him a television persona, was futile from the beginning. But his agent slash master wouldn't care. Either way he'd turn a profit in the end of this.

The evil bastard took Zeek into his slavery a year ago, after his last owners, the bigwigs at J. Hill Pharmaceuticals, apparently lost him in a researcher's ill-fated card game. Eston nurtured a lot of vices, and he was damn good at all of them.

Zeek had to admit, he thought his new Hollywood agent would be his ticket to a better life. That hope didn't last long. Like everyone in the world with a brain that still worked—fame, fortune, and adulation remained lusts worth striving toward. Only now he understood the truth.

Yet it seemed better than being in a cage, though the sound stage was most likely locked too. Of course, even if he did break free, where could he go? He might as well have been on the moon or under the sea. Despite his size and the strength that went along with it, the backlots were surrounded by the undead hordes, kept out only by the electric fences and drone-controlled machine gun bunkers (in case the adoring public got too uppity). And past the first wave of mouths were thousands, nay millions, more—an ocean of tiny ravenous jaws ready to devour him to the crunchy parts before he gained more than a few feet of freedom.

That aside, he was glad there were no more tests.

The memory made Zeek cringe—the researchers prodding, sticking, and inserting God-knows-what into God-knows-where. Even today, his pink shaven rear felt as if they'd filled it with landmines and sent a blind schizophrenic to find them with his teeth.

He should be thankful. If it wasn't for the scientists he'd still be a normal runt of a gorilla, maybe cozy in his space at the zoo. Healthy, uninfected, dumber than a rock, and more than likely, zombie food.

The wealthy had been searching for a cure, a drug to fix the virus they themselves created, to make it give them the immortality they sought without all the annoying side-effects, such as death, putrefaction, grave crotch, zombie musk, etcetera, etcetera. They'd found a way (if you had the money to afford it) to keep the brain functional enough to retain intelligence. But while it made the organism, as a whole, close to immortal, it didn't stop the virus from eating away living tissue.

So they started their trials for a better drug on animals.

The first had been Spencer, the iguana. Zeek used to pet him when they caged them together. He remembered the first series of shots they gave the poor lizard. Boy, were they in for a surprise.

That's when they learned how the new drugs also affected growth rates. Little Spencer became big Spenzilla, over three times Zeek's size now, more than a hundred back then. The media televised his rise to fame and subsequent escape. It made good TV, so who could blame them?

Next, they discovered the new drugs also amplified specific traits in their hosts. In Spencer's case, it was his predatory instincts and base aggression. The lizard managed to trash an entire city before they got him to calm down. Last Zeek heard, they'd dropped him off in Japan and he'd gotten a movie contract.

Then the scientists descended the evolutionary ladder and experimented with the serum on a moth. Damn thing got bigger than Spencer. The drugs highlighted the moth's sensory perceptions. One day, it broke free too and flew toward the sun, like most of its kind would flutter toward a campfire or a bug zapper. He made it out of the stratosphere, maybe actually into outer space.

Wherever you be, my fuzzy friend, I salute you, Zeek thought. *One of us made it to glory.*

A monkey came next. It was hard to get a chimp like usual (chimps became no longer readily available since zombie poachers were more likely to eat their finds than sell them) but the local zoo exhibits held a gorilla in wait.

From their previous failures, they'd managed to downsize the aftereffects. Zeek only grew marginally compared to the others, though still enormous by any standard. And his augmented characteristic turned out to be smarts. Lucky him.

So here he was, his last days on earth, stuck in another cage, where his choices of escape led to death and dismemberment no matter what he chose. Except this go around, because of the drug's blessed gifts, he was humanly aware of his approaching demise.

Whoopee.

"C'mon, Kong. Learn this stuff!"

Christ, Eston had him calling himself Kong now too.

"If you don't learn this, its all over. You're brains will only take you so far…"

Brains? *That's it!*

He wouldn't be able to absorb enough culinary knowledge to be convincing as a chef, but what if he gave them something better?

Sure, they'd booked him as a cook, that couldn't be changed, yet maybe he could twist the idea, morph it into something other than straight food preparation. Like Eston said, it was more about his looks, about his gorgeous cranial measurements than his skill. Perhaps there was another angle he might take it. Some shtick that carried him through this disaster, at least long enough to have a better idea in pursuit of a more concrete longevity. It worked for Tim Allen on *Tool Time*, and that bum knew nothing of fix-it; instead he got away with the lie through comedy.

Zeek knew zippo about jokes either, so what next? What did people want more than to laugh?

Fame. Fortune.

The public, despite their undead drudgery, still stared at pretty, famous faces longer than normal ones. That was why celebrities continued to exist, why television continued its rule——because the people in charge needed a method to keep the other ninety-nine point nine percent in line and quiet, catatonic and docile.

It seemed zombies were zombies' worst problem. Without some way to occupy the moronic masses' hunger for whatever they could fit into their mouths, the elite wouldn't be able to force them into the factories and utility plants, into their mills and sweatshops. The undead didn't work for any kind of wage; they simply had to have their appetites filled, then be led like lemmings. Big money came from zombie-tech, since it was the only kind of tech truly left. And television was the key.

What about the real bigwigs? They already had fame or fortune or both. What did they want? Why should they be interested in watching his show, because even they enjoyed wasting brain cells on inane crap?

Critically, they could vote his show down quicker than no ratings. He must appeal to them all.

Immortality. That was their answer.

If you have everything, you surely want to be able to keep it, right? That was how the damn zombie infection started in the first place. The rich were not happy with having it all, then dying, and having all their toys fade away. So they invented, or rather attempted to invent, something that might help them avoid sharing forever. They wanted a taste of what it was like to be a god…

Zeek snapped his fingers. A glorious epiphany burst into his head on how he could save his ass and the show. Even Eston would be proud of this doozy.

It was crazy.

It'd take a reformatting of the show entirely, though remain within the confines of his pilot commercial.

Most importantly, he'd need approval from the guys over Eston's head. From what he heard, they might not be that difficult to convince, as long as they knew there was more money in it.

No need to wait, he told himself. No better idea would ever come.

Zeek lumbered to the call button where a PA waited somewhere on the lot. He pressed it repeatedly until a disgruntled sigh came over the speaker. Every person in showbiz all wanted the same thing, so he knew just what to say to get his new best friend's help completely.

Zeek spoke into the receiver, "I need a big favor. If you help me, I think I can make you a star."

After a short pause, the voice asked, "Whatcha need?"

Zeek answered, "A miracle. And you're my Jesus."

* * *

The lowly PA had proved to be a godsend. With the promise of fame, he'd broke into the studio manager's office and got the right numbers to call. Zeek had told him exactly what to say to lure those he reached into this secret meeting. And now he stood before three of the most powerful people in television, nay the world.

The network execs of ZTV.

They were actually dumber than he thought. None of them appeared to be on a steady regiment of the drugs that kept most of the wealthy sentient. Each had a team of servants that poured bile espressos over their lips, filed their overgrown nails while their arms dangled, clipped the inch-long nose hairs that curled along their nostrils, and vigilantly kept the maggots on their waxed faces to a pristine minimum. Hell, one servant to each was simply devoted to keeping them propped upright.

If people were willing to wipe your ass, why did you need to worry about anything else, Zeek supposed. He kind of expected them to be this way. After all, he'd seen a lot of what they put on the air, even before the Apocalypse. It took someone being an absolute bonehead to make those kind of decisions in the first place.

During the wait for their arrival, Zeek had constructed a makeshift set out of the old furniture left in the sound stage from old shows and movies. The food the caterers left to hold him over the next two days, he placed out for his ingredients, using the ground up bone meal as imitation spices. He had almost everything he needed.

Zeek took a deep breath and gave them his idea.

And like clockwork, at the precise moment he'd planned from the second the PA gave his agent a ring, Mr. Hollow H. Eston burst open the sound stage doors and stomped inside.

"What the fuck is going on in here, ape—?"

Eston noticed Zeek's company and stopped dead in his tracks, so to speak. At such levels of debauchery before him, even Eston stood in awe.

He whimpered. "Mr. Execs… a pleasure to be in your presence… " He turned to Zeek. "Why are they here, Kong?"

"I called them," said Zeek. "With a little help from a friend."

Eston glared at the PA. The PA strategically scooted out of his line of view behind Zeek's enormous foot.

"And *why* did you call them?" asked Eston.

"Because I have an idea for our show."

"You should've contacted me first. Chain of command. The talent begs the agent, the agent tells the director, the director asks the producers, the producers beg the execs. That's how it works, ape."

"I may be an ape, but I'm not a damn, dirty ape, Mr. H. Eston."

"Cute pun." Eston strolled through Zeek's crude set, examining it as if he knew a thing about design. "Well, I see you learned something from the books I gave you. Maybe you're not as stupid as you appear either. But it looks like all you have is condiments and no food, all side dishes and no main course. What do you plan on using for your main ingredient?"

"It just arrived."

Eston yelped as Zeek squeezed his spine and chest between two fingers and lifted him into the air. With satisfaction, Zeek heard his agent's ribs snap, though that didn't stop his curses.

"What do you think you're doing?" Eston screamed.

Zeek smiled. "Adding the final ingredient."

* * *

Zeek was a star. Or rather, his alter ego, Kong, became a star. He had to give the late Mr. Eston some credit. The name did go better with *kooking*.

Before the scheduled shoot was to begin, the stage crew went through the last few minutes of preparation, checking the lighting to make sure his rot patches didn't attract too much attention, fixing his blush so his black cheeks looked rosy flush, re-taping his lazy glass eye to keep it staring directly into the camera. Everything had to be perfect. They shot the show live now. If something got screwed, they wouldn't have a second chance to make it work, mainly because of Zeek's holy idea, the one that propelled him and his show to the number one slot across the board.

"Do you need anything?" asked his new agent, Mr. Chris Whittaker, the former PA that had helped him so dearly. "Water? Soda? A brain sandwich with fried bananas dipped in peanut butter. I can cut the crusts off for you, the way you like."

"No, Koko." It was Zeek's affectionate name for him. "I'm fine."

"Positive? I can always get you a banana."

"I'm fine."

"Whatever tugs your tuba, big guy. I'm here for you."

Chris aka Koko gave him a wink and two big thumbs up before making himself invisible. The perfect agent.

They had to shoot the show outside; no place was big enough to accommodate him comfortably. Besides, he wanted to be near his devoted fans. They finally loved him for more than his physical assets, for more than the spectacle of his size and species. They cared about what he represented. What he had uniquely to offer.

Over the heads of everyone, he could see the fences that kept his zombie admirers from flooding into the set and devouring them all. There were thousands, the city emptying, the outlying countryside drained too. They pressed against the initial barrier fence that surrounded the more lethal electric wall like a fat lady's thighs in fishnets. He was pretty sure the ones at the front had been crushed to death—giving their all for a glimpse of him and his magic.

Why did they love his mojo? Because he shared it with them. He gave them what they wanted. And for those who already garnered a taste, he gave them the final thing they lacked.

Immortality.

He had a guest celebrity for every show currently scheduled and every show the execs could possibly give him, to infinity if his body held together that long. Jimmy Zepp, Zalle Cherry, Tim Cruz, Janzifer Haniston, Lad Zit, Rob Zombie—all the A-listers down the row begged for a sooner slot. They all wanted their fame to last forever. And they were willing to make the ultimate sacrifice to attain it.

Today's guest was Roger DiZero. Zeek planned to make his entrance into the kingdom of the eternal a tasty one too. He'd make the perfect lasagna—handmade pasta, freshly ground meats and cheeses, and a double helping of Mr. DiZero, in the role of the special sauce.

When he told DiZero about his recipe, the man practically wept, as much as the undead can ever do. Roger looked a little rubbery from all the plastic installed in his features, but once they ground him enough into powder, Zeek was sure he'd make an excellence spice.

Then the man became a legend. Then his fame would never die, never be taken from him. He'd live on forever *inside* all his fans.

And his fans would get a *taste* of what it was like to be a star.

The set cleared. The lights dimmed in ready for his introduction. The prompter counted down from ten to six then raised a hand to silently do it with his fingers.

Five.

Zeek straightened his spine and licked his tongue along the back of his teeth. He tasted Eston. After all this time, he couldn't get that nasty flavor out of his mouth. It appeared evil never did truly die. It just spoiled.

Four.

In the silence he heard the zombie masses grunt in unison. Either they grunted or that was their stomachs, in anticipation of the feast to come. Like Oprah, he liked to give out gifts to the audience. Namely the diced up celebrities.

—(the prompter was missing his index finger so the nub instead had to count for three)

The gorilla-turned-god beat his fists into his chest and his "Kiss the Kook" apron before giving the audience his new millionaire smile with the world's biggest Chiclets.

Two.

The lights erupted bright. The cameras rolled.

One.

Zeek took a deep breath.

Action!

MAX VILE
Bits & Pieces

Moody heard a loud bang from somewhere inside the museum. It startled him. His roach slipped from between his nails, landed square in his lap, and burned the holy fire out of his crotch.

He hopped off the sarcophagus replica and swatted the loose embers from his slacks.

Goddamn it. The roach ate a hole the size of a dime through the inseam, all the way to his Hanes. Eddie would be sure to take it from his pay once he discovered another pair of ruined workpants. That made two this week already.

He could always complain to the museum manager, saying Eddie was treating him unfairly, but what good would that do? Everyone knew he was a loser, even himself. His cog was so tiny they would remove him from the gears and replace him. Simple as that.

Another banging noise, followed by several softer creaks, erupted from the main hall.

Moody snuffed the roach with his heel and kicked it under the plastic tomb.

"They're playing my music, Tut," he said to the fake mummy lying in the sarcophagus. He took his security-guard hat off Tut's head. "Time to give reason to my life."

Moody clicked on his flashlight and slipped through the Egyptian exhibit toward the source of the noise. He doubted there was an intruder. It had been less than a year since he started working the new job, and a month since he'd been demoted to the third shift, but in that time nothing gave him the impression that noises equaled thieves.

During his first week on nights he heard a racket, which turned out to be a flock of pigeons that entered through a window. He left the damn thing open to air smoke from a joint, and the little pricks flew into the rafters and pooped all over the ancient-man manikins. Eventually he fed the birds crumbs with rat poison. He hated killing them, but it was either that or hand Eddie another reason to downgrade his already pitiful standing. He spent that night scraping bird shit from cavemen's foreheads.

Eddie never missed an opportunity to run his big mouth, but he never told stories about intruders in the museum, so there must not have been a robbery in his time. The man, now in his sixties, said he started around Moody's age. Long time to be nobody. Moody guessed his life was right on tract to follow in the old man's footsteps.

Moody considered the last few hours, wondering if he'd left the window open again. The thought of bird shit made him cringe. But no, he'd only smoked with his pharaoh pals in the makeshift pyramid.

It was prehistoric beast month and wooly mammoth bones dominated the front of the building. Curved tusks were angled toward all those who entered. The creaking noises might have been coming from the rigging that suspended the elephant skeleton in the lobby. If the wires snapped there would be a mess, and probably a bone or two shattered on the floor.

Of course, the bones weren't real. They were facsimiles of the true pieces the owners had locked in their vaults. Still, if any of them fell—with his record—they'd surely blame him.

"What'd you do this time, Mood?" he said to himself in imitation of Eddie. He hated when Eddie called him Mood. "You take some acid or shrooms or something? Think the mammoth was your cousin and hump it? Huh-huh, huh-huh. You're fired!"

As he rounded the hallway leading into the main lobby, he tilted his flashlight toward the floor looking for bones.

The air smelled foul, like rotten meat and sewage.

Please don't let it be the toilets, he prayed. He'd rather deal with pigeon shit than people shit. Ever since the taco place set up shop in the food-court the bathrooms were disaster zones.

Something smacked his face. It happened again, and again—followed by a buzz. He stopped walking and swatted away—

Flies. Lots of flies. His flashlight beam showed a thick cloud of them.

"Fucking toilets." He took off his hat and used it to shield his eyes. Whichever janitor Eddie hired for night-call would soon be pissed, because *he* sure as hell wasn't cleaning this one.

He kept his head down and hurried into the lobby, which was a huge, vaulted-ceiling cavity, unlike the maze of the museum. As he entered the room he could feel a cold wind, and the stench became worse. The flies thinned enough for him to uncover his face.

Saber-toothed tiger bones gleamed as he scanned his flashlight over the display, the bathroom doors, and the floor. He couldn't see an overflow of water; he'd have to look inside.

"Fantastic—"

A third loud bang echoed through the cavernous room. The noise erupted from somewhere close, in the direction of the mammoth display, he thought. A wrenching noise followed, like a spring popping.

Moody grabbed his baton, but then replaced it with his phone.

In case of an emergency Eddie had given him instructions to call, or dial 911. He didn't. Instead, he clicked on the phone's camcorder. If something was breaking he wanted proof that it wasn't his fault.

He sprinted around the displays, toward the front of the lobby. Sure enough, the back end of the mammoth skeleton was swaying from the support cables.

The flashlight beam passed through the elephant's ribs. In the crisscrossed shadows beyond, the darkness on the wall shifted. The movement made him freeze. The sound of several pairs of feet clapped across the marble floor.

Had some stupid kids broke into the museum after all?

"Hey, hold it!" he shouted, trying not to sound as frightened as he felt. He heard the feet scrambling on the far side of the display.

Maneuvering around the elephant's hind legs, he saw the great double doors of the building's entrance. One of them was ajar, and the door wedge had fallen out, keeping it from shutting completely. Must be how the flies got inside.

If it was kids, how did they get past the security system?

Might not be kids; might be worse than kids, he thought. Could it be an actual burglary?

There was enough damage to consider calling the cops. Part of the skeleton's right leg was missing. He found the femur a couple feet away from the exhibit, broken into three. Several smaller bones lay scattered on the floor, which explained the bang and the creaking.

Moody swiveled the light through the mammoth's ribs. The room was too big and open for the intruders to get far. There wasn't any place to hide, unless they fell flat on their bellies behind an exhibit.

The light illuminated a furry patch on one of the stuffed, long extinct animals that flanked the mammoth. As he moved the light beam the hairy model trembled.

Moody looked again.

The model appeared wet and dirty—patches of fur were tangled and discolored. And what was that next to it... *attached* to it?

Connected to the fur was something shiny, though rusty in spots, and painted sky blue. The top of a Volkswagen beetle was somehow melded onto the fur. Its windows were gone but the curved dome of the car was unmistakable.

"Well, that's new," he mumbled.

The car roof and the fur turned away. What came in its place made Moody drop his flashlight, and scream.

For an instant, before darkness swallowed his sight, a huge round eye peered at him through the skeleton.

On instinct, he snatched up his light and took off the way he came.

He heard bare feet racing along the marble after him. By ear, he knew they'd outrun and circle him, blocking his escape.

He tried to press the emergency code on his phone but his hands shook and he fumbled the buttons twice. *Why can't 911 be one number instead of three?* he thought.

Ahead of him, the feet-sounds stopped.

Moody screeched to a halt and lifted his flashlight, which he almost dropped again before planting the beam on the impossible thing towering over him.

Words escaped his thoughts; he couldn't make sense of what he saw. The thing was huge, standing a few feet short of the vaulted ceiling. It filled the area between the displays with its girth. Pieces of it were made of metal, such as the car top. Bits of it were furry, like the display beasts. But its head, for the most part, was a gorilla—a giant one, with a metallic jaw big enough to swallow him whole. Two massive eyes bore down solely on him, squinting. Their pupils shrank in the glare.

"Do you mind not doing that?" the gorilla said.

Moody's legs quivered. He shifted the light out of the giant's face, more from a loss of motor control than the monster's instruction.

"Much appreciated," said the gorilla. The thing's voice was hoarse and had an accent—British, maybe, like some rejected Muppet gone horror show.

Behind Moody, the doors were still open. He could run that way; however, the thing had already exceeded his speed once. This time it would have a clear sprint to snatch him up and devour him.

As if reading his mind, the monster said: "Please don't run again. I wouldn't want to be forced to eat you, if at all possible."

The rotten smell he'd mistaken for the toilets came from the creature. From a close distance the smell was like a wall of heat, making him nauseous. Flies tickled his face but he didn't dare make any sudden movements to swat them away.

"I assume you have plenty of questions, but are too terrified to ask. Am I correct?"

After a long pause, Moody realized the question wasn't rhetorical. After a longer pause, he regained control of his tongue and lips. "Uh... *maybe?*"

"Relax. I didn't mean to scare you. I simply need a few things, then I'll be on my way."

Slowly, Moody's senses returned enough for him to understand what he was being told. If running wasn't an option, what was he supposed to do? He spoke with caution and sincerity in case the monster decided it *would* have to eat him. "How'd you get by the alarm?"

"My boy. If you don't want anyone to get into this collection of relics, you should choose a keypad code other than *12345*."

Eddie should've changed those damn numbers; Moody kept telling him they were dumb.

The gorilla continued, "I could have simply knocked the doors down, but I was trying not to disturb anyone while I got what I came for."

"You need something... from the museum?"

"Yes."

"Can I ask what?"

"You may."

Moody thought about that one for a minute, then asked. *"What?"*

The gorilla began moving, but it didn't walk on two legs. It only had one: a crippled limb it dragged along. When it moved it used its two extra long arms, with its fingers propping it up high. The feet-like sounds, Moody realized, were the gorilla's fingers and knuckles.

Halfway to the mammoth, the creature paused, saying, "Are you coming?"

Now that the monster had moved, Moody could see the hallway leading to the mummy exhibit. The thing might not be able to follow him if he ran—

Moody yelped as the monster slid a hand around his torso and lifted him from the ground. It held him in one hand while dragging itself toward the mammoth with the other, leaving a trail of greenish slime on the floor. The vibrating ooze was filled with tiny worms and maggots. No wonder flies were everywhere.

The creature set Moody down beside the exhibit, then grabbed the unbroken left leg of the mamoth skeleton, yanking and twisting it until the femur snapped free. The monster made a happy noise, and shook the femur to throw off the loose bolts.

"We didn't break this one. Cheers!"

Moody dodged the limp leg as the gorilla positioned it.

It wiggled the bone against its flaccid thigh until the creature found an opening. Carefully, it slid the femur through its flesh until its upper leg went rigid, and then pushed its fingers into the hole all the way to the wrist. After fooling around inside the flesh for a few seconds it found a secure fit and removed its hand.

The monster smiled. "Much, much better. Too bad I buggered the other bone or I might have been walking out of here on my knees."

"Are you going to… eat me now?" asked Moody.

The gorilla shook its head. "No, I'm not going to eat you. I promise. You've been far too civil for me to repay your kindness by way of the tooth. Please don't be afraid."

Moody surprised himself with a laugh. When you lost it, everything must be funny, he figured.

The gorilla chuckled with him, a guffaw that echoed like thunder.

"I'm nuts!" Moody shouted.

There was no way this was happening: a giant, part-monkey, part-machine, part-fake mammoth was talking to him in the museum? There was probably angel dust in his last joint. If they didn't slap him in a coo-coo asylum he'd have to strangle his dealer.

"That has to be it," he said. "I've flipped. I'm grade-A almonds. Nuts!"

"Bananas," added the gorilla.

Moody clapped his hands together, laughing harder. He reached into his pocket for his wallet, retrieving a joint from inside. He lit it with his Zippo. *Might as well enjoy myself in this little freak-fest*, he thought.

"I'm glad to see you're in better spirits," said the gorilla.

"Me too. Any minute now I'm going to wake up on top of Mr. Tutankhamen's crypt." Moody offered a puff, but the gorilla shook its head. "By the way, you're not real."

"Really?"

"Oh, yeah."

The creature thought about that for a minute while Moody swiped flies from his face. The little pests had begun to congregate on his pants, some actually finding their way into the burnt hole in his crotch. He smacked them dead but more took their place.

Finally the gorilla replied, "But what does *real* mean? Are any of us *truly* real?"

"Touché," Moody said, as if he comprehended the creature's meaning. "So… my name's Virgil Moody. What's yours?"

"I don't know."

"What do you mean, *you don't know?*"

"I mean, *I don't know.* I don't think I've ever had one of those. I've had a lot of things, but never a name."

There was writing on the gorilla's chest, beneath the fur. No, not fur. There was dried seaweed around its sternum. The breastbone was shiny.

Moody turned the flashlight on it and read:

PROPERTY OF KONG-TV, SEATTLE, WA.

Below, several cables and electrical wires dangled like spilled guts.

The creature wasn't one, but many. A conglomerate. Nowhere, except in its face, did it have two parts that were the same. Every section of fur resembled a patchwork quilt––some grey, others mahogany, most black, a few even rainbow swathed. Between them Moody could see stitches, made partly of rope, partly of twine, partly not stitches at all but gleaming staples. Metal had also been fused to the heap of its body, some bits were unknown, others he recognized, like the car hump on the gorilla's back, the aluminum sign on its chest, the metallic sheen of its jaw.

Its face was one piece, maybe an animatronic from a giant gorilla robot. Or part of an attraction at a theme park. Its rubber and latex skin had fallen off the jaw, though the rest was intact.

"Okay, not who… *what* are you?"

Again the monster shrugged.

Moody asked, "You don't know that either?"

"Nope."

"Then where?"

"Where did *you* come from?"

"Tennessee, originally."

"And before that?"

"Uh… from my mom?"

"And before that?"

Moody paused. The gorilla's point washed over him like a cold shower. "*Whoa… I don't know.*"

"Exactly."

"So you don't remember anything?"

The giant scratched its head and pondered the idea. "I remember the sea, the crabs in my brains… fish fell from my fur, but the fur isn't mine. I use new pieces to replace those I've lost. I pick them from the sea, from beaches, from stuffed animals and dead dogs, from parked cars and amusement parks. I pick them out of trees and from under rocks. But something must have been there before, because… how did I know to replace them?"

The gorilla pinched two fingers into its side and pulled out something long. It was an oar. The wood was splintered and soft, bending from its own weight. The gorilla dropped the oar and sighed.

"Seems I'm falling apart faster than I can maintain. My legs went yesterday. At the beach, I saw the museum's flyer, and I thought I'd sneak in to get some replacements. Maybe the journey overextended my resources."

The beach was only a few miles from the museum, but it was a long walk on one's fingers.

"Can you walk now?" asked Moody.

The gorilla shook its head. "My other leg's gone entirely. I have to build it from the ground up."

Moody took a deep puff and held it. "Maybe... I can... help."

"Really?"

Moody coughed a plume of smoke. *Why the silly son of a bitch not? This is a dream, and a kooky one at that. I didn't pay for the trip, but I should get my money's worth despite the fact.*

The gorilla waved its hand to clear the air. "That's a nasty habit," it said. A finger fell from its hand. "Oh... that's not good."

"Can I give you a name?"

The gorilla picked up the lost finger and sighed. "That would be nice."

"Then I'll call you Kong." He pointed to the television station call letters on its chest.

"Brutish, but okay."

"One last question."

"Fire away."

"Did you say you're made of *dead* things?"

"Some. Some were never alive to begin with."

"Like a zombie. *Zombie-Kong.*"

"Zombie... returned from the dead. Let's hope so. By the looks of things, we may soon test the theory. Maybe you can be my Messiah? *Zombie-Messiah!*" The gorilla, now named Kong, grinned. "Enough sad talk. We're all just pieces of a whole, I suppose. If this is it for me I want to go out with a bash. You like to party?"

"Does a hooker turn tricks?"

Kong reached into the gash in its stomach. With its thumb and forefinger it pulled on a cord. "You're going to love this."

The sharp smell of gasoline bit Moody's nostrils. The rattle and hum of a motor sounded from within Kong's chest. Smoke steamed from the giant's ears, which acted as an exhaust. There must've been a generator in there somewhere.

"Cool beans," Moody said.

"You haven't seen anything yet." Kong thumped a place on its neck and the lobby filled with music, a song by the *Grateful Dead.*

"Righteous!" Moody motioned for Kong to wait. "I'm not going to run and leave you. I just need to get something that might help with your predicament. Is that okay, Kong?"

"So long as you return."

"Oh, I will." He sprinted toward the janitor's storeroom, careful not to slip in the river of maggots and muck covering the lobby floor.

Since he was dreaming, he considered pulling a Playboy bunny out of the air along with a chili-cheeseburger. Hell, two Playboy bunnies! When *whatever* flushed through his system, ending its spree, he was positive he'd pay for it tenfold. Might as well go balls to the wall while it lasted.

Behind him, Kong shouted one last thing. "If you can find bananas, much appreciated."

* * *

Halfway back to the lobby he dropped his items—mops, extension cords, and a vacuum cleaner—to the floor, and thought, *Moody… what the fuck are you doing?*

The drugs, if they ever existed, were gone. His weed high had faded too. To the best of his knowledge, he felt sober.

He looked around the janitor's storeroom: plastic jugs of detergent, rust-covered paint scrappers, piles of dirty rags, a nudie-magazine tucked behind a case of WD-40. This was reality—not the kooky idea floating around in his skull.

"I was actually going to drag this stuff into the lobby to help an giant imaginary gorilla make a new leg," he said. Then he repeated it to make sure that he understood his degree of his craziness. "I got to stop smoking."

Maybe his high school teachers were right; maybe he *did* kill too many brain cells. They said he'd end up with a job no better than this—what if they were right about everything else too?

He went to the water fountain and splashed cold water onto his face.

No, he wasn't snoozing. He was definitely awake. Could he have been sleeping before? Kong seemed so true, so vivid in his imagination, and he'd never been creative enough to envision such a thing.

Of course, if he believed Kong was real he was certifiably schizoid.

Only one way to solve this dilemma—

He pushed open the storeroom door and started toward the lobby. The music was still there, increasing in volume as he approached.

It's not real, Moody. Just ignore.

He found it hard to ignore the ripe stench of decay with a hint of ocean salt, the rotten meat, moldy wood, wet hair and musk.

His foot slipped and he grabbed the submarine exhibit to keep from falling. The thick slime now coating the heel of his boot moved. Tiny maggots fell from his boot to the floor.

You're seeing things. Ignore, ignore, ignore—

He walked around the slimy footprints that led to the storeroom. His own, from when he left the creature.

Ignore, ignore, ignore—

Moody rounded the corner into the lobby. A wall of buzzing flies slapped his face. Despite their itching wings, he did his best to obey his own instructions… but when the gigantic head of a mechanical gorilla swiveled his way—the face atop a mountain of living garbage—he heard his inner voice scream.

You're on your own for this one, pal! I'm getting the fudge out of here…

Moody began to cry.

"Please… don't weep over me," said Kong. "Or else… I'll feel worse than… I already do."

Moody didn't stop. In fact, he bawled louder. To his credit, the giant gave him several minutes before it spoke again.

"I'd be inclined to allow you… whatever you need to reconcile me… but I think my time in this world is done," it said. Kong's head slumped as if its neck could no longer hold the weight.

Moody's fit started to recede. He wiped his face. "You're… real?" he said, between sobs.

"Mostly," Kong answered. "And those parts… not for much longer."

Moody stepped closer. Why not? If he was a lunatic, why fight it?

Kong didn't appear as healthy (if that was the right word) as before. Its massive arms seemed deflated. The digits, once used for walking, were now disjointed and broken at the knuckles. Each finger crawled around in circles lethargically, gradually slowing. Kong's body had come apart too. The stitches holding together its patchwork skin had become unraveled. Its giant head was malformed, as if the metal had begun to sag. To melt.

The giant no longer looked threatening. It was falling apart.

Moody regained some of his meager courage and approached.

"Are you okay?" he asked.

"My guess is no."

"Are you… dying?"

"I don't think I was ever really alive."

As they spoke, Kong's body deteriorated quicker. The fur began to shed. The beetle's roof on its spine shriveled like a raisin, flaking into dust. Every part of the creature was crumbling or dissolving.

"What's happening to you?"

Kong's face twisted into what looked like a smile; it was hard to tell with the animatronic head folding together like Play-Doh. "Never should've taken so many different parts… this body's not good enough to survive." Kong's voice was devolving too. The syllables slurred. "I need… to find something more whole… to start… to take… need another to join with me… "

At Moody's feet, the ooze that was Kong's body lapped over his steel-toe boots. He stepped away, watching Kong's head join the mush.

Poking through the softening skull, he recognized the shape of a skull. Kong's face fell away to reveal a set of human bones, which protruded from its giant metal head.

For a moment, Moody thought he saw the skull smile at him—*but what skull doesn't smile?* he thought. Regardless, he returned a grin as if they shared some private joke.

The bones lasted no longer than the rest, and they liquefied too. Seconds later there was nothing recognizable in the debris.

Moody scanned the enormous pile of stinking compost. He blinked, then rubbed his eyes hard. The heap didn't disappear. He gave himself a couple of slaps on the cheek. Still it remained, clear as a pink slip, ruining the lobby floor.

Kong was gone. Even the flies had died and fallen to the ground, joining their lifeless babies, which were curling by his feet.

He sat on the mammoth display ledge, wiping tears from his eyes. *Hmmm?* he thought, and that was the sum of it. He felt dead from the neck up.

He pointed his light toward the center of the pile. Several bubbles popped in the shape of a circle. Below them, the ooze stirred until a thick bulge, shiny and raw, rose through the bubbles. It twitched back and forth, sprouting a long neck. The bulge and the neck grew several feet into the air, curled to the floor, and then slithered from the bubbles before the bulge—*must be the thing's head*—rested at eye-level with Moody.

It was a worm of some sort, though none Moody had ever seen, not even on nature channels. Its pink body was as thick as his forearm. *Unformed* came to mind; the thing looked like something aborted. It had no nose, no ears, no eyes, and no mouth that he could see—just a fat nub swaying on the end of a thin body. It seemed to be examining him.

Normally he would run screaming at the sight of such a thing, but after having a conversation with the giant gorilla, his threshold felt pretty lax.

The thing lowered its head toward his hand.

Moody yanked his hand away.

The creature made no effort to attack or bite (as if it could with no mouth). Instead, it waited silently beneath his palm.

Cautiously, Moody touched its head. The worm pressed against his hand. He stroked his fingers along its wet bulge. It vibrated, and Moody heard a purring sound he couldn't place.

Euphoria washed over him, inside and out. Moody smiled so wide his cheeks hurt. His pants swelled as he sported an erection—the intoxicating emotion filling him everywhere with an indescribable ecstasy. It was the best high he ever enjoyed.

He removed his hand but the feeling didn't go away. The worm cocked its head coyly to the side, and Moody, despite the lack of words, understood what the creature was saying, what it was asking—what it offered.

"I've never been chosen for anything special in my life," he said. Knowing he might feel different in the morning; he unbuttoned his shirt and opened it wide. The worm slid inside and coiled around his torso, its tail slinking down to wrap around his leg, the bulge of its head nestling against the beat of his heart atop his breastbone. Carefully, he re-buttoned his shirt and left the lobby to get a mop.

He only had a few hours to clean up the colossal mess, but he wasn't worried. There were *bigger* things on his mind.

* * *

"You gained some weight, fat boy," Eddie said. "Night shift has been good to you, Mood. It's been a couple months and already you look like the spitting image of a young Buddha."

He patted Moody's stomach, then snapped his hand away as if he'd been burned.

Moody smiled. "That's not fat. It's muscle weight."

Eddie nodded and cleared his throat. "Well, don't get your panties in a wad… and make sure you check in tomorrow a few minutes early. I'll need to show you the new security system—"

"Is the code *12345*?"

Eddie answered with a grunt, and left the locker room.

When Moody was sure he was gone he opened his locker and took out a bag of alligator bones, swiped from the museum's storage shelves. No one would miss them, at least, not for some time.

He left the museum and drove home with a grin. When he reached his shitty apartment complex he shielded his eyes from the morning sun, slipped in through a broken door, and ran up four flights of stairs to his one-bedroom apartment.

It was a tight fit. His new project had already filled his apartment to the door inside a month.

His stomach growled but he ignored it. Work first, then food.

Moody stepped over the arm of the construct—the new body he was building for his friend—and he sat beside the sack of its hand. He dumped the alligator bones on the stained carpet beside it, and he went to work sticking them inside the hand, building the new skeleton, piece by piece. Of course, he didn't know how a hand worked beneath the skin, but his friend—the worm he named Kong Junior—sent the required information to his brain.

Since Kong had disintegrated in the museum, and the worm had joined with him, he spent every free hour rebuilding. The apartment stunk to high heaven but no one complained. His neighbors were either too afraid of being deported, or too busy cooking methamphetamines in their kitchens.

For the skin and fur needed in a single arm he'd sewn together half his carpet, a dead dog, a road-kill cat, and three taxidermy raccoons stolen from the museum's prop storage. For the inner muscles of the forearm and bicep he used maggot-swollen strips of meat. For strength he added bungee cords.

Combining his determination with Kong Junior's smarts, there wasn't anything they couldn't accomplish.

The masterpiece was the head, the biggest part he would finish before working on the chest. They manufactured its face almost verbatim to Moody's memory, only this time without the animatronics. For eyes, bowling balls hung heavy in their tar-covered sockets. Other features included clothing from his closet, rubber from stolen tires, caveman dresses from the museum, leather from a cow he poisoned at a nearby farm, and countless other bits and pieces he scavenged, swiped, or skinned.

Kong Senior would've been proud.

"We're one and the same," Kong Junior said to him in his thoughts.

"I know, I know," Moody said.

The worm uncoiled from beside his intestines and poked its head through Moody's elongated navel. The bulge slipped through the buttons of his shirt, examining their work firsthand.

With his free hand, Moody petted its head.

He wondered where the worm came from, what it was, and if it had a purpose—but he couldn't answer those questions about himself either. No one could. It was better, he had found, simply to exist.

However, there was one query that just wouldn't leave him alone:

"Why a gorilla?"

"I don't know," said Junior in his mind.

"That's your answer for everything."

Junior thought a moment then said, "Don't you want to be something you're not?"

He didn't answer but both of them knew he couldn't agree more.

Once the work was completed he would add the greatest part—himself—into the cavity he once saw smiling, the creature's skull. There he'd become its brain, forever interwoven with Kong, or until it was time for another metamorphosis. By then he wouldn't care. He'd forget his name, forget his past—forget everything. He would be part of a new life, something bigger than any of his pieces... bigger than himself, larger than anything he could've imagined. Literally.

He had finally found his place in the world, a place where his life mattered—higher than he'd ever been before.

"Maybe a month or two to go," he said. "Maybe less, if we hurry."

Kong Junior didn't answer. Instead it slipped free of Moody's body and slithered into the new giant's arm by the shoulder. The construct's hand flexed, the arm tensed. Moody gave its huge palm a high five.

Kong Junior popped out of the arm and danced around the living room.

Yeah, he was happy too.

161

TREVER PALMER
Reach For The Sky

My name is Calvin Jackson. I'm eighteen-years-old and this is the story of how I befriended a giant zombie gorilla. Yeah, you read that right. What the hell? I was only twelve when it happened, so cut me some slack.

I wasn't very popular when I was in the sixth grade. Oh, who am I kidding? I'm not popular now. But none of that matters. When I was twelve, I did everything in my power to be a "cool" kid. And I darned near almost made it.

It all started in the playground. I'd stick anything in my mouth and eat it. Insects were usually the main fare. I slowly noticed that I liked the taste of grasshoppers. They were chewy, and usually excreted a taste that reminded me of candy apples. Ants didn't quite cut it, but I'd scoop them up in my hand, destroying their latest hill, and jam them into my mouth, too. There was really no taste to them. If anything, they usually left me sucking at my teeth to dislodge their squirming carcasses.

Things like eating bugs really made me a crowd-pleaser on the playground and I enjoyed the status for the few weeks that it lasted. Nobody was calling me mean names, or slapping the back of my head, or threatening to kick my ass. It was nice. But then I went and made a mistake. It's really nothing out of the ordinary for me.

One spring afternoon, while Miss Sweat's sixth grade class was out on the playground, everyone was wondering what I'd stick in my mouth next. The expectations were growing enormous. I really needed to pull out all the stops to keep up my "coolness."

So what did I do?

I hunted around the playground for something to eat. I was hoping for a grasshopper, and had that stuck in my mind, when I came upon what I considered would be my greatest achievement. Lying in the dirt beneath the swing set was a fresh pile of dog shit. Now, I wasn't crazy enough to stick the shit in my mouth. But as for those green flies buzzing around it? Well, you get the picture.

I managed to catch one of those emerald green flies. I pulled its wings off and watched it buzz around in my hand. It tickled. I turned around to the crowd gathered around me and showed them my latest acquisition. I noticed the looks on their faces, but was feeling such a rush from finding the fly that I didn't really let it register. I just popped that fly into my mouth and started chewing. For effect, I stuck out my tongue and showed everyone the messy goo that was swimming around in my mouth.

"You just ate a dog shit fly!" said Eddie Fisher. "What the hell is the matter with you? Are you crazy?"

For a moment, I just stood there with my tongue lolled out. And slowly, oh so slowly, I saw the reactions on the crowd's faces. Suddenly, the realization that I'd just gone from cool to plain ass weird hit me like a sledgehammer. Everyone was laughing and pointing at me. Quickly, I spat the remains of the fly out of my mouth. And then I began to rub what was left of its corpse off my tongue.

"What a dumbass," said Lee Edwards.

The girls didn't say anything, but I could tell from their sneers that I'd lost their support, too. Not that there had been much of it to start with. Sixth grade girls are funny squirrels. You never really know what to expect from them. But I knew what to expect now. And trust me, it wasn't good.

Eddie Fisher came over to me and punched me in the shoulder. It hurt, but I didn't cry. I held those tears back as hard as I could. Things were already bad enough.

"I should make you eat that shit," he told me. "Would you like that, too?"

I shook my head.

"Fucking weirdo," muttered Eddie. "Come on, guys. Let's get out of here."

I watched them all walk away from me. The swings fluttered back-and-forth on their rusted chains in the cool spring breeze. I was really holding those tears back. I think it hurt a lot more than if Eddie would have punched me.

Thankfully, Miss Sweat called everyone back into the class-room. I had lost everything in mere seconds on the playground. I was devastated. It was now back to a life of being a total loser. That was just fucking great.

But that all changed that afternoon as I walked home.

I could still hear Eddie Fisher laughing in my ears as I turned the corner onto Rogers Street. I lived in the last house on the left. Before you got there, however, you had to pass by the home of my next-door neighbor, Arthur Foreman. Only I didn't call him Arthur or Mr. Foreman. Instead, I referred to him as Charlie. For some strange reason when I was a little boy, around three or four, I took to calling him Charlie because that's what his white mutt of a dog was named. Why that stuck is beyond me, but it did.

As I got to Charlie's house, I could hear him in his backyard. It was more laughter, but light and fun unlike that of Eddie Fisher. I stopped for a second, listening to it, before I finally decided to cross Charlie's yard and peek around his house. I'd seen Charlie skin rabbits in his backyard before, and he often got to laughing whenever he was drinking. It wasn't going to be a surprise if he was covered in blood and sitting there waving around a buck knife with a bloody rabbit crusting in his lap.

However, what I saw made my jaw drop.

Charlie was standing in his backyard, hoisting a bunch of bananas to a giant gorilla. The gorilla was tittering around on its paws, playfully growling as it snapped the bananas away from Charlie and popped them into its mouth like grapes. Charlie continued laughing as the gorilla did a wild jig about the yard.

"Hey Charlie," I called out. "Who's your new friend?"

Charlie turned and looked at me. Amidst the laughter, there was a large smile on his face. He titled back his greasy John

Deere ball cap and winked at me. He waved a hand in my direction.

"Come here," he said. "And meet him."

I crossed the backyard, soon finding myself in the gorilla's shadow. Strangely, I wasn't afraid of it. It stood maybe twenty feet tall, but it didn't scare me. I guess after the day I'd had there wasn't much emotion left in me. But as I stood there gazing, and feeling its eyes appraise me, a jolt of enjoyment coursed through me.

"What's its name?" I asked.

"Bobo," replied Charlie. "What do you think of him?"

"I think he's great!"

Charlie pulled out the makings of a cigarette. He rolled the Bugler together and stuck it between his lips. He lit it with a kitchen match and puffed out a smoke ring.

"I think he's great, too," replied Charlie.

"Where'd you get him?"

"Sorry," said Charlie. He winked at me. "If I told you, I'd have to kill you."

I knew Charlie was kidding, but still felt a tingle of cold sweat trace its way down my spine. Sometimes I wondered if Charlie was joking or not.

"You can't keep an gorilla in your backyard," I told him.

"Sure, I can. Who's going to complain? Besides, he's as docile as a lamb. I've got him trained."

"How did you train him?"

"Well," said Charlie, "it wasn't really me that trained him. It was the people I got him from that turned him into a zombie, you see."

"It's a zombie?" I asked. "You mean it's really dead and eats people?"

Charlie laughed. "No. You've seen too many movies. I mean a zombie like in Haiti. It's under a spell to do anything I ask."

"Oh." I looked into the gorilla's eyes. It bared its fangs at me and I could see the ends of its mouth turn up into a smile. "Can I pet it?"

"Sure."

I walked over to Bobo, keeping my eyes on its face. I tentatively reached out a hand and stroked it. Bobo's fur was coarse and thick.

"And you can't tell me where you got him?" I asked, again.

"Nope," replied Charlie. He puffed on the last of his Bugler. Then he dropped it to the brilliantly green grass, the color of a billiard table, and smashed it out beneath his heel. "I'd just as soon tell you where I got that piece of Stonehenge."

I kick myself for not having asked him about that rock from Stonehenge he supposedly owned. But I guess that's another story.

As it stood, I couldn't keep my eyes off of Bobo.

"I think he likes you," Charlie told me.

"I sure do like him."

"Stay outside and play with him. I'll go and make us some lemonade." Charlie smiled. "I think you two are going to be good friends."

And that's how my too short relationship with Bobo started. It was there in Charlie's backyard on a warm spring afternoon that I found what would become my best friend ever.

Oh, I didn't get to do much with Bobo. Heck, there wasn't that much to do. It wasn't like we could go to the movies or arcade together. At first, Charlie didn't like the idea of Bobo leaving his backyard. But he eventually warmed to the idea when he saw how Bobo and I got along so good. We'd take walks down to the Rough River and simply hang out. We'd lie on our backs on the banks and stare up at the sky. And it was then, during simple trips like these, that I learned what Bobo wanted the most out of life.

We'd lie there, basking in that warm sun and he'd reach his arms up towards the sky. It was like he was reaching for the clouds. Even someone as tall as Bobo was going to fall short there, but I still got a kick out of it. Bobo made me laugh a lot during those days.

We spent a lot of time together. Sometimes, sitting in Charlie's backyard, I'd climb up onto his back and just hang there. It was something out of this world.

But, as per the usual with me, something went dramatically wrong. Like being cool for a few days before swallowing a handful of green shit-flies, I went and fucked everything up. It was just par for the course, I guess.

One Saturday morning Bobo and I were hanging around Charlie's backyard. Next door, I could see my Dad mowing the grass. And I knew my Mom was washing her car. Yeah, yeah, I know. Those are jobs the kid is supposed to be doing, but my parents were cool. They let me hang out with a giant gorilla, didn't they?

Anyways, we were hanging around the yard when Charlie came out the backdoor. He had another one of those Buglers perched inside his mouth with a cloud of smoke forming a halo over his head. He stopped next to me and reached out a hand, patting Bobo's side. He smiled down at me.

"What do you two guys plan on doing today?" he asked me.

"I don't know," I replied. I reached out and petted one of Bobo's long toes. His skin was warm and hairy. "There's not much to do."

"Well," said Charlie, "I'm sure you'll think of something." He dropped the Bugler to the ground where it smoldered. "I'm going to the liquor store. I'm fresh out of spirits. You two behave yourselves. And if you take Bobo off, don't forget to have him home before dark."

"I won't," I said.

Bobo softly growled.

I watched Charlie walk to the small pick-up truck in his driveway. In just a few short years he would be killed inside that truck. After running a red light he'd be crushed beneath a cement truck. And yes, they say he was drunk at the time.

"What do you want to do, Bobo?" I asked.

The gorilla reached out and gently nudged me with a fingertip. I laughed, grabbing onto it. I reached it up to my face and feigned picking my nose with it. Bobo let loose with a grunt and the sides of his mouth curled up.

"Want to see where I go to school? I know it sounds boring, but they have a playground, too. We can climb on top of the monkey bars, or something. What do you say?"

167

Bobo tilted his head, the edges of his mouth still curled. I took that as a "yes."

"Come on," I said. "Let's go."

Charlie never kept Bobo chained up. Since the gorilla was hypnotized to follow his every order he never had the need to. And that was just fine with me. It must've suited the neighborhood, as well, because nobody ever complained. Yeah, I find that funny, too. But truth is stranger than fiction, or so they say.

It wasn't a long walk to the Ratliff Elementary School. As usual, I had the sidewalk to myself as Bobo walked along aside on the road. The streets weren't busy with traffic on the weekends, so we rarely had to move for a passing car. Sometimes you'd see a Soccer Mom passing in a minivan, her mouth agape and eyes bugging out of her skull, but that was about it. Nobody ever bothered Bobo and me.

Until that Saturday, that is.

We reached the school and gravitated immediately towards the playground. As I had mentioned to Bobo, I thought the monkey bars might be a fun place for us to hang out. Bobo could climb on top of them and sit. It'd be nice.

Or so I thought.

I walked us over to the monkey bars. Bobo immediately climbed up, reaching his paws towards the sky. He let out a growl that I took as pure happiness. I didn't follow him up, instead giving him all the room he needed. And he simply stood there, arms outstretched.

And that's when I heard the voices.

No, no. No voices inside my head. I heard Eddie Fisher and the rest of those guys coming to the playground.

"What the hell is that?"

My stomach turned as I realized that Eddie had spotted us. He didn't know about Bobo, and I wanted to keep it that way. I was selfish. And I sure didn't want to share with a bastard like Eddie Fisher.

"Come on, Bobo," I said. "Let's get out of here."

Bobo dropped his arms and looked at me. There was a puzzled expression on his face.

"It's time to go. Come on!"

Before he could climb down, though, Eddie Fisher and his gang were atop us. And they weren't empty-handed. In their grubby mitts they were carrying a cache of rocks which they immediately began throwing at Bobo. The giant gorilla let out with a roar that made them take a step or two backwards, but it wasn't enough to get them to stop throwing the rocks.

"Quit it!" I said. "You're hurting him!"

"Any friend of yours has to be a loser," said Eddie. "And that's one ugly friend you've got there. Where'd you find him, at the zoo?"

"If you don't stop…"

"You'll what? Cry on me?"

Suddenly, Bobo jumped down from the monkey bars. He landed between Eddie and me. For a moment, I was blinded. All I could see was Bobo's butt. And that's when I heard the scream. It was Eddie, and he was crying bloody murder. I ran around Bobo and saw that he had picked Eddie up. Eddie's arm, up to the elbow, was buried inside Bobo's mouth, his fangs working feverishly to chew through the muscle and bone. I felt hot bile rise in my throat as Bobo spat the gory appendage aside. And Eddie, and all his loser friends, shrieked. Some of them picked up rocks and began to pelt Bobo with them, and he knocked them all aside, letting loose with a guttural roar.

As for what I was doing? I was simply standing there, mouth wide open, watching the entire episode. I didn't know the first thing to do.

But I did hear the woman's scream over Eddie and his friends yelling, and Bobo's growling. There was a subdivision behind the playground, and I turned around to follow the direction of the scream. I saw her standing in her backyard, hands to her face, screaming as she stared at Bobo. For some reason, I screamed myself when I saw her dart inside her house. I don't know why, but I knew it couldn't be leading to anything good.

Rooted to the spot, I watched as Bobo tossed Eddie away. He landed like a ragdoll in the dirt and crumpled up into a fetal position, crying his head off. The other boys stopped throwing rocks and turned away to run. They simply left Eddie there to tend to his own wounds. I felt a rush of hot anger at that. The fucking cowards!

I didn't linger on Eddie long, though. We can't forget that I practically hated his guts. So I turned my attention to Bobo. The large gorilla roared and beat his chest. Then he walked away and returned to the monkey bars. He climbed to the top, still roaring, and beat his chest, again. Then he raised his arms to the sky. I couldn't see his eyes very well, but I had the strange sensation of knowing that he was crying. The big guy didn't really mean to hurt anyone. He just wanted to reach the sky. He just wanted to be free of Charlie, Eddie, and probably, if truth be known, even me.

And I couldn't blame him.

I took a step forward, reaching a hand towards Bobo, when two police cruisers skidded to a halt on the edge of the playground. The policemen threw open their doors quickly, taking position behind them, guns drawn and aimed directly at Bobo.

"No! Don't hurt him!"

But the police ignored me. I was just some dumb kid to them. And there's no telling what that distraught housewife told them. She'd seen Eddie's arm hanging out of Bobo's mouth, and she had heard all of our screams. To the police I was probably just another little kid in a shit heap of trouble.

I started to run towards Bobo, who returned his attention to me. And I could see those glistening tears in his eyes.

He just wanted to reach for the sky.

Bobo threw his arms up, again, and that's when the police let loose with their gunfire. The bullets tore into Bobo's hide, spitting flesh and blood everywhere as he tumbled from the monkey bars. He slammed down on the ground, just a few feet away from where Eddie was still crying, and I knew he was dead. The thought that he might have survived that barrage never entered my mind.

I walked over to his corpse and knelt down. I ignored the warnings from the cops to stay away from him. Instead, I knelt beside Bobo and took one of his large hands in my own. It was already cold.

TW BROWN
Iced

1

"…erratic behavior of the Gulf Stream has brought unseasonable weather to most of the UK—

Click

"…scientists continue to insist that this temperature anomaly, seen in parts of China and—"

Click

"…section of ice the size of the state of Georgia has broken free—"

Click

Brett Urban switched off the television and tossed the remote on the conference table. A dozen well-aged men in near-identical suits stared back expressionless. He took a deep breath and considered his next words carefully. "The Athens camp is believed to be in that section of ice." Brett leaned forward, placing both hands flat on the polished mahogany.

Looks were exchanged, but he didn't think it had quite sunken in. Then, like somebody switching on a bank of lights, eyes began to widen.

"Mister Urban," one old man said, peering at Brett over his thick glasses, "are you telling us that the expedition team is—"

"I'm not saying anything yet," Brett interrupted. "But I need to be on a plane now, before any of the media, or worse… the environmental activists groups… get on scene."

"Have all traces of that camp sanitized, Mister Urban," another old man hissed.

"The last thing we need is this administration getting wind of our operation," a third added.

Brett leaned down and grabbed his case. "Give me twenty hours and tell your friends to keep the satellites away from the area until you hear from me."

As he left the room and closed the door behind him, he heard the buzz of conversation kick in. The old codgers were, without a doubt, on the phone to various contacts within—and on the fringes of—the government.

DECC Corporation was funded by some of the wealthiest men in the world, and when a geological report arrived claiming that a microbe, previously unknown to man, had been discovered in a glacial ridge in Antarctica, a team had been dispatched immediately. Unlike most government research teams the expedition had the best equipment money could buy.

Less than two weeks later, DECC's headquarters received confirmation.

Within a month, experimental stations all over the Antarctic began encountering *problems* ranging from equipment issues to a mysteriously sudden termination of funding.

One outpost—funded by a joint China-Russia Intel organization—proved tougher to deal with. Their power generators suffered a catastrophic fire. By the time an evacuation team arrived all the members of the outpost were dead. Frozen.

Brett walked onto the tarmac and crossed the expanse to board the waiting plane. He sat down, strapped on his headset, and nodded for the pilot to take off. Conversation wasn't necessary. Vic Brady, the pilot, knew where to go. He flew Brett wherever the corporation needed his special talents.

Brett opened his case and read from the folder that had been waiting for him in the conference room. The microbe was perplexing, with one curious finding: there was something in the genetic makeup suggesting a loose relation to primate DNA.

Initially, the board at the DECC Corporation had been furious. After years of raping the Amazon in search of the "one thing" that would offer them a miracle cure for everything, they believed their payday had come.

Brett did not want to be in Rachel Redding's shoes. Doctor Redding had insisted that the seemingly mundane finding by a third-rate geological team was indeed the break they'd been looking for, being one of the first to examine the sample in a DECC lab.

Brett had been along when the doctor's handpicked team was sent down.

He, along with Vic, were the only outsiders that knew where the site was located. Even the construction company that assembled the facility had been handled; an unfortunate plane crash ensured nobody would find Athens. The men who ran DECC didn't even trust each other with the knowledge. Each of them owned well-known, multi-billion dollar companies, credited with something mankind could not live without—from technology to snack foods—and each of them had stolen the core idea from a friend, family member, or colleague.

Brett read from his notes as land vanished beneath him, replaced by the waters of the Atlantic.

His mission was simple, his objective clear: take possession of samples, notes, and research; destroy all other evidence; eliminate all persons, and the destroy Athens facility.

* * *

Vic Brady's voice sounded in Brett's headset: "Mister Urban, we should be in range for the beacon, sir." It was the final fail-safe of the Athens facility, built to blend in with the environment. Even if a satellite passed overhead it was unlikely to see anything.

Brett flipped open his laptop and brought up the tracking screen. The central beacon, indicating the facility, appeared as a red square. All members of Athens were medically fitted with a tracking chip, and blue dots indicated personnel. By clicking the blue dots Brett could bring up a person's dossier. Or if he typed in the name it would highlight the corresponding dot.

"I should have us on the ground in twenty," Vic announced.

"Mmm-hmm," Brett acknowledged, his eyes fixed on the screen.

What he was seeing had him perplexed. And Brett Urban didn't experience that feeling very often.

* * *

Swirls of snow and ice-crystals made it difficult to see, but Brett had seen enough during the descent to know there were problems, aside from the huge sheet of ice that had broken free and was slowly drifting north. Current projections had it on a collision course with Africa. Given the degree of melt between now and then it would still be the size of Georgia when it arrived, and having it collide with *anything* was bound to have consequences. He needed to get in and out so the proper authorities could avert the potential crisis.

But back to the problem at hand: the residents of Athens were not where they should be. Almost half of them were two miles east of the facility. From what Brett could see there was nothing that direction aside from a nasty wall of ice. Truth be told, it looked like the Cliffs of Dover. Strange how he hadn't noticed it when he'd dropped the research team off, or during any of his three subsequent visits.

Nope, he thought, *there had not been a cliff over there. No wall of ice… or whatever it was.*

The members of the research team were divided into two clusters of six and eleven. The group of eleven was bunched together on the far side of the camp, like they were locked outside, trying to get in. The other group was halfway between them and the facility. A single member was inside the building, and if the overlay was accurate he was in a storage closet; it looked like he was hiding.

Brett checked his computer and discovered the man in the closet was Matt Whitehurst, biochemist.

There were three people in sickbay—again, bunched together at the door. The rest were scattered in singles and doubles throughout the facility, exhibiting a disturbing lack of movement.

He'd located Doctor Redding.

She was alone in one of the facility's recreation centers. Like the others, she wasn't moving much, until the airplane circled the complex and touched down. Then some of the scattered members showed activity, but not the mob on the far side of camp, and not Matt Whitehurst.

Something about this was very wrong, but for the life of him, Brett couldn't figure what.

2

Doctor Rachel Redding heard the droning sound of an approaching aircraft, knowing it would come sooner or later. Now all she had to worry about was their intentions. She held no illusions about their mission, and it didn't take a paranoid conspiracy theorist to assume that the DECC wasn't exactly above board. If a single radio message had been sent out in regards to what was going on, there was no telling what the response would be.

Doctor Redding, known by her colleagues as the no-nonsense type, prided herself on being an atypical woman. She felt no ticking biological clock as she passed forty, and while her looks—wavy brunette hair just past the shoulders, a curvy, athletic body, hazel eyes—turned heads, she found little desire to copulate. On the rare occasion that the urge arose she was quite adequate at dealing with it herself.

The events of the last four days made her angry; there was no logic for what she'd seen. She knew there was a misguided and ridiculously delusional section of society that reveled in what she'd witnessed, but even after witnessing it firsthand, her mind was not able to accept it.

The dead do NOT get up. They do not eat the living.

The organism they had been sent to investigate baffled everybody. When one of the biologists came back with evidence linking the sample to primates, nobody was thrilled. It did not explain the cellular activity seen under the scopes.

Then an unlikely error produced interesting results: Doctor Jane Reason nicked her hand while dealing with a sample; she didn't report it until later that afternoon. The sample, now contaminated with her blood, would have sent a buzz throughout Athens had it not been for the massive ice slide, and subsequent fissure, that allowed a state-sized section of eons old ice to break free.

After that, it was one unbelievable event after another: the team that had been at the site of the original find came on the radio, hysterical. There was a great deal of screaming. Then… silence. Attempts at hailing them were unsuccessful, but later that night two members of the team arrived at Athens with fantastic stories.

Everybody listened but nobody believed the stories, which were dismissed as delusional rants by individuals cracked under the pressure of isolation in a desolate environment. There could be no truth to their tale of a fifty-foot-tall white gorilla breaking free of the ice that cascaded down the Ronnie Ice Shelf.

The debate was heating up, and the two "obviously crazy men" were being restrained when Doctor Jane Reason stumbled into the room.

And here's where things became difficult for Doctor Redding: take the possibility of Doctor Reason being a walking corpse out of the equation—the human jaw should not be able to exert the amount of pressure necessary to bite into somebody's neck and tear away a chunk of flesh. Also, evolution has rendered man's incisors useless when it comes to ripping and tearing. Yet, there she was, falling on top of one of Athens' support staff (a fancy label for the cooks, repairmen, and janitors), and biting a hole in his neck. During the struggle, just about everybody involved came away with an injury, be it scratch or a bite. And just as things seemed under control, the man with his throat torn open defied logic and sat up.

The scenario played out all over again.

By the time Doctor Reason and Harold Clemmons—the staff member with the gaping hole in his throat—were secured, over a dozen people were injured.

Nobody expected the injured to suffer the same fate that night.

As people slept, the injured died. Odd, considering none of the injuries appeared serious.

Worse, nothing seemed to be able to bring down the walking dead.

Rachel had seen one of them shot with a flare gun at point-blank range. The casing lodged in the man's gut. The smell—

A scratching, pawing, pounding on the thick, metal double doors to the Athens recreation center made her jump. One of *them* was outside the door.

How was she going to make it to the plane?

3

"Fuel it and I'll meet you shortly." Brett opened the cargo hatch and pulled out a footlocker.

"How long you gonna be, boss?" Vic asked.

"Long as it takes," Brett shrugged. "Something's not right here…" His voice trailed off as a peculiar sound wove itself into the edges of the howling wind.

A pair of dark figures stepped away from the shadows of the closest building, slowly making their way against the wind towards the landing strip. Brett flipped open the trunk and pulled out his silencer-fitted Beretta.

"May as well start now."

"Didn't you say something felt wrong here?" Vic placed a hand on Brett's arm.

"Yeah. So?"

"They don't look dressed for the weather."

Brett took a closer look. Sure enough, neither of the approaching figures wore a stitch of exposure gear… not even gloves. Maybe that explained the pained, awkward way they fought through the wind and swirling ice-crystals.

What happened to this place? he wondered. *Had something gone wrong when the ice separated?*

Oh well. Perhaps the clean-up job would be easier.

He fired three quick shots into the center mass of each body.

They barely twitched.

"What the—"

The two figures stepped into the light, one of them female. The three bullet holes in her chest were the least of her problems. Her lower lip and a chunk of her left cheek had been ripped off, exposing dark-stained teeth in an exaggerated and hideous perma-grin.

The other looked as if his ample gut had been the site of a barbecue.

The howl of the wind changed as a new sound joined in. Brett did his best to categorize the sound, but all he came up with was the peculiar roaring of the unseen creature in the television show *LOST*.

The approaching individuals, now less than ten yards away and closing slowly, paused at the sound. Their heads moved in awkward fits, cocking towards the low mewling before returning to Brett and Vic.

"Boss?"

"What the fuck is going on?" Brett asked, inspiring no confidence in Vic whatsoever.

"I was so hoping you were fixin' to tell me!"

4

Rachel lay flat on the floor, peering under the tiny slit between the door and the floor, fairly certain there was only one set of feet on the other side. Problem was, she had no idea what to do. She'd seen some of her colleagues try to subdue the...

Well now, she thought, *that's the first problem. Just what am I dealing with exactly?*

"Zombies?" she scoffed.

Feet shuffled and the pounding at the door resumed.

"Shit!" Rachel squeaked, instantly angry at her frightened response.

Climbing to her feet and dusting herself off, she took a quick inventory of her possibilities. Her gaze lingered on the mop closet. An idea came; it was a bit more "action hero" than she liked, but considering the circumstances it would have to do.

Taking a deep breath and clutching the doorknob, Rachel turned the knob and yanked. The young woman standing in the hallway was Donna Noble. Rachel hated her, and she was a mess. There was so much blood it was hard to tell which bite killed her.

The mess, formerly known as Donna, stumbled into the rec-room. Her arms were outstretched in a sleepwalking parody; her dead, filmed-over eyes were wide open. She was obviously aware of Rachel's presence.

"That's right," Rachel sing-songed, backpedaling towards the closet. "Follow me."

5

A loud rumble shook what amounted to their whole world. It was enough to cause the small aircraft to bunny-hop sideways a few feet and cause a stack of steel drums to topple.

Brett grabbed Vic by the collar just in time to keep Mister Barbecue from getting a hold of an ankle. Changing magazines quickly and letting the slide load a new round, he shoved the pistol's muzzle against the back of the dead man's head and fired.

The body dropped like the proverbial sack of potatoes.

"Well how do you like that," Brett said with a smirk.

"What's that?" Vic asked, still looking at the woman who should not be getting up, but was nonetheless.

"Those terrible movies!"

"Excuse me?"

"All those films with the word *Dead* in the title."

"Still not following you, sir."

"Shoot 'em in the head," Brett put a round in the woman's forehead, sending her toppling over backwards beside the big man.

The rumbling sound came again. It was much louder this time and coming from the east. Seconds later, slow and rhythmic vibrations began.

"Something tells me this job just got a lot harder." Brett began sifting through the footlocker.

6

Rachel slammed the closet door and allowed a smattering of nervous laughter to escape as she leaned against the wall.

There was a sudden shudder. All the lights flickered and went out and Rachel found herself on the floor with a sharp pain blooming in her left arm.

Her arm was visibly broken just above the wrist.

Holding back the tears, she climbed to her feet as the lights came back on. She heard, before she saw, the trio of zombies up the hall. They were lying on the ground like flipped over turtles, struggling to regain their footing.

After taking a deep breath, Rachel ran as fast as she could manage across the rec-room, out the door, down the hall, and past the undead threesome. Taking her first left, she stopped short when she saw more walking dead pawing at the glass window in the door. The women's locker room was to her right, so she ducked inside. There would be an exit leading outside, she only hoped there would be some protective gear too. Otherwise, unless the plane was parked outside the door, she would die of exposure within minutes.

She rummaged through a bin and came up with a suit, one glove, and a facemask. It wasn't ideal, but it was certainly better than nothing.

A peculiar, rhythmic vibration came; it was strong enough to cause the overhead fluorescents to flicker.

The swelling above her left wrist was tremendous. She tried her best not to dwell on the odd angle her arm was bent as she slid it into the sleeve of the exposure suit. Sitting on a bench, she slipped her feet into a pair of boots that were at least two sizes too large. The door to outside needed to have a pass code typed into the panel, which she did before opening it to the howling wind and deadly cold.

7

Brett shouldered the pack and flipped the chest closed. Vic still stood like an idiot staring at the most recent improbability making itself known.

"Is that…?"

"A giant snow-white gorilla tall enough to overlook the two-story light tower?" Brett tugged at his facemask, keeping the flap over his mouth. He didn't want the freezing air to reach his teeth, worried that the warmth of his mouth, combined with the temperature of the air, would cause his teeth to fracture and shatter like hot glass shoved in a freezer.

"Just wanted to know I wasn't seeing things," Vic nodded.

"Take these." Brett held out a green burlap carry bag. "Inside are two dozen affixable explosives."

"Okay…" Vic said, fixated on the enormous primate.

"Around the buildings you'll find black squares painted on structural keys. Place the devices on the squares." Brett spun Vic to face him to ensure he was being understood. "Then get your ass back here to refuel. Be ready for immediate departure."

"Y-y-yeah," Vic stammered.

"Oh," Brett said, glancing at the fifty-foot gorilla that was reaching the far side of the complex. "And try not to let *that* see you."

"Thanks for the safety tip," Vic grumbled as Brett jogged towards the main building.

8

Rachel froze in her tracks. After all she'd seen the past two days she thought she was ready for anything. She was wrong.

Across the open expanse of ice, moving into the dazzling white light that was illuminating from one of the light towers, the giant gorilla stood. Only, in the light, Rachel could tell there was something wrong with the behemoth. It took one ponderous step forward, and in that instant she knew what was wrong: the monster and her coworkers were suffering from the same affliction. With one giant arm the beast swiped the light tower aside and took another step. Its giant head jerked, and the beast altered its course away from the landing strip.

Making certain that her mask was in place, Rachel made her way along the side of the building. She saw a couple colleagues as she passed by doors and windows. All of them were in the same state: bloody, filmed over eyes, and obviously dead.

An odd moaning howl made her glance over her shoulder.

The enormous gorilla held an unknown someone in one of its huge hands.

"Oh my God." She watched in horror as the person was stuffed—kicking and screaming—into the gaping maw of the undead gorilla.

A bearded man wearing a clear faceplate stumbled around the corner and Rachel froze, fearing he was one of her recently deceased colleagues.

"Holy crap!" the man exclaimed, stumbling back a step.

"Who the hell are you?" Rachel demanded, her eyes drifting to the peculiar device he was holding.

"Vic Brady, ma'am." Vic quickly regained his composure. He was pretty sure that Brett's job included killing all the residents of Athens, but that wasn't his assignment. "And who might you be?"

"My name is Doctor Rachel Redding," Rachel did her best to sound authoritative… and unafraid.

"You mind telling me what that is?" Vic said, pointing towards the giant gorilla, which was at the far side of the facility pulling apart a storage hangar.

"I'm guessing it's a relic from when this place was known as Gondwanaland."

"Huh?" Vic didn't consider himself stupid, but that last statement went straight past him.

"History lesson later." Rachel glanced over her shoulder. "I'm guessing you came in the aircraft I heard? Maybe we should get on it and leave."

Vic slapped the device in his hand on a black square painted on the building that Rachel had never really noticed before. It didn't take a lot of mental ability to figure out what was going on. The guy was probably from DECC Corporation, and they were taking care of their mess the only way they knew how.

"Got two more of these to put in place," Vic said, pulling another device from the burlap bag he had slung over his shoulder.

"Then we can go?" Rachel prodded.

She didn't ask what he was doing. *Smart gal,* Vic thought, *too bad the odds of her joining them were unlikely.* He moved past, heading between a pair of buildings at a jog.

Glancing one more time monster tugging at the roof of one of the buildings, Rachel shivered and took off after Vic.

9

Brett pushed the zombie back and watched it struggle before coming at him again. He wondered why the damned thing hadn't frozen solid. Well, he wasn't a scientist; he was a "fixer" working for some very wealthy, powerful men. He didn't have time to waste.

After bringing up his pistol, he shot the man in the face. Then he opened the flap of his tablet and selected the dot: Greg Meyers, nutritionist—the last target inside.

One of the dots had taken off in a hurry.

Great, Brett thought, *a survivor.* Or as the men at DECC would see it… a witness. This one had been on a beeline for the landing strip, but suddenly changed directions. He didn't want to go chasing all over, and hoped that this "Rachel Redding, biochemist"—according to what came up when he'd selected her dot—would make his job easy and be waiting by the plane.

The ground shook.

That… *thing*… was on the move again. It must've gotten tired of ripping apart the storage hangar.

Time to go, Brett holstered his pistol and closed his tablet. With any luck "Rachel Redding, biochemist" would be at the plane.

A single shot would finish the job, and then they could be on their way.

Speaking of *on their way*—if Vic had no problems finding the squares he'd soon be done his task, but he still needed to top off the tanks, which gave Brett time to get a closer look at the giant gorilla.

Photographs and a video might come in handy. You never knew when you'd be asking for a pay raise, or or leak something. Brett Urban didn't know what was going on, but obtaining footage was the correct thing to do. He was a businessman.

He set his digital camera in the window. A look through the viewfinder made it clear that it was almost impossible *not* to have the massive beast in the shot.

He began his narration: "You are seeing some sort of giant, undead gorilla. I didn't know about the undead bit until I ran into a few people here at this remote research station. I've already shot footage, demonstrating that these things can take a fatal amount of gunfire, and that a headshot is the only sure way to put one down. If you'll take a look—" Brett zoomed in on the primate. There were huge rakes across its chest and a fatal slash across its throat. The wounds looked ancient; the meat was dry, no blood. "This bastard was in a fight. I'd hate to see what did that sort of damage to old Bonzo there."

The gorilla scuttled into the open area of the complex.

Brett paned up and down before zooming in on its face, making sure the filmed-over eyes could be plainly seen.

"There is no doubt that the people I showed you earlier suffer from the same disease," Brett narrated.

184

10

Vic activated the pumps and made sure the plane was topped off.

He said, "So Doctor Redding, you're saying that unknown *thing* is a prehistoric ancestor of the gorilla."

Rachel nodded.

"And it became stranded on the Antarctic after the continents broke apart, then after years inside the ice, global warming set it free?"

"That's a simple way of looking at it, yes. The sample found by the survey team likely holds the key to whatever is causing the dead to get up. It's why the giant primate is not just another frozen sample, like that mammoth discovered a few years ago."

"Huh?"

"Never mind," Rachel shook her head. "I don't mean to sound ungrateful, but when are we leaving? That thing is moving into the complex. Granted, it's slow… but it won't take long for it to reach us if it sees—"

A flash and a boom cut her off.

11

"You'll notice that an RPG to the torso has left a hole." Brett zoomed in. "Well… a nick maybe. Like monkey-boy cut himself shaving. Still, if you'll look… there's no blood."

A moaning howl made the ground vibrate.

Brett clicked off his camera.

Something had the monster's attention and it wasn't Brett. It only took him a second to realize that its head had turned towards the airstrip. Grabbing his bag and stuffing the camera inside, Brett pulled his face-shield down and ran. He wasn't concerned about outrunning the beast, but he didn't want to hamper their chances of leaving. Besides, once Vic became airborne he would flick the switch and the plate of ice they were standing on would be history. The giant beast would sink to the bottom of the ocean.

Brett ducked around a corner and sprinted up the corridor.

He was confident Vic would have everything done and be ready to go as soon as he reached the aircraft. As for that one dot... well... "Rachel Redding, biochemist" wouldn't survive the blast. If she did, she'd end up at the bottom of the ocean.

12

"We don't have a choice," Rachel insisted. "If that thing sees us, or smells us, or does whatever the hell it does... we don't have time to wait for somebody who may or may not show up!"

"Ma'am, you don't know Brett," Vic interjected. He tossed the nozzle aside and placed the last device on the square painted on the giant storage tank. "He'll be here any second."

"I've been meaning to ask," Rachel said suspiciously, "just where exactly is your... friend?"

Pop.

Vic blinked, surprised.

A hole appeared in Rachel's facemask. Darkness spread and a tendril of steam wafted out of the hole. Then the doctor's knees buckled and her body collapsed to the ground.

"Don't stand there gawking!" Brett tucked his gun into its holster. "Let's get this bitch in the air before it's too late."

Vic scrambled aboard and hurried through the preflight checks.

Brett stood in the hatch, watching the mountain of simian flesh draw near. He flipped open his tablet and glanced at the prone figure at the base of the ladder leading to the aircraft. He selected the dot, confirming what he was already almost certain of.

"Checks are done!" Vic announced.

Brett tugged the ladder, which also brought the top half of the hatch closed. He took his seat as the plane swung around and pointed its nose up the runway. The whine of the engines increased as the aircraft began to make its way up to speed. They endured a brief stomach lurch as the bounds of gravity were broken.

Brett looked out the oval window as he pulled a handheld device from his case. With the press of a few buttons a flashing green light came on. Still watching, he typed in one last code. The rising ball of flame engulfed not only the giant ape, but the Athens complex as well.

Funny, Brett mused, *that thing didn't look so big or scary from up here.*

After one pass, it was clear that there was nothing left. The plane banked and headed away leaving the glow of flames behind to vanish into the sea with everything else.

13

Two months later:

Brett scooped up his case. The board at DECC had summoned him once more. This time he had no intention of answering the call. He knew damned good and well what this was about.

Walking into his living room, the television was still on. The talking head doing her best to not look skeptical as she spoke.

"…appeared yesterday at Tierra del Fuego. While it is being described as a giant ape by witnesses, there seems to be something drastically—"

Click.

WILLIAM MEIKLE
The Dreams That Stuff Is Made Of

"Make it realistic," they said. "This is 1953, not 1933."

What they expected him to do with a three thousand dollar budget was a mystery to Doug Turner. Originally he had planned to do it in stop-motion, but the bean counters were having none of that.

"Harryhausen is finished," they said. "Audiences want more realism. And make it big. People like big."

After a bit of head scratching he took them at their word. He even took the quest for realism a bit *too* literally. Buying forty gorilla pelts on the black market cost nearly half his budget, and some sleepless nights wondering whether the authorities would find out about the museum in Rhodesia that had been pilfered to fulfill his order when they came up short on live catches. Then he had to get the wardrobe people to work overtime to stitch it all together. He had to call in every favor in his book for that one.

By the time he'd organized a midnight raid into the country to steal enough straw to stuff the sewn skins he was starting to feel more like a criminal than a FX specialist. And after three more days trying to get the head—and the mouth in particular, right, he was starting to feel he should be *anything* other than a FX specialist.

But when, right on schedule, the bean-counters turned up to view the star of their new movie, Doug was sure they'd be impressed with the fifty-foot *monster* that stood on the soundstage.

He didn't get the expected reaction.

They laughed.

Then they berated him, long and hard, for wasting their money. Doug was told in no uncertain terms that his future in the business depended on him getting it *sorted*. Quite how that was to be done was never mentioned, but they were most insistent on the matter.

Doug took to the bottle for the weekend.

* * *

Once he got sober the situation looked no better. He was on the verge of walking away from the job completely when he had a visitor.

At first Doug was lost in his own reverie, staring at the sad sack of straw and hair that stood in the otherwise empty soundstage and wondering just how he'd ever convinced himself that it would work. It looked less like a monster than he'd hoped, more like an oversized stuffed toy. The eyes looked exactly like what they were; globes of plastic stuck on with glue, one slightly askew giving the giant gorilla a comical squint. One of the false teeth he'd had mocked up out of papier-mâché had already fallen out leaving a gap on the left hand side, and the bottom jaw hung open just *too* far, making the beast look more imbecilic than frightening.

He was on the verge of setting fire to it when a hand touched his shoulder. There was a small man at his side. His skin looked like old polished leather that had been left to age, and he looked so thin as to be almost skeletal. But his blue eyes danced with life and his laughter echoed loudly around the soundstage when he looked at the gorilla.

"So *this* is why my prize exhibit was stolen? I must say, it looks better here than in a museum."

Doug was at a loss how to reply.

"I guess there's no use denying it," he finally said resignedly. "How much do I owe you?"

The little man laughed again. It was so infectious that Doug couldn't help but join him.

"Nothing," the little man said. "As I said, it looks better here. But it would look even better in motion."

Now it was Doug's turn to laugh.

"That *would* be a good trick. Sadly it is only a dream."

The little man put a hand on Doug's shoulder again.

"Then a dream it shall be. But you must dream through African eyes."

Doug blinked.

* * *

He was surrounded by greenery, and rain pattered down to drum on leaves the size of dinner plates. He swung, fluid and effortless, through branches of tall trees, roaring his joy at life, at freedom.

* * *

Doug blinked again.

The stuffed gorilla had moved. It now no longer stood upright. It was bent over, knuckles balancing it in a pose that looked almost belligerent. The squint was gone. Even the gap in the teeth looked more *natural*. The fur seemed to bristle, as if ruffled by wind.

"What just happened?" Doug said.

The little man laughed again.

"You dreamed the African dream. The gorilla pelt from the museum wasn't *just* a pelt. It was once a man, a great sorcerer and shape-changer. The pelt remembers. The pelt *dreams*—of past glories, and freedom."

Doug laughed.

"That's the best pitch I've heard in years. Seriously… what kind of whammy did you put on me?"

The little man showed Doug a smile. There was a gap in the top row that made the grin look lopsided.

"There is no *whammy*… just faith. Gorillas are made to be free. Watch and learn."

The man started to hum; a deep bass vibration that rattled Doug's teeth. He lifted an arm.

The gorilla responded.

A huge hairy arm raised high above the gorilla's head. The little man started to walk forward. The gorilla rose from the sitting position and walked across the soundstage. This was no thing of skin and straw. Muscles bunched beneath the skin and although the pelts seemed to hang slackly off an emaciated body, there was more than enough animal power on display to send Doug shuffling backwards quickly, looking for the exit.

The gorilla stopped at exactly the same time as the small man who stood beneath its swollen belly, dwarfed by the upright creature. The man seemed unconcerned. He opened his arms wide then slapped at his chest with his palms, a quick drum-roll. The gorilla followed suit, at the same time *bellowing* a roar of defiance across the soundstage.

Doug stopped being frightened. He was looking at the *gorilla*, but in his mind's eye he was seeing the movie, the beast rising up out of thick jungle to terrorize a terrified group of intrepid explorers.

This just might work.

He stood and moved to the small man's side, trying to ignore the creature above them.

"Can you do that to order?" Doug said.

The little man smiled, showing the gap in his teeth.

So did the gorilla.

* * *

It took Doug a couple of days to set it up. He had to take out an overdraft to pay for the foliage he wanted, and even used up all the money in his wallet to get some extras onto the soundstage and primed.

During the whole two days the stuffed gorilla sat in the corner of the soundstage, head bowed as if asleep. At times Doug wondered whether he'd dreamed the whole earlier experience, or whether he was finally succumbing to the *delirium tremens* his alcohol consumption surely merited. The small man, who eventually introduced himself as Mr. Mkele, put paid to that idea. All it took was for him to place a hand on Doug's shoulder, and he was back in the jungle again.

Running free.

As the deadline to the screen test grew closer, Doug's anxiety levels grew in proportion, but the little African man was never far away, and always willing to allow Doug access to the dream. It became the one place where he could feel no pressure, no worry, just the joy of rain in his face and a freedom of action unconstrained by money and bean counters. The dream sustained him through to the Friday morning on the soundstage, and the arrival of those bean counters to see the *gorilla*.

When Doug saw the mass of foliage arrayed across the set, and the extras dressed in pith helmets and khaki, he actually smiled and started to relax.

There's no way this is going to fail.

The screen test itself went like clockwork. The drummer, who Doug persuaded to work for a pack of cigarettes and a fifth of rye, set up a rock-solid beat as the *explorers* entered the *jungle*. Mr. Mkele added some verisimilitude by raising his voice in a singsong chant that seemed to vibrate through the whole stage and set the foliage rustling as if in wind. Right on cue the *gorilla* rose up out of the greenery, s*lapped* its palms against its chest and *bellowed*.

An extra fainted, the bean counters applauded, and everyone said all the right things.

Two hours later they axed the movie, killing the project stone dead.

"We want to do something with tentacles, something in stop motion. Harryhausen is hot this year."

* * *

Doug went home and made a start on drinking himself to oblivion.

"Those men are wrong," Mr. Mkele said. He sat across the table, not drinking, but not stopping Doug from doing so. "Your city needs to see what the jungle is like. Your city needs to see freedom. *You* need to see freedom."

Doug took a swig direct from a bottle of rye; his third, or maybe it was his fourth—he was already starting to lose count.

"Freedom seems a heck of a long way away my friend," he said.

"That is because you have forgotten the dream."

Doug slugged down more rye.

"Not forgotten," he said. "But what good does it do me now?"

Things started to get foggy, but he heard the little man's words well enough.

"You just have to have faith in the dream. There is still time to show them the power of the free."

* * *

Doug opened his eyes to a wash of fuzzy green that only slowly came into focus. He was lying in thick foliage. As his eye focused he realized he was back on the soundstage, in the artificial jungle.

I really tied one on this time.

He stood, shaky on unsteady legs.

A janitor was sweeping the set, an older man that Doug barely knew. He had his back turned, lost in his brushing.

"Hi," Doug said. It came out as a deep rumble. He cleared his throat. The old janitor turned, looked up and fled, screaming. It was only then that Doug started to suspect something wasn't *quite* right.

He seemed to be too big, too bulky. He raised a hand towards his face, and screamed at the sight of a broad hand, covered in thick coarse hair, with broken dirty nails. That wasn't the worst part—the hand was nearly three feet across. He screamed again. It came out as a *bellow* that echoed around the soundstage. A security cop arrived at the door and immediately raised a pistol and fired. Doug saw the flash, but felt no impact.

He missed.

But he was wrong in that. He looked down to see a hole in his side, pieces of dry straw poking out of it.

"Hey," he shouted.

The whole set vibrated, and the security guard dropped his gun. He too fled.

193

Doug lumbered towards the door. He was too big to fit through. He put up a hand to push the tall sliding door aside. It fell away into the road outside with a *crash*.

Somewhere people started to scream but Doug scarcely noticed. Something was *very* wrong. He seemed to be inside the *gorilla*.

Living the dream.

A *nee-naw* wail heralded the approach of several police squad cars that screeched to a halt out in the lot beyond the soundstage. More shots rang out and *puffs* of straw flew. Doug yelled again.

"Hey, stop shooting at me!"

It came out as a roar that shook the whole street, and several of the police officers backed away fast. Doug took his chance and broke into a run but, uncoordinated as he was, and unused to the sheer bulk of this body he stumbled into one of the patrol cars. He swatted it with a hand and the car flew ten yards in the air before landing with a *crump* of glass and metal. The shooting got more intensive.

Doug fled in the opposite direction from the gunfire—and straight onto the exterior set where they were filming a western. He stumbled, almost fell, and demolished the whole façade of a street, the thin wood splintering beneath him. Horses whinnied, women screamed, and more police cars arrived.

This isn't going to end well.

Doug had no plan beyond escaping the shooting policemen. He bounded through the western set, scattering film crew and extras to all corners, before he realized that continuing in that direction would take him to the heart of the city.

He stopped running, but that allowed the police to blow more holes in his body. Straw flew everywhere. He was seriously considering just standing still, letting them take him down, when he heard a *singsong* chant that he recognized. It seemed to come from the hills to the east of the city. Doug turned in that direction and broke into a run. More shots followed behind him but none hit him, at least none that he felt. He bounded through suburban streets past the shocked faces of homeowners and children, knocking cars and trees aside if they got in his way. All he could think of now was the song.

It led him high to the hill overlooking the city, to the large letters of the HOLLYWOOD sign. There was a car parked beside the sign, and a small man stood beside the open driver's door. He was the source of the song. As Doug slowed from his headlong rush he saw another person, slumped in the passenger seat.

That's me!

Mr. Mkele's song rose to a crescendo.

Doug blinked.

* * *

And woke up sitting in the car, staring out at the HOLLYWOOD sign, and a giant gorilla trying to tear it apart.

"Quick," Mr. Mkele shouted. "The sorcerer has been awakened. We do not have much time."

Doug pushed himself groggily out of the car. The little man was already running, not away from the gorilla, but towards it. He was carrying a bulky kerosene container. There was another on the ground beside the car, and Doug immediately saw the intent.

He means to burn it.

Mr. Mkele had reached the sign and had already started sloshing kerosene around as Doug lugged the other can over towards him. The gorilla paid them no attention, seeming intent on tearing the HOLLYWOOD sign apart. Even as Doug arrived beside the smaller man and joined him in pouring the kerosene the gorilla managed to tear the leftmost O from its moorings and threw it, like a discus, down towards the city where it swooped away out of view. The beast roared its defiance and slapped at its chest, but now that he was closer Doug could see that it was already badly damaged. Several large rents ran down its left side, straw having already fallen in a pile at the gorilla's feet. Enough had escaped to make the body look strangely deflated.

And that was not all. One of the stitched seams in the head had split and more straw was already falling from it. The beast was not finished yet though. Even as Mr. Mkele flipped a lighter and tossed it at the creature's feet it had torn the H from the sign and was using it to beat the rest of the sign to a broken pile of wood and plastic.

The flame took it fast. With one last statement of defiance the gorilla stood tall, slapped its chest, and roared, long and loud before falling in on itself in a shower of flaming straw that danced away in the wind.

* * *

Later, on their way back down the hill, and while the Army and police were headed up in the other direction, Doug finally decided to ask the question that had been bothering him.

"What just happened?"

He got an answer, but maybe not the one he was expecting.

"The city has seen," Mr. Mkele said. "And you have shown your skill. I believe your *bean counters* will now be more than keen to procure your services. And I shall be more than willing to help you. For you see the sorcerer could take more forms than just the gorilla."

The little man laughed, showing the gap in his teeth.

"Would you like a crocodile skin?"

T. A. WARDROPE
The Upright Gorilla

"You're the one writing the movie about the Tortuga Go-rilla?" The woman on the phone asked in a breathless voice. Jonas looked at the number on the phone; this was certainly not anyone he knew. He wasn't nearly famous enough to have a fan stalker of any kind. In a perfect world, she would be a reporter for Variety asking about his script deal.

"I am working on the screenplay, whom am I speaking with?" he asked. Instead of an answer he heard the dull rumble of background traffic and the hiss of dead air on her cell phone. This was the kind of prank that his half-wit roommates would think was really funny. Maybe if they'd stop wasting their time on this kind of shit they might finally get a break.

"They will kill all of us if you make that movie," she said. "I know you aren't going to just take my word for it, so I'd like to explain it all to you." Jonas looked around the bar's patio for a manic looking lady on a cell phone. This was the part where she was supposed to say she was right behind him. He didn't see any women on the patio at all, besides the waitress heading toward him with another bottle of Miller Lite. If it wasn't a prank, the woman on the phone could be just the kind of crazy that could spice up the script that was going nowhere. He wasn't getting any writing done, hadn't in a few days. He could tell her that he hadn't actually written anything; that would get her to go away.

"Okay," he said, "how about in an hour?"

"Where do you live?" she asked.

"I'd rather meet in public."

"No, no," she said. "It's not safe at all."

197

"We're not meeting at my house, I don't even know why I should meet you in the first place."

"Okay, come to the LA County Natural History Museum, come to the Exposition side of the building and knock on the single door staff entrance in the southeast corner," she said. "I'll be there at 5 p.m. to let you in."

"Today?"

"There's hardly any time," she said. "Finding you took too long."

Metro and a bus got him through the early rush hour traffic just in time to be at the door at 5 p.m. She hadn't given her name, but as she opened the door, she said, "Jonas" very clearly. The woman was about ten years older than Jonas, much more physical then he assumed she'd be, and dressed in casual work clothes. Her hair was a tangle and mess. A laminated ID badge hung from her pants.

She led him through two security doors and into a small conference room lit by an overhead fluorescent bulb. She closed the door behind them and sat down at the scratched and stained wooden table.

"Sit down," she said. Jonas pulled out the closest chair and sat in it with a loud creak of wood. She didn't look all that crazy, maybe she had a few more wrinkles and grey hairs than a woman her age should, but that was all. He hoped she wasn't going to bring up the Illuminati, that was so two years ago.

"You didn't tell me your name," he said.

"Precaution. Couldn't risk it until I met you face to face," she said, as if he'd understand. "I had to know you weren't one of them."

"You found me, you know who I am. Who are you?" he asked, but he really wanted to get to whom exactly "them" were.

"My name is Alex," she said, as she folded her arms on top of the table. "What is it going to take to just abandon the project completely, pretend you never heard of it?"

He laughed loudly. Two years of menial, ambition killing servitude and his rookie agent had finally managed to get him some sort of script gig. A first draft of a film that was destined for straight-to-video if it ever even got produced. If he could work his way through it, he'd have a check, a credit, and a membership in the Writer's Guild. Nothing this woman could say would get him to throw that away. Especially since he was a month's rent away from moving back to Ohio with his tail between his legs.

"I don't think you can do that, um, Alex," he said.

"Was this idea your own, the idea to write this movie about the Tortuga Gorilla?"

"No, not at all. A producer needed it written and I was lucky enough to get the job," he said. He wanted to tell her that he received a vision from an alien life form, but decided not to confuse her any more. He didn't tell her he never had any interest in monster movies of any sort. He wanted to write crime, thrillers, and the dark human drama that didn't need some hokey rubber suit to realize on screen. So, the complete writer's block that followed was not a surprise. Alex might be able to give him some new angle on the story. This could work out well.

"What did they tell you about the gorilla?" she asked as she dug through a file in the corner of the room.

"Well, the producer heard a legend about a group of scientists who found a giant gorilla on Tortuga Island, tried to study it, but wound up angering it and setting it on a path of total destruction. They want a final scene where the gorilla swims ashore at Miami and wreaks havoc. They kill him with an air strike that levels half the city. You know, like *Cloverfield*," he said with a grimace.

She slid a photo in front of him. The photo was out of focus, and looked a little bit like one of those pictures of Bigfoot. Instead of a loping human shape, the large subject was clearly a gorilla. An adult tree stopped short of the gorilla's blurry chin.

"Did your producer show you this?" she asked. He felt like he was being cross-examined.

"No," he said, and then he decided to take the bait. "What is this?"

"This is a photo of the real Tortuga Gorilla."

"There are a hundred ways this picture could be faked."

"I was there when the picture was taken and I can assure you it was very, very real," she said. Could she hear what she was saying? Did this whole situation strike her as being natural and acceptable? She had a job at the museum so she couldn't be a total nutjob. NASA had their burnouts that believed in UFOs; maybe Alex was the biologist's equivalent. Even so, why did she want him to not write about the gorilla? Shouldn't she want to expose it to the world?

"The producer heard the legend somewhere and he'll just find someone else if I don't write it," Jonas said. "I don't see the danger. Who's going to kill me?"

"Fifteen years ago," Alex said, as if she didn't hear him at all. "I went with a natural history exhibition to visit Tortuga. Because it's an island that has been mostly left alone, the nature preserve in the center of the island presented unique opportunities. There were five of us selected from a few universities and museums in California. None of us knew about the legend before we got to the island. We only knew about the pirates."

Pirates, now that was something that could sell some scripts. Jonas wanted to take out a notepad, but knew Alex wouldn't like that. Alex did not want the movie made at all, certainly not with her crazy story as part of it. He had to listen and remember the key points. At the least it could give him some story ideas, and might even get "based on a true story" tag out of the whole deal. Not that he'd tell Alex about it.

"We took this picture when he crossed right in front of us, didn't notice us or care we were there. We just stood there, dead still in the jungle, and watched this three story gorilla disappear into the lightless depth of the trees. We argued for maybe an hour, to decide if we should follow it or not. How could we not follow it?" she asked.

Jonas realized she really wanted him to answer. "I don't know."

"We tried to follow it and got nowhere. That gorilla was moving fast. We got ourselves lost and then found ourselves surrounded by some sort of local native people. I have to admit, I didn't know who they were, didn't even know there were any native people left on Tortuga. I know now they were a twisted splinter group from the Caniba tribe, but anyway, they looked about as surprised to see us. Both groups tried to communicate, but that went nowhere, so they pulled out axes and knives and pushed us along the trail away from the direction we came from."

Scary jungle natives were a real tough sell, especially considering all the cultural sensitivity criticism that was always aimed at Hollywood. He'd have to find a sympathetic character among them. Maybe Alex could be plied for more detail?

"They led us into a cave hidden under a cluster of tall trees. The cave was lined with torches and the floor was worn smooth. We whispered to each other about running, but mostly we were curious to see what there was to see. So, they took us down a spiraling tunnel and eventually we were led into a massive central cave. The cave had a stone table in the center, and all around it were several rows of carved wooden benches, all facing center. There was a fire pit filled with ashes directly underneath the stone table.

"I noticed that the walls of the cave were lined with human skulls, ribs and limbs. Arnold, from UCLA, joked that it was like something from a 1930s serial. Some sort of shaman stepped out of a cavern and looked us over. He was naked, except for a collection of red stripes on his upper body and dark circles tattooed in his eye sockets. He shook his fist violently and then walked directly to us.

"Ronald took out a piece of paper and drew the best gorilla he could. He drew a tree next to it for scale. The shaman grimaced and he pointed fiercely at us. He yelled a command and the men at the top of the cave surrounded us. He shouted another order and then led us into another tunnel. We walked upwards, on a route lit by torches. The tunnel was marked on both sides by paintings, markings, and all kinds of art— drawings of a giant gorilla. This was a ceremonial journey we were taking."

"What do you mean?" Jonas asked.

"They were taking us to meet their god," she glared at him as if he was a child. "We walked toward bright outside light and found ourselves standing on a stone ledge that overlooked a narrow green valley. The leader raised his decorated arm and pointed to the valley. I followed the line of his finger and saw a large, dark, and hairy body, lying among the rocks and trees. The giant gorilla looked quite dead."

The producer had not included this part of the story when he gave him his background notes. Alex's version of the legend was filled with great details. He wished he had brought an audio recorder. He had to remember as much as he could, get some more details, but not look like he was interested. He leaned back and crossed his arms in front of him—the universal gesture of disbelief.

"The gorilla was dead, like it had just died of a heart attack. The leader pointed at us, more exactly, he pointed at Ronald. Ronald reddened and took a step back. I didn't know what I could do… don't think any of us did. Three of the Tortuga Caniba walked forward, and pulled Ronald closer to the edge. We all knew what was going to happen next, but we couldn't think of a way to stop it. I suppose we didn't believe what was happening."

Alex paused, allowing her full meaning register with Jonas.

He nodded, he got the point, and he should believe what had happened and avoid their mistake. Alex didn't understand subtlety in the least, which was good because neither did his producer.

"The men pulled Ronald's arms behind his back, and the leader drew a three bladed weapon from a pouch and held it out for everyone to see. He pointed it at Ronald, and then used his free hand to pull grey powder out of the same bag and throw it over the edge. The powder drifted into a cloud on its way down. Without any warning, the leader raised the weapon and slashed it across the lower part of Ronald's throat. His blood came out like a fountain, and the leader guided Ronald's body over the edge of the rock. The leader watched the body fall. We couldn't see over the edge, but it didn't matter, we couldn't really see anything after we saw Ronald get murdered, we were blind with shock. The rocks under us shuddered."

Jonas waited, looking down at the picture on the table. There wasn't much of a story here. The damn gorilla was dead.

What was she thinking? No matter how big it is, who cares about a dead gorilla? Dinosaurs are pretty big too, but they aren't a big mystery. He was wasting his time.

Checking his watch, he realized that his next bus was in five minutes.

"The gorilla rose slowly, and stood at its full height. From the ledge it was easy to see the creature was huge, fifty feet. We knew it was tall, though, so that wasn't that main shock. The horror was discovered as the gorilla turned to face the shaman and our group. It was so close, and so still... we could see its facial features. The skin was draped across the bone, torn in places so the rotten meat was exposed. The giant eyes were opaque and unmoving, insects swarmed over its skin, and the massive stench of a hundred dead animals drifted off of his fur. A stain of fresh blood coated his dead, limp lips. The creature opened its mouth and roared out a shattered and wheezing noise. Half its teeth had fallen out; the tongue was blackened and full of holes. The gorilla was dead, but still moving.

"You're telling me this was a goddamn zombie gorilla?" Jonas blurted out.

"I'm telling you that the gorilla was dead, yet it was animated. I don't know what to call it."

Jonas pulled the photo closer, trying to distinguish the decay she was talking about. There was too much blur and grain to see that kind of detail. Even so, the photo could have been altered. The producer was not going to go for this story, at all. Maybe there was another twist. He decided to wait for the next bus, but he needed answers real fast.

"Even if everything you say is true, Alex, I don't understand how you made it here to tell me about it," Jonas said.

"The gorilla turned away and moved toward the thicker jungle. The Tortuga Caniba walked us back to Bodden Town in silence. Of course, we were in all kinds of shock, so the walk back was a total blur. We went back to our hotel, went to our rooms, and spent a couple of days to ourselves. Eventually we met in the hotel bar, wanting to create a believable story in regards to Ronald's death. We all agreed that it had happened, we all remembered the gorilla, and we even agreed that it looked like it belonged in the ground… not above it.

"Arnold had been nodding along, but he finally spoke during a sustained pause. During the time we were apart he found someone in town that knew something about the Caniba. Legend and hearsay said these Caniba had worshiped the giant gorilla for centuries; they sacrificed anyone they could to keep the god's favor. One day, the gorilla died. Scores of islanders died as the Tortuga Caniba piled on the offerings to the dead god. Finally, they sent a shaman to Haiti, and he came back with the secrets of re-animation. They brought their god back from the dead, and continued their sacrifices, but not to gain his favor, but to keep the gorilla from destroying the island."

"Didn't anyone notice the smell?" Jonas asked.

"Their god was too terrible for many of the Caniba. They fled the jungles and the island, only the most fervent stayed with the tribe. The group's numbers diminished until they were nothing more than a circle of fanatics bringing sacrifices to the gorilla. We had the misfortune of meeting those few that remained," she said.

"I don't understand why the island would put up with them if they are carrying on with these sacrifices," he said.

"This sect of Caniba are a doomsday cult. They believe that on the day they run out of sacrifices for the god, he will leave the island and go out to destroy the world. If they are threatened, they will cease to appease the gorilla with sacrifices. The dead gorilla *will* destroy the world. They must be left alone."

"Right," Jonas said. He took one last look at the photo and then pushed it towards Alex. He pushed his chair back as if he was about to leave. The visit had been interesting, but didn't really do much for him as a practical matter.

"You tell a great ghost story, Alex," Jonas said. " I don't know what any of this has to do with my screenplay or movie gig. I can't even use this stuff you're telling me because I can't see not getting laughed out of the office."

Jonas stood up and pulled on the office door. The door didn't move, he pulled it again, hard, and the door didn't open.

The knob didn't turn. He faced Alex; she was still sitting on the table as if he was supposed to sit back down.

"I would like to leave now," he said.

"If anybody on that island sees or hears about your movie, they will come and kill us," she said. "Or the Caniba will release the gorilla. You cannot write that movie."

"If I don't, they'll find someone else. Are you going to track them down too?"

"Yes, until this story is buried… where it belongs," she said.

Jonas jerked the door hard for emphasis.

"Fine, let me out, so I can go home and erase the script," he said.

"Do you believe me?" she asked.

"Yes," Jonas lied.

* * *

The bus ride away from the Museum gave him time to do research with his iPhone. In the time it took to get home, Jonas determined that there were five people on her team, like she said. He found a photo of the group in an academic journal— saw a younger Alex, Ronald, Arnold, a woman named Jennifer, and a man named Fredrick. There was no mention of Ronald's disappearance, or of the giant gorilla, just that their expedition was cut short due to weather. The article also said the group was planning to return at an undetermined time.

Arnold's name popped up a few lines lower on his search results. Jonas popped that article open, saw that it was from the same journal, but published two years later. The photo showed Arnold standing alone on a wharf outside of Bodden Town with a few bulky bags next to him. Four paragraphs explained that he returned to the island to pick up where the earlier expedition had failed. Why hadn't Alex mentioned this? Jonas scanned further and further through the search results and found no mention of Arnold's return or his findings.

By the time Jonas sat back down in front of his laptop, he had worked out the steps he needed to take to get to Tortuga: flight to Haiti, short boat trip to Tortuga. He could be on the island in less than a day. The flight would shave a bit off the top of his advance on the script, but it was a reasonable expense for the kind of research he could do. If he could wrap his script around a "true story" it would be easier to market. A giant gorilla story with even the slimmest of facts behind it was much better than one that was total fiction.

Jonas packed his bags for a short trip and stuck a note for his roommate to the refrigerator. Sixteen hours later he climbed out of the rusty boat that took him from Haiti to Tortuga, and set his bags down on the rickety wooden dock. The sun was toward the center of the clear blue sky, the heat was well into the 80s and a thick wash of humidity stuck to him. No one met him on the dock, and as he looked down the length of the wharf, he couldn't see anyone at all. He wrapped his bags over his shoulders and marched through the port of entry. No one checked his passport; no one offered to carry his bags, and no taxis waited.

He walked over a rough open patch that might have been a building once, and stepped into a three-way intersection. The main street ran from northeast to southwest, and it was empty in both directions. None of the feral street animals he expected could be seen either. Dry roads and dirty buildings were neglected to near collapse. A few dirty, parked cars sat on the street; many were covered with palm leaves and debris from the overhanging roofs. The island was nearly silent; there was barely a breeze to make any sound except his footsteps. Jonas double-checked the map he had printed out, then crossed the street to follow the third road to the southeast.

Building after building went past without any sign of residents or merchants. Weather-damaged aluminum lay amid broken glass and splintered wood on the street. Bodden Town was abandoned or deserted, and had been for sometime. Why hadn't the boatmen told him? Were they so desperate for fares that they didn't want to scare him off?

He reached his destination, and saw the sign for Fort des Trois Hotel swinging loose. He wondered how soon he could catch a ferry back to Haiti, as there was little hope of getting anything out of the trip. He wanted to spend as little time as possible in the ghost town.

Forty feet from the front doors of the hotel, he heard the distant squawk of an AM radio sending reggae into the empty street. A drifting hint of pipe tobacco. A wisp of smoke floated out of the front windows of the Fort de Trois.

Jonas kept his distance, looking into the hotel without standing in front of it. The glass was broken out, or maybe had never been there, so the raw light of day poured into the entire lobby. The lobby was small: a front desk, a collection of coffee tables and chairs, a single elevator in the far dark corner. What had been a lush carpet was water damaged and peeled at random squares. A shadow of a man sat near the front, smoked a pipe and stared at the street.

Jonas stepped closer to the man, but stayed outside of the hotel itself. The man at the table was shirtless. He had a series of red rings painted up the lengths of both arms. Three small stripes sat on each cheek. Jonas noticed that his sockets had been filled in and darkened with black paint, making his features resemble a living skull, rather than a human face. Still, the man looked very much like Arnold.

"Arnold?" Jonas asked.

The man stared at Jonas over the top of his glowing bowl. He rolled the pipe stem against his teeth, kept his eyes locked on Jonas. The man was impossibly lean, as if his thin muscles were stuck right to the bone, with a shortage of skin pulled tight over it. He hardly resembled the photo taken before his solo expedition.

"Arnold? Is that you?" Jonas asked again.

The man set his pipe down, but left his mouth slightly open—open enough that his cracked lips showed yellow and jagged teeth. The teeth moved up and down as his jaw quivered, like he was trying to speak but forgot how. A scent of rot drifted off of the man.

"There are so few of us left," the man said.

"Where did everybody go? What happened?" Jonas asked. The man didn't seem to hear any of the questions.

"I wasn't expecting you. It's a shame there is only one of you. Not what we need. Not that I am ungrateful, the course was set sometime ago, and what must be must be. I'll give you the choice of who goes first, though. It's all I can do," he said.

"What do you mean?" Jonas asked. Something awful had happened to the island, he wondered how much Arnold knew about it. Jonas wasn't afraid of the skinny man, but what if there were more dangers in the shadows of the alleys outside? What if the Tortuga Caniba were real?

"When the time comes, I can go first if you want," he said. "Or, you can go first, I would understand completely." The man picked up his pipe again and drew in a massive cloud of smoke. He exhaled and watched the whirls of smoke twist in the sunlight. A strong breeze destroyed the cloud and brought a stronger scent of decay into the room.

"I don't understand what you are asking," Jonas said. He knew this was almost a lie as he said it. He had a growing fear that there was a fatal result of going first, something at the hands of the Tortuga Caniba. Maybe murder-suicide. Whatever it was, Arnold assumed Jonas would be more than willing to cooperate. He was wrong, in a few minutes Jonas planned to steal an abandoned boat if he had to and get back to Haiti.

"We could flip a coin, I guess," Arnold said. He reached into his pocket fiddled with loose change. A pair of rumbles moved through the floor, making the tables and chairs vibrate. The sound could have been some massive machine moving down the street toward them. The sound could've been a low-grade earthquake. Arnold set his pipe down and glared at Jonas.

"Or, there's no rule that says we couldn't go at the same time. Not like we'd be too much for him, right?" Arnold cracked a slightly off-kilter smile. "He's got two hands."

A trio of rumbles, strong and deep. Jonas wanted the noise to be the tremors from an approaching quake. An exploding gas line would be possible too. There were so many things the noise could be made by. A stronger wind blew into the room; it carried an overpowering stench of mold, spoil and compost. Whatever was going to happen, Arnold was content to die. Jonas didn't want to believe that a giant dead gorilla was working its way towards them. Whatever it was, it was coming, and he had seconds to flee into the maze of one and two story buildings that sat between him and the shore. He had to get what he came for, first.

"Arnold, why did you come back here, why did everyone else stay away?" he asked. Arnold stood up, wiped a streak of sweat off of his face and looked at somewhere far beyond Jonas' shoulder. Four impacts, very close, the walls of the hotel shook.

"Once you've seen the god, you can't go back to the regular old world," he said. "This is the only miracle I've ever seen. Besides, the Haitians stopped picking people up from this island a long time ago. They think it's cursed."

"Alex and the others went back to normal," Jonas said.

"Really?" Arnold asked. "She got you out here, didn't she?" Arnold shrugged hopelessly and walked slowly out of the hotel and onto the uneven asphalt. The ground shook as something heavy shifted its weight. The thick reek of decay was almost too much to take; Jonas covered his face with the lower part of his shirt. Some part of him wanted to go out into the street and see the thing, to prove to himself it was real. He knew he should be running away, dashing through the streets to get to the wharf and a boat. Despite the smell, he stood and watched Arnold.

A shadow fell over half of the entire block and covered Arnold in thin darkness. Arnold closed his eyes and stood still in the street, head down to the ground. Jonas wanted to grab him and pull him back to safety, maybe for kindness, maybe so someone could verify his story. The thing pounded the ground again, just outside of the hotel, and the tables and chair bounced on the floor beneath.

Jonas gagged on the odor, turned away from Arnold and the street. He ran to the back of the hotel. As the kitchen door swung shut behind him he heard the grotesque sounds of bones snapping and skin bursting, then a muffled scream, which trailed off into silence as its source flew higher into the air.

He pushed open the back door. The smell of weeks-old kitchen trash drove away the other stink. He ran past the trash and followed a dirt path that served as an alley. A tall man stepped into his path, blocking the way forward. The man was thin like Arnold, but had long black hair, tan skin, and the eyes of a native South American—not Haitian at all. His skin was covered with scores of the red circles and there were more than twenty red marks on his cheeks and face. His eye sockets were painted a deep black.

Jonas' breath left him as he searched for something to say to the shaman. He raised his hands, from instinct, and waved them in the place of words. The shaman drew a triple blade from behind his naked torso and held it between the two of them. Jonas raised his arms to block a strike, but the blade flashed past them and sliced into his throat with a deep stinging cut. His blood splashed out and warmed the front of his shirt. He clutched his throat and fell to his knees.

The shaman bent down to meet his eyes. He put a hand on his shoulder; the feeling was faint and fading. Darkness reached out from the edge of his vision, added to the spots dancing in his sight. White eyes and a face that was coated in red paint consumed his line of vision.

"Either he was going to come to you," the shaman said, "or you were going to come to him."

The face was swallowed in darkness, the warm ground hit him, but it felt distant, like it hadn't really happened. There was a feeling of safety as Tortuga Island and its gorilla moved further away. He forgot where he was, what he was doing, why he was there.

Then, everything ended.

About the Authors

DR. STEVEN RUTGERS is a physician executive with significant accomplishments in developing management care strategies, integrating delivery systems, improving quality and utilization management programs, and coaching medical staff on healthcare business and practice issues. Being fictional, he rarely writes fiction.

JAMES ROY DALEY is a writer, editor, and musician. He studied film at the Toronto Film School, music at Humber College, and English at the University of Toronto. He is the author of *Terror Town, Into Hell, 13 Drops of Blood*, and *The Dead Parade*. In 2009 he founded *Books of the Dead Press*, where he enjoyed immediate success working with many of the biggest names in horror. Anthologies he has edited include *Best New Zombie Tales, Best New Vampire Tales*, and *Classic Vampire Tales*.

SHELLEY ONTIS is a full-time freelance writer who also writes fiction and poetry. Sometimes people publish it. She is also a caped superhero. Okay, not that last part.

DAVID NIALL WILSON has been writing and publishing horror, dark fantasy, and science fiction since the mid-eighties. An ordained minister, once President of the Horror Writer's Association and recipient of the Bram Stoker Award for poetry and short fiction, as well as being nominated for long fiction and non-fiction, his novels include *Maelstrom, The Mote in Andrea's Eye, Deep Blue, the Grails Covenant Trilogy, Star Trek Voyager: Chrysalis, Except You Go Through Shadow, This is My Blood, Ancient Eyes* and the upcoming supernatural mystery novel *Vintage Soul: Volume I of the DeChance Chronicles*. The Stargate Atlantis novel *Brimstone*, written with Patricia Lee Macomber was published in 2010. He has over 150 short stories published in anthologies, magazines, and five collections, the most recent of which were *Defining Moments*, published in 2007 by WFC Award winning Sarob Press, and the currently available *Ennui & Other States of Madness*, from Dark Regions Press. His work has appeared in various anthologies and magazines. David lives and loves with Patricia Lee Macomber in the historic William R. White House in Hertford, NC with their children, Billy, Stephanie, and Katie, David's mother Jean, and occasionally his boys Zach and Zane.

SIMON McCAFFERY is a former magazine editor who sold his soul to high-tech corporate America. He lives in the Tulsa, Oklahoma area with his wife Angela and his three amazing children. Writing and selling fiction since 1990, he owes his love of zombies, science fiction, and things that go bump in the day (and night) to his father, James McCaffery, who taught Simon to read at an early age and gave him a box of paperback books when he was eleven. *Something Wicked This Way Comes* was among them.

STEVE RUTHENBECK works in communications and has twice won the Minnesota Society for Interest in Science Fiction and Fantasy Short Story Award. His favorite writers include Richard Matheson, Ray Bradbury, Seigbert W. Becker and discovering new or previously unheard of authors in anthologies. He lives in the country, close to the family farm. His World War II action/horror novel, DogSS of War, is currently available on Kindle.

ADRIAN LUDENS is a radio announcer living in the Black Hills of South Dakota. He is a member of the Horror Writers Association. His fiction has appeared in *Morpheus Tales, Alfred Hitchcock's Mystery Magazine* and others. Recent anthology appearances include *The Mothman Files* (edited by Michael Knost, Woodland Press), *D.O.A.* (edited by David C. Hayes and Jack Burton, Blood Bound Books), and *Blood Lite 3: Aftertaste* (edited by Kevin J. Anderson, Gallery/Pocket). Adrian is currently polishing a short story collection. Visit him at curioditiesadrianludens.blogspot.com

AMANDA C. DAVIS is a combustion engineer who loves horror fiction in all its forms. Her work runs the gamut of speculative fiction and has appeared in *Shock Totem, Redstone Science Fiction, Goblin Fruit,* and others. You can follow her on Twitter at @davisac1 or read more of her stories at amandacdavis.com.

MARK ONSPAUGH sat too close to the TV as a child, and now needs glasses. His young brain was irradiated with monster movies, sci-fi and Looney Tunes. DC Comics took care of the rest. Today, he is the writer of the film *Kill Katie Malone,* a co-writer of the cult fave *Flight of the Living Dead,* and has several scripts in development. He has sold numerous short stories and essays. He tells people he was raised by wolves, but his parents were nice people who onlyeviscerated the occasional wayward traveler. You can visit him at www.markonspaugh.com and on his Facebook pages, including *Out of My Mind – Fiction and Film from Mark Onspaugh.*

GUSTAVO BONDONI is an Argentine writer with over eighty stories published in ten countries and four languages. A winner in the National Space Society's *Return to Luna* Contest, and the *Marooned Award for Flash Fiction*, his fiction has appeared in three *Hadley Rille Books Anthologies, The Rose & Thorn, Albedo One, The Best of Every Day Fiction*, and others. More recently he has published his first reprint collection, *Tenth Orbit and Other Faraway Places* and his short novel *The Curse of El Bastardo.* Visit him at: www.gustavobondoni.com.ar.

REBECCA SNOW is a Virginia writer whose short fiction has been published in a number of anthologies. She can be found online at cemeteryflower.blog.com and on Twitter @cemeteryflower.

MEGAN R. ENGELHARDT wanted to be a writer since she was old enough to make marks on paper. Over the years she dabbled in politics, law, and librarianship, but kept finding her way back to made-up worlds and crazy, fantastic ideas. She loves the Internet and thinks Internet people are some of the most creative folks around. iTunes tells her that *Steam Powered Giraffe* and *House of Heroes* are her favorite bands, and that *The Lord of the Rings: The Musical* is her favorite musical. Her bookshelves indicate that she loves *Terry Pratchett, Neil Gaiman*, teen fiction and books about fairy tales. She lives in northeastern Ohio with her husband Lucas, an economist and the straight line to her squiggle.

TONIA BROWN - is the author of *Lucky Stiff* and lives in NC with her husband of many years. She shares her home with a brood of moody cats, and her likeness with an identical twin sister. She likes coffee and fudgesicles, though not always together. Her next novel, *Badass Zombie Road Trip* will be released by in early 2012 by *Books of the Dead Press*.

MICHAEL O'NEAL works as an actor out of Los Angeles and Las Vegas in film, commercial, and live theatre and also writes horror, fantasy, and speculative fiction for various publications. He is the fiction editor of *Dark Moon Digest* and a freelance editor for all formats of writing from novels, flash fiction, short stories, memoirs, scripts, obituaries, and any other obvious lies that are too good not to write down on paper. Dozens of his own stories have been published in magazines and anthologies abroad, mainly because he's good at tricking people into believing his fibs by scaring them into submission, if you'll pardon the pun. For inquiries, he can be contacted at devilsplayground@live.com. By reading this excerpt, you are now under the curse of Pharaoh Tut'is'Own-horn. You must tell ten people you know and ten perfect strangers about Michael O'Neal, or else a monster will come out from under you're bed tonight and eat you, toes first. You have been warned.

MAX VILE is a prolific author of horror and the erotic & his works can be found in numerous publications and sometimes scrawled on dirty bathroom doors. He currently resides in Sin City but has been known to travel out of body for his many spiritual quests, or often just to scare the crap out of folks that pissed him off (if you see him in your dreams tonight don't be afraid; he's just glad you read his story and wanted to ask you a few questions about its review). His artwork can be found on FineArt America or if you just Google his name, for the lazy. He can be reached for info, requests, fan mail, contracted work, personal attacks, and spam at meat4thebeast@live.com (be warned spammers: he has a way to retrace the spam to your account and will infect you with more than a computer virus). His blood type is AB- but he loves the taste of O+, for anybody who might be interested in a donation...

TREVER PALMER's mother gave birth to him on April Fool's Day while watching *Creature from the Black Lagoon*. Since then, he's held jobs in a slaughterhouse, mental hospital, and porn theater. He now lives with thirteen cats that tell him what to write. He is the author of the novella *Different Seasons,* the collection *Smells Like Fish*, and has authored numerous short stories.

TW BROWN is a member of the Horror Writers Association and the writer of the *DEAD* Series (*The Ugly Beginning*, *Revelations*, and *Fortunes & Failures*) as well as the *Zomblog trilogy.* He is the editor for May December Publications and oversees the selection team for the various anthologies under that label. Notreebooks, Pill Hill Press, and others have published his work but this is his first appearance in a *Books of the Dead Press* title. Besides zombies, he is a fan of all things pertaining to the American Civil War and Seattle Seahawks football. In what little spare time he can find he plays guitar and tries to train his Border Collie to do silly tricks.

WILLIAM MEIKLE is a Scottish writer with more than ten published novels and over 200 short story credits in thirteen countries. He is the author of the ongoing *Midnight Eye* series, and his work has appeared in numerous anthologies.

T. A. WARDROPE resides in Minneapolis, MN where he tends to his own private bestiary, which does not include any gorillas. He has a M.F.A. in Creative Writing from Hamline University and is a graduate of Borderlands Press Horror Writer's Bootcamp. His science-fiction novel, Arcadian Gates, will be available from Amazon in early 2012.

Great titles from:
BOOKS OF THE DEAD